THE
doctor

A NASHVILLE NEIGHBORHOOD BOOK

NIKKI SLOANE

Appendix Edition

ISBN 978-0-9983151-8-8

FOR NICK

ONE

NASHVILLE IN THE SUMMER WASN'T FOR THE FAINT OF heart—the heat and humidity were oppressive. Preston had invited our friends over to hang out by his dad's pool, and when we ran out of beer in the cooler, I volunteered to get the other case from the fridge in the garage. I did it because I needed a break from everyone.

Preston Lowe and I had been together for more than three years and had started dating the summer before our junior year of high school. Since then, we'd done almost everything together. All the school dances. Family vacations. Our first year of college. Hell, our senior class even voted us 'Most Likely to Marry Their High School Sweetheart.'

I'd loved him so much, I'd given him my virginity.

But . . .

Preston had changed. I didn't know if there was a turning point, or a single event that made him different, but he wasn't the sweet, caring guy I'd known. We'd gotten comfortable with each other—maybe too comfortable. He'd tell me anything, including when he thought I looked like I wasn't 'trying' anymore, or acting like a bitch.

It was June now, and we were both home from Vanderbilt University, but I saw my boyfriend less this summer than I did when we were at school. We had jobs, sure. But today he made it clear he was more interested in hanging out with our high school friends than he was with me.

God. We'd been best friends, and now we didn't really talk anymore. No deep conversations, or playful teasing, or anything. Preston only called me when he was horny. That's what I'd become to him.

Cassidy Shepard—Preston's release valve.

I tucked my phone into my swimsuit top and played my favorite song by *Joven* as I walked through the house to the garage on the far side of the home. I opened the door and padded down the two steps into the cavernous garage, not bothering with the overhead light. The cement floor was cold on the soles of my bare feet, but the music was awesome, and in the dark space, I tried to let go of my annoyance with Preston. Maybe I was just in a bad mood and needed to shake it off.

I did that.

Literally.

I closed my eyes and danced to the song playing from between my boobs, not caring about the grimy floor, or how I was cold in my damp swimsuit. I tried not to care about anything, and it kind of worked. I swayed my hips to the music. I put my hands in the air and waved them around and couldn't stop the idiotic smile from warming my lips.

It felt good to dance like a fool, lit only by the light coming from the open door to the kitchen. Since I knew every word by heart, I sang along and, as I hit the chorus, I really let go. I swiveled around, swinging my hips as I belted out the lyrics—

A startled sound choked off in my throat as I jerked to a stop.

Dr. Lowe stood in the doorway, and judging by his expression, he'd been there awhile.

I was surprised to see him for a number of reasons, but the biggest was Preston's father was a trauma surgeon at Davidson County Hospital. He was usually on-call and wasn't around much. He was always there for the things that mattered, like birthdays and graduation, but most of the time, Preston and I were alone in the house.

Why had his father kept such a big home when his son went off to college? It was strange. Dr. Lowe barely used it.

Preston's dad looked younger than he was, at least in his face. There were faint lines at the sides of his eyes that hinted he was forty, but the lines made him look smart. Distinguished. His dark brown hair and short beard were threaded with a few strands of silver, and the afternoon sunlight coming from the nearby window highlighted the gray. It was a good look.

In the series of pictures we'd taken before our senior prom, there was a shot of Preston and his dad, and my friends drooled over Dr. Lowe. I'd made fun of them, but I understood. My boyfriend's dad wasn't just attractive—he was fucking hot.

But rather than smile at him like I usually did, I went wooden.

Was it possible to die of embarrassment? My knees turned soft, but my spine snapped straight and my face flushed to a thousand degrees. I dropped my gaze to the cement floor and tucked a lock of my long, dark hair behind my ear, trying to play it off like he hadn't just caught me dancing and singing like a crazy idiot.

"Uh . . ." I stammered. I dug the phone out of my top and shut the music off. "I was just getting another case of beer for the—" Shit! What was I doing? Preston's friend Mike was the only one of us who was twenty-one. "I meant Coke."

It was the worst 'save' in the history of 'saves,' and all Dr. Lowe did was chuckle. It was a deep, pleasant sound that filled the spacious garage. It drew my gaze up to him. He had his hands resting casually on the sides of the door frame, and his expression was faint amusement.

But he blinked it away and straightened. "Preston sent you to get his beer?"

I shrugged, pulled the fridge open, and stared at the nearly empty shelves. At least the cold air coming from the open refrigerator calmed my heated face. "I offered."

The cardboard creaked when I grabbed the case's handle and lifted the twenty-four pack off the shelf. I tried to focus on the heft in my hand and not the man in the doorway, since it was the second time this summer he'd caught me.

The second time he'd seen me doing something he shouldn't have.

Oh my God, don't think about it.

Lord knew I'd spent enough nights fantasizing about that day, so I plastered on an indifferent expression and lugged the beer toward the door. Every step brought us closer, and yet Dr. Lowe didn't move. His maple brown eyes sharpened on mine until I pulled to a stop. He was blocking me.

"Are things okay with you two?" he asked, full of concern.

I nearly dropped the case in surprise. Preston seemed oblivious to the divide growing between us. How the heck did his dad see it?

"We're . . ." I wasn't sure what to say, or how to say it. "I think it's school. It got us out of sync."

Dr. Lowe nodded slowly. Preston had struggled with his new freedom as a college freshman, and he'd found going to class on a regular basis a challenge. His grades hadn't been good, and it was a sore spot between him and his dad.

I forced myself to brighten. "I'm sure we'll be fine."

His expression didn't change. He looked at me funny, like he was worried or upset, or as if he didn't believe me. But he nodded once more and stepped back to let me pass. I was halfway through the kitchen before he spoke.

"Cassidy." His voice was quiet, yet strong. "I don't know if I ever said it, but thank you for everything you did with Preston."

Confusion made me slam on the brakes. "What?"

Dr. Lowe shifted on his feet, visibly uncomfortable. "When he came to Nashville, it was hard on him. You made it easier." He balled his fists, set them on the kitchen island, and leaned forward, pressing his knuckles into the granite. "You made him a better person, and I'm grateful."

The cardboard was cold as I clutched the case closer to my body, stunned.

Growing up had been complicated for my boyfriend. Preston's parents had him young and never married, and he didn't talk much about why he'd lived with his mother in North Carolina until he was sixteen.

I didn't know what kind of relationship he'd had with his father before he arrived in Nashville, but it sounded nonexistent. The story I'd pried out was he'd been hanging around with a group of kids his mother was scared of, and like the Fresh Prince of Bel-Air, she'd shipped him off to live with his dad, determined to keep him away from their bad influence.

When Preston and I started dating, we both joked it was because I was the first girl who was nice to the new kid in town. My smart, somewhat nerdy friends became his friends, and eventually, his mother's plan seemed to work.

I squeezed the beer in my arms, not sure how to respond to his father's gratitude. What was I supposed to say? *You're welcome?* "That's really nice, but I didn't do anything."

A faint smile lifted at the corner of Dr. Lowe's lips and spread wider as he spoke. "Well, I'm thankful either way. Sorry about interrupting whatever that was you were doing a minute ago."

His light teasing brought on fresh embarrassment, and I pulled my shoulders back. "Hey, I couldn't help it. I really like *Joven.*"

"I agree they're good, but they don't," his smile widened, "give me seizures."

"Ha, ha," I said in a flat tone. "I'll have you know I'm normally a great dancer. I didn't know anyone was around." I shot him a pointed look.

He lifted his hands in mock surrender, but his smile didn't fade. "Well, I don't really have room to talk." He hooked his thumbs back at himself. "World's Worst Dancer right here."

"I don't know. Your son might have you beat."

Preston spent most of the school dances hanging out on the side of the dancefloor. Whenever he did dance, it was like he was mimicking those inflatable windsock men outside of used car dealerships—all flailing arms and spastic hips.

As I left Preston's father and went down the stairs to the basement, I couldn't shake the feeling he'd given me. A warm tingling in my chest that felt all sorts of wrong, but good too.

It was two more weeks with Preston before I reached my breaking point.

As I sat in my sweltering car, parked in the Lowe driveway, grief swept through me. I mourned the death of our relationship. I missed the guy I'd loved, but knew he was never coming back.

My grandmother passed away last week, but Preston didn't come to the funeral. He'd had to work, he said—which was fine. But he didn't come to the visitation either. He didn't stand beside me or hold my hand as I'd cried while staring at the casket. He'd left me on my own to field the incessant question from my family, "Where's Preston?"

"Sick," I'd lied.

I found out from our mutual friends he'd forgotten and gone to the movies. That made it obvious how little I mattered now.

A frustrated sigh slipped out as I reached across the seat and snatched up my backpack. I'd brought a swimsuit and towel over, knowing I was going to need to work up to the moment I told him it was over between us. I'd never broken up with someone before.

I didn't ring the bell. I climbed the front steps and pushed open the unlocked door, comfortable walking into the Lowe house unannounced. Would this be the last time I did it?

The wind sucked the door shut behind me with a loud slam, and heavy footsteps pounded on the hardwood floor until his dad stepped into view.

"Cassidy?" The momentary confusion on his handsome face was replaced with an easy smile.

I froze in place. "Hey, Dr. Lowe. Didn't he tell you I was coming over?"

He shook his head. "I think he's in the pool already."

"Oh. Okay." I headed toward the door to the basement, but only made it a few paces before the toe of my sandal caught the edge of the entryway rug. "Ah!"

Like an idiot, I stumbled forward on shaky legs, fighting not to go down, and instead tumbled right into Dr. Lowe.

He grunted softly as I collided with his hard chest. I knocked him back a half-step, but then his steady hands locked onto my waist. Embarrassment flickered through me, but as I lifted my flustered gaze to his, the emotion burned away.

Oh.

The sensation of his hands on my body made my breath catch in my throat.

There'd been concern for my near-fall in his expression seconds ago, but it evaporated as his hold on me tensed. Something gathered in his brown eyes—something that looked a hell of a lot like heat. The muscles running along his jaw tightened and flexed.

I had to be imagining it. There was no way he was looking at me like he was thinking about sliding his hands around my back and drawing me closer. My body hummed from the contact, and the buzz grew louder and more frantic the longer we remained motionless.

His embrace put me far more off-balance than tripping on the rug had.

We were standing too close, but he was magnetic. The pull toward him was a force I struggled to overcome, even when I knew I had to.

His voice came out strange and uneven. "Are you all right?"

"Yeah," I breathed. Why hadn't I noticed how deep and beautiful his eyes were before?

Abruptly, he released me, his hands coming off my waist as if I were a hot stove. Shame flashed through his expression and then it went blank. "Sorry."

He turned and strode quickly away, leaving me to stare at his broad back as he went. What was he sorry for? Keeping me from falling? Touching me? Or the way he'd stared at me like Preston used to, with a gaze that teemed with desire?

I'd had impure thoughts about Dr. Lowe before. I couldn't help myself and tried not to feel guilty about them. They were just harmless fantasies, I'd justified, and were kept safe in my own mind. Any shame over thinking about my boyfriend's dad was about to be moot anyway.

Outside, the stone patio led to the shady back yard and the bright blue pool was surrounded by a decorative black, wrought-iron fence. The pool wasn't enormous, but nicely proportional to the sprawling home. It was large enough for either of the Lowe men to swim laps if they wanted, which Preston appeared to be doing now.

He must have sensed my arrival because he stopped mid-stroke, pushed his wet, dark hair back out of his eyes, and flicked the water away with his fingers. He stared at me and raised an eyebrow.

"You're not in your suit?" No greeting. Just his annoyed tone.

"I've got it in my bag." I glanced over at the empty lounger at the side of the pool. Maybe I should tell him I didn't want to swim, sit down there, and find my way into the difficult conversation we needed to have.

He swam to the edge and propped his arms on the stone ledge. "Get your sexy ass changed, then. It's hot as balls out here, and the water's great."

It felt like an order. I bit my bottom lip as I tried to muster the courage to say no.

But I failed miserably. I turned around and went back into the house, stalling. I plodded through the large media room and into the spare bedroom Dr. Lowe used as his home gym. The only other rooms downstairs were the bedroom Preston used while home from college, and the bathroom, both of which were disasters. He left his clothes *everywhere*, and it was easier to change in here.

Calling this room a home gym was probably too fancy. It had a treadmill and an all-in-one weight machine. The futon Preston used mostly as a couch at college was pushed to one corner, and I dropped my bag on it with a sigh.

As I changed, I reminded myself of my goal. I wasn't happy with my boyfriend, but that didn't mean I wanted to hurt him. I hoped to break up with him in the least painful way for both of us.

I stacked my clothes on the futon, grabbed a beach towel out of the hall closet, and forced myself back outside.

His gaze lifted to me, and he blinked. Then his eyes hazed as he scanned my body, clad in a simple, black string bikini. "Is that new?"

My mouth went dry. What had I been thinking, bringing this swimsuit? I hadn't been, really. I'd grabbed the first thing that would work and had shoved it in my bag. Wearing the bikini had been a bad idea.

"It was on sale at Target," I croaked.

His expression was thick with lust as he pushed off the side. "I like it." He swirled his hands beneath the water, floating closer to me and the shallow end. "C'mon in."

Preston's intentions couldn't have been more obvious if he'd tried. He wanted to fuck. Was it the only reason he'd called me over? I hurled the beach towel down onto the lounge chair and twisted my dark brown hair up into a bun.

I didn't want to get it wet, because it'd take forever to dry, and I might need to leave in a hurry if things became too emotional.

Reluctantly, I went to the stairs at the front of the pool and took my first step into the water. I only made it halfway down before his cold, wet arms were wrapped around my body, and he was pulling me deep into the center of the pool.

"Wait," I said with forced casualness, struggling against his embrace. I wanted to get in under my terms, and I didn't want him so close. I needed distance to do what had to be done.

Whatever disconnect was going on between us, it seemed to get wider every time we were together, and Preston ignored my protest. His mouth crashed against the side of my neck, planting kisses. It'd always been the surefire move to turn me on, the fastest way to get in my pants, but things had changed between us, and this was one of them.

"Preston," I said, pushing away and finally getting out of his hold.

He turned and looked up at the huge arched windows on the back of the house, then focused on me. "What? Are you worried about my dad? He doesn't care what we do."

Oh, God. A shiver ran through me, but since most of my body was underwater, it was unlikely my boyfriend could see it.

Like a fool, the first weekend home from school I'd tried to bring Preston back to me and used the only tool I could think of—sex. The back yard beyond the fence was surrounded by woods, so no one could see us as we went skinny-dipping in the middle of the day. There weren't people around to witness how he'd set me down on the thick cushion of the lounger, knelt between my parted legs, and thrust inside me.

I'd let him fuck me while I thought no one was watching, but I'd been wrong. As Preston's tempo increased, I'd turned my head to the side and saw a figure at the window.

TWO

DR. LOWE VANISHED FROM VIEW THE MOMENT OUR GAZES locked, and Preston mistook my gasp of surprise as pleasure, too into the moment to think it'd be anything else. I didn't tell him what I'd seen, and Dr. Lowe never said a word about it. Not to me, and probably not to his son either. He was excellent at pretending it hadn't happened.

But I wondered how long he'd stood at the window.

How much of my naked body had he seen, writhing on the deck chair? Should I have felt unease? Disgust? I didn't. All I felt was odd and jittery, like I'd been left under a heat lamp too long. Whenever I thought about it, my skin glowed hot and was stretched too tight.

"I just got in the water, give me a second," I said, stalling for more time.

Preston shot me a helpless grin. "Sorry." Although his tone said he wasn't. "You put on a bikini. How am I supposed to keep my hands to myself?"

Six months ago, I would have found his comment playful and charming. Today, it turned me off.

He leaned back in the water, floating near me, and his brown eyes looked richer with the water reflecting in them. He was cute when we'd first started dating, and he'd since filled out as he grew into a man. Like his father, he was handsome. Preston's hair was short on the sides and long on top, and lighter in color than his dad's.

My stomach hurt with worry as I watched him glide through the water, carefree. He had no idea I was about to drop a bomb.

"Hey," I started, my voice already wavering. "We need to talk."

The patio door opened with a noisy slide, drawing our attention. Dr. Lowe stepped outside, carrying a pitcher in one hand and two plastic cups in the other.

Preston grinned widely, and he asked his dad teasingly, like it was some joke I wasn't in on, "What's that?"

"Fresh lemonade," Dr. Lowe answered quickly. Too quickly.

Preston laughed. "Poor Judy. Maybe I should go over there and tell her you hate the taste of lemon. She could make those cookies again. Or the brownies. Those were awesome."

I wrinkled my forehead in confusion. Preston swam close and circled me in his arms.

"Our next-door neighbor got divorced, and now she wants my dad. Bad. Up until today, she's been trying to seduce him with baked goods." He squeezed tight, and it felt constricting. "Hey. How come you don't bake stuff for me anymore?"

"Probably because I'm busy and we hardly see each other?" My tone was more pointed than I'd meant for it to be.

Dr. Lowe walked toward the glass table perched under the umbrella and set the pitcher and cups down. "Well, enjoy."

"You think she roofied it?" His son said it as a joke, but Dr. Lowe's gaze narrowed suspiciously at the pitcher.

"I'm sure it's safe," he said, then disappeared back into the house.

"What a glowing endorsement," Preston joked.

Under the water, his hands began to wander, playing with the strings at my hips. I squirmed away, but he didn't get the message, and my irritation reached critical mass.

"I didn't come over to have sex with you."

He shot me a confused look. "Then, why did you?"

Oh my God.

His simple question broke the last piece of my heart. He couldn't see any other reason I'd want to be here? I wasn't his friend anymore—I was just someone to stick his dick in. The realization was incredibly hurtful, and tears sprang into my eyes. My voice went shallow. "Preston, I can't do this anymore. It's over."

"What?" He went wooden, his shoulders snapping stiff. But judging by his reaction, he'd heard me loud and clear.

"You've changed. We're different people now."

His shocked expression was frozen on his face. It was painfully tense, and the only sound was the water quietly lapping at the edge of the pool. That was, until the sliding patio door rang out a second time.

"Not now," he growled at his father.

It didn't slow Dr. Lowe down. He had a cordless telephone in his hand. "It's your boss. He says you're not answering your cell."

"Fuck," Preston muttered as he swam to the edge of the pool. "My battery ran down." He stretched up a hand and took the receiver. "Hello?"

He paused, listening to the other side, and contorted his face with an annoyed look.

"No, I'm not coming in today. I don't work again until Wednesday."

My gaze locked onto Dr. Lowe's, and the thought seemed to hit us at the same time. Today *was* Wednesday.

"Shit," Preston said into the phone, scrambling toward the steps. "Yeah, of course. I'm so sorry. I'll be there in fifteen minutes."

He flew up the stairs and out of the pool, dropping the phone on the chair cushion and grabbing the towel there. My towel, because he'd forgotten to bring one out.

"I gotta go," he said, scrubbing the water off his skin. No idea if he was talking to me or his father. "I'm already late."

Dr. Lowe crossed his arms over his broad chest, visibly displeased, and Preston noticed.

"Yeah, I know," he said, banding the towel around his hips and hurrying toward the patio door. "I screwed up. Sorry."

Again, no idea who this apology was directed at. I was glad to be in the cool water at that moment, because my blood boiled. He didn't give a thought to staying and talking. He didn't say anything to me—including goodbye. As he ducked into the house, I was left floating both physically and emotionally.

My frustration got the better of me. "How did he not know it was Wednesday?"

The summer had him all screwed up, but this was his job. Waiting tables wasn't life or death, but Preston acted like having spending money for his upcoming sophomore year was.

Dr. Lowe sighed loudly. "I'm sorry about him. You know you're welcome to stay as long as you want."

Um, unlikely. "Thanks."

He hesitated. "And there's fresh lemonade."

"I know what you're doing," I said. "You're just trying to unload that on me."

He smiled and nodded like he'd been busted. "I feel bad pouring it out. If you like lemons, I'm sure it's good and probably not drugged."

I squeezed out a smile, meeting his. We held each other's gaze for a long moment. Long enough for the smiles to end and be replaced with something different. He gave me a look similar to the one earlier and it made my pulse pound in my throat.

What the hell? I stared down at the ripples in the water, blinking rapidly. Maybe I wasn't imagining things.

"Do you want some?" His deep voice sounded unsteady, and his question threw me.

What exactly was he offering? "Some?"

"Lemonade."

Right. I was an idiot, projecting things that weren't there. "Oh. Sure."

He picked up a cup and poured from the pitcher, and my focus was drawn to his hands. They weren't just beautiful, they were talented and worth a lot of money. How many lives had he saved with them?

Off on the far side of the house, we heard the garage door go up, a car back down the driveway, and tires peel out.

"Here you go," he said, bending down over the edge of the pool to pass me the cup.

"Thank you." I took a sip, and he gauged my reaction. I puckered my lips. "Ugh. Don't feel bad about pouring it out. It's too tart."

I set the cup on the side of the pool and turned my gaze to the steps. I couldn't stay here. I climbed out of the water as Dr. Lowe gathered up the cups and pitcher.

He paused when he noticed me standing beside the railing, my arms crossed over my chest. It was warm outside, but when the breeze blew, it was chilly. I was drenched and wasn't going to go inside the house to change until I at least stopped dripping.

"You forget to bring a towel out?" he asked lightly.

"No," I said. "Preston did, and he took mine."

He shook his head and muttered something under his breath as he went inside the house, taking the gross lemonade with him. He reappeared thirty seconds later with a folded towel and passed it to me.

"Thank you," I said. "I didn't want to go in and drip all over your carpet."

"Because you're capable of thinking of someone besides yourself."

It had to be a dig at Preston, and I had absolutely no response. I wrapped the towel around my body and pressed my lips together.

Dr. Lowe's expression wasn't exactly frustration—it looked like he wanted to say something else, but instead he held it back and just frowned. His brown eyes filled with disappointment.

"Can I get you anything else?" he asked, hovering awkwardly. Almost as if he hoped I'd start a conversation. I searched the back of my brain to find something, but couldn't.

"I'm good," I eked out.

"All right. I'm . . . going inside."

He turned swiftly and disappeared into the house, moving so fast he didn't see my mouth fall open. The man was a surgeon. He oozed confidence and always seemed calm in a crisis. When Preston had totaled his car two years ago, his father had been concerned, but never lost his cool throughout the ordeal.

Seeing Dr. Lowe unsure? It made me nervous.

THREE

AFTER I'D DRIED OFF ENOUGH, I LET DOWN MY HAIR, grabbed my phone, and padded back into the house, shivering in the air conditioning. The enormous television was on, showing some news program, and the volume was so low I could barely hear it.

Dr. Lowe didn't seem to be watching.

He sat casually on the large sectional couch, one arm thrown over the back of it, and gazed vacantly at the coffee table before him. The angle of his body and his form fitting t-shirt showed off his toned frame. His jeans clung to his powerful legs, and I lingered inside the doorway, gawking weirdly at him while my toes burrowed into the plush carpeting.

My desire to talk to him was strong, but I shouldn't. He was Preston's father. I couldn't exactly ask him for advice on what I should do now, could I? I cinched the towel tighter around my waist and made my way into the spare bedroom where I'd gotten changed.

After I shut the door, my disappointment made me move slowly. I dropped my phone beside my stack of clothes and sighed. What was I going to do? Wait for Preston to call me? Technically, it was done. I'd told him we were over.

Knuckles rapped softly on wood. "Cassidy?"

I went motionless, and my heart skipped a beat faster. "Yeah?"

"I . . . need to say something," Dr. Lowe's voice came from the other side of the door. "Can I come in?"

I clenched a hand tight on the side of my towel. I hadn't started changing, and he'd seen me in my swimsuit a minute ago, but that had been beside the pool. It was stupid, but I felt more exposed now that I was in the house. I pushed the thought aside. "Yeah."

He stepped into the room, shut the door behind him, and when he faced me, his shoulders sagged. Whatever he was about to say, it seemed deadly serious, and he'd struggled with the decision.

"What's wrong?" I whispered.

"I shouldn't be saying this, and it's not my business, but Preston—" His eyebrows pulled together. "You should end it with him."

I nearly fell over. "What? Why?"

It took him a lifetime to say something. Every rise and fall of his chest as he breathed made it harder for me to do so. I ran a list of reasons in my head of why he'd ask this, and one of them was absurd.

"Because," he said, "I've watched the way he treats you, and it's not right. He's at a point in his life where he's extremely selfish, and he's not going to get better. Not for a while." Dr. Lowe's expression was resigned. "Not until he learns to stop taking things for granted, and I'm unfortunately speaking from experience. When I was his age, I was the same way."

It was a lot to process, and I swallowed thickly. It was hard to think around him. Maybe the lemonade had been drugged.

I opened my mouth to tell him I'd broken it off with Preston five minutes ago, but he kept talking.

"I know this all sounds terrible. What kind of dad am I, telling you to break up with him?" He shook his head at his own question. "I don't want to see either of you get hurt, but I think that's bound to happen, no matter what you do. I'm probably going to walk out of this room regretting I said any of this, but I want to be clear, this is on him, not you."

He rubbed a hand on his defined jaw, and the whiskers scratched against his skin.

"You're a great girl, Cassidy, and frankly, you deserve more than my son can give right now."

"Wow." It was a breath, rather than a word from me.

Dr. Lowe's face twisted with embarrassment, and his shoulders straightened sharply. "I'm sorry. I really shouldn't have said anything."

"No, wait," I cried as he turned toward the door. "I just broke up with him."

"You did?" He stilled. "Why?"

I dropped my gaze to the carpet. It was too hard to look him in the face as I told him his son was less than perfect, even when Dr. Lowe seemed to know Preston was human. "For the same reason you just said. Preston and me, we're different people from who we were three years ago." My gaze crawled up Dr. Lowe's body until I could meet his eyes.

"I'm not sure the new me likes the new him all that much," I admitted.

"I get it," he said, and he genuinely seemed to. There wasn't defensiveness or anger in his eyes. It looked mostly like relief. "I grew up a lot when I was in school. I did stupid shit until I figured out how to be an adult, and I'm guessing that's where he is right now."

"Still figuring it out?" It was a half-question, half-statement, because I knew it was true. Preston couldn't get a handle on all the freedom of college life, and he'd gone overboard.

"Yeah. He's got a ways to go," his father said.

"I'm sorry."

Confusion flooded Dr. Lowe's face. "For what?"

I shrugged. "I don't know. That I couldn't make it work."

He looked at me like I was being silly. "Don't do that. This isn't your fault. Things don't work out sometimes, and that's just life."

I took in a deep breath. It was strange to talk about it with him, but it felt good too. It was nice to hear I wasn't to blame. He was always so good at knowing what to say or do, and with that thought, I grew sadder than I'd been all day. "It sucks. I feel like I broke up with you too."

The second it was out of my mouth, I wanted it back. His eyes went wide.

"I mean," I sputtered, "because we won't see each other again after this. Like, do we say goodbye?"

I'd been a huge part of Preston's life. There were pictures of me with my boyfriend sprinkled throughout this house. I'd even gone on vacation with the Lowes last summer.

I wasn't overly emotional, but I blinked back the threat of tears. "Is it weird to say I'm going to miss you?"

Dr. Lowe's face was heartbreaking, and the gravel in his voice matched. "No, not at all. I'm going to miss you too."

As I swallowed the lump in my throat, he moved toward me, his arms spread open for a hug. I stepped into it eagerly and let him crush me against his chest. If he didn't care my swimsuit was wet, I didn't either.

He was warm and solid.

His arms wrapped tighter, holding me, and it brought on a fresh threat of tears. I didn't want things to change. I didn't want this part to be over.

My cheek was pressed to his chest, and I could hear the hurried beat of his heart inside. I closed my eyes, squeezing back the tears as his hand smoothed down the hair on the back of my head. How long would he let me stay like this?

His warm palm was on the small of my back, and once again, the contact of it against my skin left me breathless. He moved, shifting the position subtly, as if settling me into his embrace, and unexpected pleasure jolted through me. It was instantly followed by a wave of shame. He was only offering advice and comfort. This was the *most* inappropriate time to get turned on.

Yet I grew heavier each moment I was in his arms, wanting to get closer to him. He smelled like wood and leather, and the scent was enticing. His muscles under my hands flexed and tensed, like whatever this strange thing happening between us was, he could sense it too.

The hand in my hair moved, and he cupped the side of my face, drawing me back enough so he could peer down into my eyes. The way he gazed at me, it sucked the last of the air from my body. Made every nerve ending tingle.

His look was intense. Wild. It announced he was considering doing something very, very bad.

We stood as two people on a crumbling cliff, afraid to move or the ground would give way beneath and make us fall. Only our shoulders lifted with our hurried, uneven breaths. His palm seared against my cheek, and my eyes hooded.

When his gaze slid down to my parted lips, I knew we were doomed, and the worst part was I didn't care. I wanted it to happen. I tilted my chin up to meet him as he lowered his mouth to mine.

FOUR

WARNING SIRENS BLARED IN MY MIND, BUT IT WAS USELESS. HIS gentle, hesitant kiss roared loudly through my body, drumming back any other sound. His soft lips moved against mine, cautious and testing, and I answered back. Even more, I encouraged. I opened my mouth to welcome his seeking tongue.

He drew in a sharp breath through his nose as our reckless kiss deepened, but it didn't stop his exploration of my mouth. Behind my back, his palm urged me into him, and his grip on my face firmed. His lush tongue dipped past my lips, slid against mine, causing goosebumps to burst down my legs.

I couldn't think, breathe, or even move as he kissed me, because I worried I'd break the spell.

Dr. Lowe used the hand cupping my face to tilt me further up, enough to break the contact of our lips, but his mouth was still on my skin. It moved hurriedly over my cheekbone, streaming down the side of my neck.

I shivered.

My skimpy swimsuit was still wet, and the air conditioning was blowing on us from a vent overhead, but the tremble that shook my shoulders had nothing to do with that. It wasn't the cause of my hardened nipples jutting out beneath the triangles of my bikini top either.

Dr. Lowe was.

I nearly lost my balance as he moved in, walking me backward toward the wall. He drew the hand away from my back and threw his palm flat against the wall by my head.

His haggard breathing filled my ear. "What the hell am I doing?"

Was he thinking out loud? Because he didn't stop. His damp lips skimmed over my neck and closed on a spot where it met my body, giving me another wave of shudders. When he sucked lightly, a sharp bolt of electricity shot straight between my legs. I had my arms wrapped around his waist, and I clenched his t-shirt in my hands.

I wasn't supposed to like it, but it felt so damn good.

I leaned my head into his hand, giving him more room on the other side to kiss my neck, and I closed my eyes.

"You mean, what the hell are we doing?" I murmured, because I was just as much a part of this as he was.

When I threaded my fingers through his thick hair, the thought pounded in my mind. *Is this cheating?* No, it couldn't be. I had ended it with Preston. We needed more closure, but I *had* ended it.

My heart lurched into my throat as Dr. Lowe's hand slipped down the wall and came to rest on my shoulder, the edges of his fingers beneath the black string holding my top in place.

The room was steamy hot and frigid cold in the same instant. I was feverish and shivering while the war between my head and body intensified. His mouth journeyed back up the slope of my neck until it sealed over mine.

He was twenty years older than I was. My boyfriend's— *ex-boyfriend's*—father. What was wrong with me? With us? We had to look insane. He had me pressed against the wall hard enough my swimsuit left damp triangle shapes on his shirt.

I liquified under his lips. The way his mouth moved against mine wasn't just seductive, it enslaved. His greedy kiss made me thirsty for more.

"We shouldn't be doing this," I whispered. My words said one thing, and my body another. I bowed off the wall, arching my back, causing his hand to creep lower. His fingertips inched along my skin, heading for the curve of my breast.

"I know," he groaned into my mouth. The sharp edge of his teeth glanced off my bottom lip as he nipped at me.

Down his long, deliberate fingers went, following the string until it met fabric and began to widen into the cup of my top. It was amazing the way the cold swimsuit rubbed against my sensitive nipples, and I ached for more.

His voice was strained. "I'm going to keep going," he took a shallow breath, "unless you tell me to stop."

Was he warning me, or pleading with me to do that?

My throat closed off. I didn't want him to stop. I was out of control and only thinking about myself. I was too focused on how different and exciting this experience was.

He must have figured out I wasn't going to say anything, because his fingers trailed down the edge of the cup toward the center, all the way to the bottom string going across my ribcage.

I gasped as he slid the triangle of fabric to the side, exposing me, and I moaned quietly when he palmed my naked flesh. To go from the wet, cold fabric suddenly to his warm grip was sensual.

Our kiss had started out tame, but as we learned each other, it grew bolder. He plunged into my mouth, his tongue stroking sinfully over mine. It teased as his fingers traced and plucked at my nipple.

I sighed as the sensations heated me to a thousand degrees. There was an insistent throb in my core, growing louder and needier by the second. It went nuclear as Dr. Lowe shifted, moving his leg between my knees.

The towel unwound from my waist and fell to our feet, but I barely gave it any attention. No, my attention was on the man who used the top of his thigh to put pressure where my ache was acute. His kiss conquered me. Before Preston, I'd kissed a few guys, but I'd never had *anything* like this.

"Oh," I moaned. White-hot pleasure flashed along my spine from the grind of his leg against me.

He lifted his mouth away from mine, and when he drew back, I could see how hazy his eyes had become. His expression dripped with desire.

"Jesus, Cassidy."

His tone was heavy and sexual, and it was shocking. Three years I'd known him, and never heard him sound like that. I shuddered, enjoying it, unable to stop myself.

"Shit," I gasped, sagging against the wall. I always tried not to swear in front of him, but right now I couldn't control my mouth. My legs were so weak, I was about to fall. "Dr. Lowe—"

He must have known. His hands tightened on my hips, steadying me as he pulled back. "Greg."

I was breathless. "What?"

"Greg. My name."

I knew that, of course. Yet he wanted me to call him by his first name? He was an *adult*. So much older than I was. I'd only known him as Dr. Lowe, and Greg sounded like—

A stranger.

I struggled to form the word. My mouth fell open to speak his name, but nothing came out, and the room grew colder every moment his mouth wasn't on me. The temperature plummeted further as lust drained from his face and was replaced by an unreadable expression.

Was he realizing the gravity of what we'd just done? Before I could say anything, a phone rang. The ringtone playing from the back pocket of his jeans was one I was familiar with. It was his special one, exclusively for the hospital.

His muscles went rigid as I flinched, and we both turned to stone. It wasn't something he could ignore, no matter how much the look on his face said he wanted to. "I'm on-call. I have to get—"

"I know you do." I nodded quickly, tugging my swimsuit back in place and trying to act as if it were no big deal. Not like we'd just been making a huge mistake.

It was cold when he took the heat of his body away. He dug out his phone, answered it, and as the person on the other side of the line spoke, he paced, listening thoughtfully.

He asked a question about the patient, but I was still hazy, coming down out of my desire, and my gaze lingered over him. He didn't just have beautiful hands—his forearms and biceps were perfect too. All tight and toned without being bulky.

Once the call was over, he gave me a somber look. "I have to go. I'm sorry."

I didn't ask him what exactly he was sorry for. That we'd been interrupted, and he had to leave? Or the things we'd done before the phone call? I couldn't find my voice, anyway. Words wouldn't even form in my head.

"Cassidy." He looked pained. "What just happened . . ."

For the first time, he didn't appear to know what to say. I stared up at him, unable to do anything but breathe shallow breaths.

"It was my fault," he said.

I blinked. What was he talking about? He hadn't coerced or persuaded me. I'd kissed him. The whole thing had been mutual. I opened my mouth to say something, to defend him, but my vocal cords didn't work, and my brain was mute.

His eyebrows pulled together, creating a deep crease between them. The painful quiet grew acute, and the longer the silence stretched, the more hurt he looked.

Then, it became clear he couldn't wait any longer. His patient needed both him and his scalpel.

"My fault," he repeated. "You say that to Preston when you tell him about this."

He marched to the door, yanked it open, and disappeared before I could do anything.

FIVE

IT HAD BEEN A WEEK AND I HADN'T TOLD A SOUL WHAT happened. Not even my new best friend Lilith, who I saw every day as I interned at the animal hospital.

I tried not to think about Dr. Lowe and what we'd done. Instead, I thought about Preston. He hadn't bothered to call or text, and anger rose inside me each day he remained silent. It was easier to focus on that. How did he not need closure? Ten seconds was all it took to undo three years.

Unless this was a power play on his part. Maybe he was waiting for me to call.

And maybe I'd been avoiding it because of what I'd done with his father. Would any good come from telling him? The relationship between father and son was okay, but not great, and I didn't want to be part of the wedge that drove them further apart. I was being a coward about it, but I also saw no upside to confessing my sins. All it would do was cause pain.

Preston might not have needed closure, but I did, and couldn't put it off any longer. On Friday, nine days after our breakup, I texted him.

> Cassidy: Are we going to talk
> about this?
>
> Preston: Talk about what?

Was he fucking kidding? I wasn't going to get into everything via text.

> Cassidy: What I said in the pool. What
> are you doing right now?

> Preston: Playing Call of Duty.

I gnashed my teeth. Of course. He was just sitting around playing video games.

> Cassidy: Is your dad home?

> Preston: No.

The tight breath in my lungs relaxed. I could do this. Get in and get out, even though the thought of not seeing Dr. Lowe again brought on a surprising sharp pang of disappointment.

> Cassidy: Can I come over?

> Preston: You horny?

What? He thought I was asking about his father being gone so we could fuck in the house? Un—fucking—real. Was this how he was handling the breakup, like it had never happened? The three dots blinked across the screen.

> Preston: Yeah, you can come over.

My stomach churned and roiled as I drove to Preston's and parked in the driveway. I shut the car off and stared up at the dark windows of the house, working up the nerve to do what I needed to.

Like last time, I went in through the front door without knocking. There was no point. Preston would be in the basement and wouldn't hear me. My flip-flops slapped against the soles of my feet as I marched through the living room and turned left, heading toward the basement door. I was so focused on my goal, the movement didn't register until he spoke.

"Cassidy?"

Oh, Jesus. My mouth went dry as a desert, and my brain quit working. "He said you weren't here," I blurted.

Dr. Lowe's face contorted into a strange expression. Guilt, confusion, and hurt. Perhaps a little fear too. It made me feel like garbage, and my gaze dropped down to see the stack of mail he was sorting in his hands and the plastic bag of takeout resting on the breakfast bar. The faint smell of garlic lingered.

He pulled his shoulders back. "I just got home."

"Oh." It was barely a whisper from me. "Sorry."

He tilted his head slightly and scrutinized me. "What are you doing here? I thought you and Preston . . ."

"We did. I'm just here to talk to him." *And make sure he understands we're over.*

Dr. Lowe was dressed casually in jeans and a form-fitted t-shirt, and I forced myself not to think about what he would look like without them. I sucked in a deep breath and lifted my gaze to meet his.

"You haven't told him," he said in a low voice, "about what I did."

"What we did," I corrected, "and I'm not going to."

Why did he look upset? Wasn't he supposed to be relieved? "Why?"

"Because it won't change what happened. All it's going to do is hurt him, and the way things are between you two . . ." I didn't want or need to say that Preston's relationship with his father was fragile. "I don't want to jeopardize what you have."

Dr. Lowe put his hands on his hips, and his shoulders sagged in defeat. "I appreciate that, but—"

My phone chirped with an incoming message, interrupting us. I dug it from my purse and looked at the screen.

> Preston: I think my dad's home. I heard
> the garage door.

Great fucking timing, Preston. I put my phone away and shot Dr. Lowe a determined look. "I don't want to hurt him. And telling him what we did?" I shook my head. "I can deal with it if he hates me. But not you."

Before he could say anything, I put my hand on the doorknob and pulled open the door. Sounds of simulated gunfire echoed from the base of the stairs and grew louder as I hurried down, passing pictures of Preston and me hanging on the wall.

When I hit the bottom of the steps, I skidded to a stop.

Preston wasn't alone on the couch. His friend Colin sat on one side, and Troy on the other, all three clutching controllers and focused on the TV screen. I balled my hands into fists at my side. Why the hell didn't he tell me his friends were over?

Colin glanced my direction for a microsecond and flashed an easy smile. "Hey, Cassidy."

Preston couldn't be bothered to look away from the game. "What's up?"

Anger tightened my vocal cords, but I choked it out. "We need to talk."

"Yeah. Lemme finish this level, and . . . I'll be right with you." It was loaded with innuendo for his friends' benefit, and they snickered.

My mouth fell open. Who was he these days? Just as I was about to snap, all three guys swore at the screen.

"Fucking shit," Troy groaned, and his annoyed gaze rolled to his friends.

Preston stood and dropped his controller on the couch cushion. "I'll be back in a few."

"Only a few, huh?" Colin turned his gaze to me. "Poor Cassidy."

Preston wasn't amused. "Shut up, dude."

He probably thought my icy expression was for Colin, when it was meant for him. I stayed silent as I followed him into his bedroom. I'd barely shut his bedroom door before his hands were on me, and I spun away.

"What are you doing?" I shrieked.

Preston wore a look of pure confusion. "Come on. They're playing the game. They don't care what we get up to in here."

Did he think I was shrugging him off because I was embarrassed his friends might hear us? "Have you lost your mind? We broke up."

He scowled. "You were serious about that shit?"

"Yes." Very much yes.

My gaze left his and moved across his messy bedroom, and everywhere I looked, there was another painful reminder of what I'd brought to an end. The poster tacked to a wall was from the exclusive Black Keys show we'd gone to at the Ryman Theatre last year. A mason jar mug rested on his bookshelf. Our school had given them out as party favors at our senior prom. Taped to the mirror was a picture of us and our friends in the stands at the homecoming game.

Preston blinked, and his confusion evaporated. It shifted to irritation. "You're going to end things with me just because I didn't drop everything for you?"

Now it was my turn to be confused. "What?"

"You asked if you could come over and I said yeah. Troy and Colin were already here when you texted. What was I supposed to say? Get lost, because Cassidy finally wants to hang out with me? The world doesn't revolve around you."

"Are you kidding me?" I gasped. The audacity of his statement blinded me with rage, and my sarcasm was thick as syrup. "I know it doesn't, because the world clearly revolves around *you*."

He rolled his eyes, put his hands on his hips, and I was struck by how much he looked like his father. Only he was a spoiled, selfish version, and the opposite of the man upstairs. I couldn't stay in this stifling room another moment. I needed to get away before my mind went to other comparisons I shouldn't make.

His indifferent attitude was too much, and I felt gutted. I barely choked it out, "Goodbye, Preston."

I flung his door open and fled through the living room, keeping my head up and ignoring the two guys playing on the couch. But Preston went after me, grabbing my shoulder and turning me to face him. "This is stupid," he said. "Calm down."

The TV went silent. One of the guys must have paused the game, either so Preston and I could hear each other, or so he could listen to our second breakup play out. I wasn't going to put a show on for them, but my anger wasn't going away either.

"Don't touch me," I hissed.

His face turned sour. "You know what? You can call me when you've calmed down."

If Preston wanted to wait for a phone call that was never going to come, so be it. My expression was firm, masking how wounded he'd made me feel. I'd been determined to end things with him but had prepared for a struggle. It had been wasted. He wasn't going to fight for us. He turned on his heel, went to the couch, and grabbed his controller.

After everything, that was how he treated me.

I wiped at my eyes as I climbed the stairs, brushing away the angry tears. He didn't care about me, so why should I care about him? I wasn't going to waste any more time on him.

Dr. Lowe was washing a dish in the sink, and when he heard me at the top of the basement steps, he cast a glance over his shoulder. His eyes widened. The water was shut off, and he hurriedly dried his hands on a dishtowel, stepping toward me. "Are you okay?"

"I'm fine." My tone was clipped. I wanted to run, but also to stay right where I was. A big part of me wasn't ready for him to be gone.

He slung the dishtowel over his shoulder and crossed his arms, perhaps to stop himself from reaching out for me, and leaned back against the kitchen island. His eyes were full of sympathy. "That was fast."

"Yup." I tried to force my feet to move, but they wouldn't. "Three years, and it's no big deal." My voice broke. "I mean, he's just down there playing video games, so . . . he's fine."

I was swept up into his hug so abruptly, it squeezed the air from my body, and in my weakened state, I softened into Dr. Lowe. His embrace was fierce, and perfect, and exactly what I desired.

"I'm sorry," he said.

Since I had my forehead pressed against his collarbone, he couldn't see me twist my face into displeasure. "Don't. It's not your fault."

"I know, but I'm sorry anyway."

We fell silent. The only sound in the kitchen was the faint ticking of the clock on the far wall. I turned my head and pressed my cheek to the flat plane of his chest, and in response, his arms shifted and settled around me. Neither of us made an effort to step away.

I was greedy. I knew it was selfish and wrong to want his embrace, but I did regardless. It felt like I belonged here. His chest lifted as he drew in a deep breath, and I rode the rise and fall with my eyes closed, hoping the hands on the ticking clock would freeze and go quiet.

But they didn't.

Each second built in my body like a timer counting down, and anxiety swelled, dreading the moment he'd let me go and it'd be time for me to leave. I'd do anything to prevent it.

So, it was a desperate measure when I lifted on my toes and tilted my head, moving to slant my lips over his. I caught him by surprise, but only for a moment, and then his mouth softened to welcome my reckless kiss.

I shivered as he took over and drove away all thoughts. My arms wrapped tighter around his waist, holding on as his dominating mouth pressed to mine and pulled a sigh from my body.

"Wait, wait," he said, abruptly yanking his head back and breaking off the kiss. "I've been waiting here, washing the same damn dish for the last five minutes, hoping when you came back upstairs, I'd find an excuse to talk to you. We need to, Cassidy."

"Oh," I whispered.

The blood in my face heated to a million degrees. I didn't want to talk about it, but it didn't matter. I wasn't going anywhere. Plus, I was certain I'd do pretty much whatever he said, as long as his arms were around me and the buzz from his kiss lingered on my lips.

"I can't stop thinking about what would have happened if the hospital hadn't called."

The way he said it made it impossible to tell if he felt regret or relief. I swallowed the thick knot in my throat. "Me too."

The scenes that had played out in my mind over the last nine days were dirty and wrong. More fantasies, ones that had me putting a hand down my pajama pants late at night just to relieve the ache.

"We have to stop," he said. But he made no effort to release me.

"I know."

"We can't do this." His words were as hollow as my agreement had been.

Dr. Lowe smelled like the fresh, clean dish soap he'd been using, but underneath, I caught the hint of leather. The scent caused the memory to flash white-hot in my mind, reminding me of his hands on my breasts, and I shuddered.

The struggle in his eyes made it clear he was losing whatever fight the sensible side of him was waging.

"Shit." He yanked the towel off his shoulder and tossed it down on the island countertop. "I don't know which is worse. How wrong this is, or the fact I can't stop." His voice dipped so low, it was barely audible. "I shouldn't, but—*fuck*, I want you."

My knees threatened to give out.

I was vaguely aware I was a mess. Hurt and angry at Preston, but I needed Dr. Lowe's mouth on mine again, and like him, I didn't care that it was wrong. I didn't give a fuck how Preston was only one floor below us and could come upstairs at any time.

I pressed into him, like I could burrow deep into his chest. "Dr. Lowe."

His embrace hardened, locking me tightly with bars made of muscle and bone. "Greg." The word was a plea and an order. "Say it."

I tipped my chin up and peered into his eyes. Saying his name would be permission. It'd break the feeble lock we'd put on our restraint, unleashing everything. Uttering it would be a promise of more.

I swallowed a breath and found my voice. "Greg."

SIX

GREG LOWERED HIS MOUTH TO MINE, AND THE MOMENT OUR lips touched, every inch of me exploded with longing. This kiss started tentative. Controlled and aware. But I was engulfed by it, consumed by it, and the sensation drove me crazy.

A single breath was all it took for us to find our rhythm. His lips were pliant against mine as I matched him and charged forward, slipping my tongue into his greedy mouth. This kiss was passionate and dangerous. It built, layer upon layer, until we were both breathless and urgent.

He seized my hips in his sure hands and steered me around, pressing me back against the kitchen island, where the edge of the cold granite bit into the small of my back through the thin cotton tank top I was wearing. Neither of us let up, though. I was wild and out of control, too wrapped up in this thrilling kiss to care.

It was almost brutal, the way he attacked my mouth. I moaned and clutched fistfuls of his t-shirt, wanting it gone between us. Our kiss was even more reckless, but beautiful too. The need between us was so powerful.

He let out the softest sigh when I gave up on tugging at his shirt and slipped a hand under the hem, resting my fingers on the warm, hard ripple of muscles across his stomach. The sound of his affected breath shot straight through me.

It was a live wire. A jolt of electricity, spurring him on. His hands on my hips slid forward, focusing on the snap and zipper of my shorts.

"I'm going to put my hand down your pants unless you stop me," he uttered in my ear.

I wasn't aware of anything but Greg.

Subconsciously, I knew Preston and his friends were downstairs, and how terrible this would be if we were caught. There were consequences, and Greg's were much worse than my own. But it wasn't revenge that allowed him to undo the metal snap of my shorts with a silent click, or drop my zipper, one slow tooth at a time. I didn't care about my ex-boyfriend. Every nerve ending in my body clamored for the man before me. I clung to Greg, not saying a word, but urged him onward with my eyes and the arch of my back.

Also, the fourth step from the top had a terrible creak in it, so we'd hear anyone coming, and he'd positioned his broad back to block me from view.

Once he had my shorts undone, he left them sitting there open and hanging low on my hips. I had on black silk panties trimmed with white lace, and his fingertips traced over the sensitive skin at the top edge while his mouth latched onto the side of my neck.

I shuddered.

How could I not? Greg's delicate strokes at the lace over my belly promised pleasure, and I was fucking eager for it. I craved release. All the tension between us had been winding the last nine days until I was so tight, I was going to break wide open. I was grateful for the counter at my back so I could use it for support.

"Stop me," he whispered. "Please. Tell me you want to stop."

He was begging me like it was his only way out, but I wasn't in control any more than he was. How could I tell him to stop? I wanted him to do it. I *needed* him to. The fire inside me was insatiable.

When fooling around, I'd always been quiet, but Greg made bold and powerful thoughts bubble to the surface. It unhinged the filter on my mouth. "Do it," I whispered. "I want you to."

Surprised pleasure snapped through him. "Yeah?"

He didn't wait for an answer. His fingers curled into a half fist and inched below the lace trim. The hard edges of his fingernails scraped lightly as he raked them down into my panties, working deeper until he found the spot he wanted.

I rose onto the balls of my feet, my flip-flops squealing against the tile.

We both exhaled loudly at the same time. I was wet. So fucking wet, I was drenched, and his chestnut-brown eyes hooded with lust. His other hand went behind my back to support me as he buried his thick fingers beneath my clothes. His touch was pure bliss. I leaned on the island, my elbows slamming into the polished stone counter, and threw my head back until I was staring at the decorative lighting fixture positioned overhead.

I gripped the edge of the counter and moaned as he stirred careful circles over my clit. The tiniest touch from him caused me to flinch and shiver. Ecstasy rocketed up and down my spine like lightning. His mouth was pressed against the side of my neck, and my hair fluttered with his rapid, uneven breathing.

Like last time, I was both feverishly hot and frigid cold. My nipples tightened and protruded through my unlined bra and tank top, as if wanting to be closer to him. It sent me into chaos. The way his skillful fingers stroked and touched me, I was going to melt into a puddle.

It felt dirty, but in a good way. Like when you went off to summer camp and they took you on a mud hike, encouraging you to smear the thick, cold mud on your skin. Years of programming had told me not to get my clothes dirty, but it was freeing when I finally got to let loose.

That was how I felt now about what I was doing.

I reveled in the wrongness of Greg.

I marveled at how perfectly his hands sizzled across my nerve endings and brought me closer to the brink with every twitch. I shook with desire and lust, throwing aside insecurities and rules, and surrendered to my most basic craving. Was I going to come? Panic simmered toward a bubbling boil. I'd only orgasmed a few times with Preston, and I'd felt weirdly embarrassed about it. Enough that whenever it happened, I did my best to stay quiet and not let on. I wasn't comfortable having him watch me when I was so vulnerable and out of control.

With what Greg was doing now, staying quiet seemed like it'd be fucking impossible. His pace increased, and I swallowed a ragged breath. I was half out of my mind, not even sure I was speaking, or what I was saying. "Oh God, I'm going to . . ."

Greg's lips moved against the base of my neck, his stubble faintly dragging over my skin. "Mm-hmm," he mumbled.

Like this had been his master plan, and he was just letting me in on it now. As if he were giving me permission to come, to fall to pieces in his arms.

I did.

And I did it with as quiet of a whimper as I could. I turned my head blindly into him and groaned, letting him hear the ecstasy ripple through my body. His arm around my back tightened at the same instant his fingers stopped moving and pressed against my throbbing clit. It lengthened my pleasure until it was so strong, I could barely breathe.

The orgasm receded, but Greg did not. He held me still and sure, dropping kisses against my parted lips. As the sensation drifted away, I felt both relaxed and twitchy. Anxious with need for something I couldn't quite figure out. Just wanting . . . more.

I pushed off the counter as his hand withdrew from inside my shorts, and before he could do anything else, I palmed the large bulge straining down one leg of his jeans. Air left his lungs in a burst and his hips moved instinctively, pushing forward into my touch.

I was a tit-for-tat kind of girl with the boys I'd been with. Always reciprocating, even if I wasn't that into it. But today was decidedly different. I wasn't touching him out of obligation, I was rubbing his erection through his jeans because I fucking *wanted* to. My fingers ached to learn the feel of him.

"Jesus," he said. He pumped his hips again, urging me to move along his length, and then abruptly froze. His eyes cleared of fog as he blinked, and his pupils focused on me. "Go get in your car."

I turned into a statue and nearly shrieked it. "What?" He was kicking me out?

"Move it down the street," he said, hurried. "The house for sale at the end of the road has been vacant and on the market for six months. If you park by the garage, no one will notice."

I stared up at him. My brain was so clouded with lust, I was slow to keep up with what he was telling me to do. He wanted me to move my car, so when Preston's friends left, no one would see it.

No one would know I was still here.

Greg's voice softened until it was silk. "Come up the balcony stairs on the side of the house."

Because the balcony was attached to his bedroom.

Panic burned slowly and grew in his eyes when I hesitated. Did he understand what he was asking? Us in his bed was a very, very bad idea.

He put his palm over my hand still cupping him through his pants and pressed, molding me to his erection. "Feel how much I fucking want you, Cassidy. Please say yes."

"Yes." It came from me instantly, no time to think about it.

He gave me a rushed kiss and stepped back, releasing me.

My flip-flops squeaked on the hardwood floor as I turned and went for the front door. The orgasm still lingered, buzzing in my system, and fueled me as I stepped outside into the late afternoon heat and propelled myself toward my car.

I focused only on my task, rather than why I was doing it. And as I parked in the driveway down the street, my car tucked behind the garage and hidden from view, the alarms in my head jumped to full volume. They were so steady and consistent, it made them easier to tune out.

As I walked back to the Lowe house, I distracted myself by staring at the dark storm clouds off on the horizon. Thunder growled quietly in the distance. The air was heavy with humidity and charged with electricity. It only added to the vibrating feeling coursing through me.

I took the wrought-iron stairs on the spiral staircase one step at a time. All I did was put one foot in front of the other until I reached the small landing at the top, and the door swung open.

My breath stuck in my lungs at the sight of him. His dark eyes studied me like I might not be real, and I felt a little like that. What was I doing here? How was it possible this gorgeous man wanted me, when he shouldn't?

I wasn't able to move from my spot on the landing, but when Greg curled his hands around my waist and walked me into the room, my body followed him willingly, and his gaze never left mine.

His room was dim. Deep blue paint on the walls, dark furniture, and the overcast light from outside didn't seem to breach the two windows on either side of his enormous, four-post bed.

Oh, God. There it was. *The bed.*

SEVEN

IT WASN'T THE FIRST TIME I'D SEEN HIS BED. I'D BEEN IN GREG'S room a few times over the years. During the Lowe's family Christmas party, we'd put our coats on it. But I looked at the gold textured duvet now with new eyes.

He made his bed perfectly. There weren't piles of shirts or dirty socks on the floor, or empty Mountain Dew cans on the bedside table like Preston's room downstairs. This was the room of a man—a precise adult—and it wasn't surprising. I'd known since the beginning how Dr. Lowe liked everything in its place. He lined the cooking utensils up in the drawers in the kitchen like they were his surgical instruments.

The room smelled like him.

Greg's grip on my hips softened, and his hands slid up my back, so slowly it felt like he was going one vertebrae of my spine at a time. Heat rose along with his hands, and goosebumps pebbled across my thighs.

He didn't kiss me. Instead, he hovered, his breath rolling over my lips as his eyes searched every inch of my face. I hungered for his mouth on mine but felt strangely too shy to take what I wanted. So, I waited, balancing on the edge for him to move. To close the last inch of space between us and claim me.

Please, a seductive voice in my mind whined. *What are you waiting for?*

Could he read my thoughts through my eyes? "If I kiss you," he said, "that's it. I don't think I'll be able to stop."

I exhaled softly and stared at his lips. I was here, ready. Desperate. "Then, kiss me."

He moved fast, sealing his mouth over mine and stealing all the air from the room.

The kiss was explosive. Heat flared from where his lips met mine, spreading outward like wildfire, engulfing me. I cased his neck with my hands, pretending to steady him when I was really stabilizing myself. Everything went weak inside me. My bones turned to jelly.

I was cold when he peeled the tank top up over my head and dropped it to the floor, but then his hands were on me, his fingertips tracing the lines of my bra. My hands found their home back on his neck, and I could feel his hurried pulse beneath my palms. The thin fabric of my delicate bra was all that stood in his way, but he seemed to enjoy touching me like this. Skirting the edge before diving in.

His soft tongue slid into my mouth and caressed, and instinctively, my hand grabbed a fistful of hair at the base of his skull. I wasn't going to be able to stand much longer if he kept kissing me like that. I pulsed with need.

Fingertips worked the clasp of my bra, and it popped loose, sliding down to catch on my elbows. I tossed it aside and reached for the hem of his shirt, but he beat me to it. Up the cotton t-shirt went, and then it was cast off, bringing his solid form into view. I wasn't prepared for how good he looked. Greg was all hard muscle twisted over his frame, a patch of hair covering his chest and arrowing down to disappear beneath his jeans.

I swallowed hard when he pressed our warm, naked skin together. If it was supposed to be wrong, why the hell did it feel right?

Somehow, between our passionate, greedy kisses and wandering hands, I found myself backed up to the bed, where the duvet touched the backs of my thighs below my shorts. His hands cupped my breasts and pushed them together, making it easier for him to run his lips and tongue from one aching nipple to the other, and back again.

Shivers shook my shoulders. I skimmed my hand over the waistband of his jeans, lingering at the button. Just enough to threaten what I was thinking about doing. How much further I was willing to go.

It was challenging undoing the button at the top of his jeans, but he held still and let me. I clawed my unsteady fingers at his zipper, and then shoved the pants down over his hips.

For a split second, I marveled at how soft his underwear was. Rich, black fabric covered him, but did nothing to hide his dick straining beneath. He gave a quiet hiss of pleasure as I smoothed my palm over the long, thick length of him. Jesus, he was big.

I was excited, but also nervous. Would I be able to give him as much pleasure as he had given me? I squeezed, stroking up and down, and satisfaction burned on his handsome face. I didn't get more than a few pumps before he attacked my shorts, wrenching them down my legs.

He stepped out of his jeans as he lifted me up, seating me on the edge of the high bed, and my shorts were a puddle left on the floor.

The tension between us grew infinitely greater and more serious. We were both down to just our underwear. My heart threatened to beat out of my chest, but I didn't care. All I needed was his mouth fused to me, his bare skin touching mine.

With a light shove, he pushed me down on my back, and the comforter felt cool against my heated skin. He stepped between my legs and followed me down, trailing kisses over my throat and down between my breasts. All while he ground his lower body against mine, and sparks of pleasure roared from the contact.

Desire hazed the room.

It took control of me and sent my hands roaming over his skin. His back was strong, and I loved skimming the muscles and the hollow of his spine. He was so fucking powerful. So different from anything I'd had.

It seemed like Greg wasn't sure what to do next. Not that he was hesitant, but more like he wanted to do everything all at once. He glided the length of his erection over the damp crotch of my panties, and I arched, bucking up into him.

He straightened, smoothing his hands down my curves until they came to a stop on the sides of my panties. His gaze traveled the length of my body, lingering on my exposed breasts before settling back on my eyes. The connection between us was sharp and taut.

"Stop me," he said, making it clear this was my last chance.

I bit down on my bottom lip and gave the tiniest shake of my head.

"Fuck." He whispered it as he began to drag the panties down and nuzzled his face into the cradle of my lap.

"Oh my God." I gripped his broad shoulders. His lips followed the descent of my underwear, kissing each new spot of my flesh he revealed.

I was going to explode. Burst into a million pieces and flutter to the ground like burnt confetti. His mouth inched along the top of my slit, and something like panic gurgled in my system. I wasn't supposed to do this, but dear God, how I craved the slippery slide of his tongue, desperate for him to go lower.

I moaned and bowed off the bed as I got my wish. The tip of his tongue brushed over me. Cautious. Curious. My reaction must have left no doubt in his mind what I wanted, because his second pass wasn't hesitant. The full sensation of his tongue against my clit tore a gasp from my lungs.

He looked amazing as he hunched over me and delivered his wicked, intimate kiss. Pleasure was so sharp and overwhelming, it made me unable to do anything but stay there and take it. It had never felt like this before. Was this how it was supposed to be?

Preston had been the only guy to go down on me. He'd done it a few times, usually when I wasn't turned on enough to have sex, and although he'd never said it, his attitude always left me feeling like he was doing me a big favor. So, really neither of us liked it all that much.

Greg didn't act like what he was doing was a favor. I kneaded his shoulders as I shook and watched him through my barely-open eyes. His were closed, but his expression made it seem he was enjoying it almost as much as I was.

His tongue was so soft. It caressed and stroked, sending my heart rate into overdrive. I grew lightheaded from how hard I was breathing and the waves of heat that traveled up my body. Pinpricks of bliss crept over my skin.

A low, deep groan came from him. A bolt of white-hot pleasure seized me as his lips closed and sucked. My hands flew from him to go to my sides, and my fists tightened until my nails dug into my palms. The stroke of his tongue was insanity. He used his lips, his tongue, and even his teeth—just a faint hint—to tease, and torment, and please.

I swallowed huge gulps of air, struggling to keep up with him. His tongue lashed at my clit, and he made every muscle in me shake. I was going to rattle apart. The sight of his mouth working over me was so sexy, I moaned.

"The noises you make," he whispered, "they're driving me crazy."

His statement earned him another whimper.

Heat crawled over my skin as I grew closer to satisfaction. His fluttering tongue was building me into a frenzy. I threaded my hands through my hair and shut my eyes tight, squeezing back the urge to let go. If I did, I worried I'd be loud.

My challenge increased dramatically when his mouth paused, and he stirred two fingertips over my clit. I opened my eyes and peered at him, which was a huge mistake. His raw, hungry expression made another moan fall from my lips.

The fingertips drifted down, and one began to press inside me. My mouth rounded into a silent "oh" as he slid deeper. Just one thick finger intruding, but my body threatened to break apart.

I clutched at the comforter beneath my body—like having a physical handle on something would help. The sensation was too intense. I wanted to control it, but I'd have better luck holding back the waves of the ocean. He had his mouth on me, and part of him was inside my body.

Claiming me. It made me want more. I shouldn't, but I wanted all of him.

This thought was my undoing.

"Shit," I groaned, locking up as the orgasm surged. Heat flooded through my veins, searing my nerves. I fell into a million pieces while pleasure roared up and down my body, leaving me cold and flushed as it subsided.

I blinked my sluggish eyes, staring up at the ceiling as the blood swooshing in my ears began to slow. My mouth was no longer attached to my brain, and the words stumbled out of me.

"I didn't know it could feel like that."

Embarrassment screwed my eyes shut tight. Why the hell had I just said that out loud? There wasn't anywhere to hide, but with my eyes closed, I could pretend he wasn't staring at me.

He leaned over, and his kiss began at my collarbone, skimming up. Our mouths fused, and when our lips and chests were pressed tight together, there wasn't room to feel anything else but him.

I hooked my legs around his waist, locking my ankles together behind his back, and sank deeper into our kiss. It was full of fire.

"Do you want to stop?" His voice was strained with need. "Because I want something I shouldn't." Our foreheads pressed together. "It's all I want whenever you're around."

My mouth fell open on an audible gasp. How was I supposed to react to that? It made my already racing pulse leap faster. All I could see were his dark, gorgeous eyes.

A warning sliced through my mind, sharp and white-hot, but I shoved it aside. I'd always done the right thing. I'd been the selfless one in the relationship with Preston. For once, I was going to do what I wanted, and what I wanted was Greg.

"I was thinking about the same thing when I just . . ."

His eyes went heavy. "When you came?"

We were too close for him to see it, but with our foreheads together, he had to feel my subtle nod. It sounded like I punched air from his lungs.

It set him into motion. The tip of his tongue skimmed down the slope of my breast, keeping contact even as my chest rose and fell with my deep swallows of breath. I was a live wire beneath him, and I swiveled my hips, rubbing my arousal against his. Our groans came out in the same pitch, low and soaked with desire.

"Cassidy." He whispered it at the base of my neck. "I want to feel you all around me, even if it's just for a few seconds. Is that okay?"

Oh, God. The muscles deep in my belly clenched in response, so tight it was almost painful. Lust wrung the word from my lips. "Yes."

He took the heat of his body away as he straightened, leaned over to the side, and tugged open a drawer on the nightstand. Were his hands shaking? No, I had to have imagined it. He dealt with life and death situations every day on his operating table and had a steady hand there. There was no way fooling around with me could affect him like that.

I lifted my head to gaze at him as he pushed down his underwear, and I pressed my lips together to stifle the whimper. His dick was long and thick, so hard it had a slight upward curve to it. I stared while he tore open the condom, and as he rolled it on, tension tightened in me until I was one compact cord, too twisted to move.

His eyes were hungry and full of longing.

"Have you thought about this?" I asked abruptly. No idea where the question came from.

He slowed. His expression clouded with hesitation, or maybe shame, and then disappeared.

"All the time." His measured gaze worked along the length of my bare body, lingering over my nakedness. I felt flushed and breathless. "Jesus, Cassidy," he continued. "After that day I saw you and Preston on the lounge chair . . . I couldn't stop thinking about you."

I closed my eyes as my heart skipped. His admission seared into my center, and desire reached fever pitch.

He pressed the fingertips of one hand to my clit, shooting sparks of pleasure down my quivering legs, and used his other hand to stroke himself. His hooded gaze traveled to where he was touching me, and he looked mesmerized.

"What about you?" His tone was tight. Desperate to know, but trying to hide it. His fingers teased my most sensitive spot, causing me to gasp and squirm. "Did you think about this?"

I gripped the comforter at my sides and nodded vigorously. It was hard to say it out loud, and what he was doing made it impossible to speak, anyway. Need choked in my throat as a soft, sticky lump.

His expression was relief at first, pleased he wasn't the only one between us who had these wrong fantasies. His face then heated with pleasure, and a finger speared into me as a reward.

"Tell me," he pleaded. "Tell me what you thought about."

I bowed my back, clenching at his invasion and loving it at the same time. How was I supposed to tell him? How was I going to think about anything but the way his finger pulsed in and out, stretching and preparing me?

I threaded my hands through my hair and shut my eyes tightly. "This," I breathed. "Every night since we kissed." A second finger joined the first and I moaned, clenching fistfuls of my hair. "Oh, God, every night."

His sigh was heavy. "Did you touch yourself?"

"Yes." I moved my hips to match his lazy tempo.

His expression was indescribable. If I'd had to label it, I'd have said he looked fucking thrilled. "Did you get off thinking about me?"

My desperation burned away any shame. I was suddenly eager to say it, hissing it out. "*Yes.*"

He had me writhing on his bed, my toes curled around the edge of the bed frame. His powerful body stood between my bent knees, his fingers fucking me exactly how I'd spent the last nine days fantasizing he would.

"You don't know what you're doing to me," he whispered, yet it sounded like he was thinking out loud. Saying it more to himself than to me. "No fucking clue how much I want this, even when I shouldn't." His fingers pumped deeper and faster. "But you want it too?"

"Yes." I was losing my grip on any sense of consequence.

His fingers retreated, and he slicked them over his cock, wetting it with my own arousal. It was erotic watching his beautiful hand work himself over. And then he slid his forearms under me, his hands on my thighs, and jerked me closer to the edge of the bed.

My heart stopped, but when the hard tip of him brushed against me, it restarted in overdrive. I hooked my quivering legs around his warm hips. He leaned over, setting a hand on the mattress beside my head as he steadied himself with his other.

"I'm not supposed to," he murmured, delivering a brutal kiss. "Just for a second. Just so I know what it would feel like with you."

He was right at my entrance and began to push, easing inside. I locked my legs around him so tightly, his hipbones dug into the insides of my thighs. Greg's eyes were as dark as coffee, and the color deepened as he advanced. He watched intently, studying every breath I swallowed as he claimed me.

Oh, shit, the uncomfortable stretch felt good. A delicious shiver tore through my body. I reached up a hand to cup the side of his face and held on to him, even as my lips rounded into a silent moan.

"Fuck," he uttered so quietly, it was a ghost of a word.

His slow push kept going. Deeper, wider, harder. I whimpered as it felt even better and more uncomfortable. I'd only been with one other person before, and even though Greg had done his best to prepare me, it still was a tight fit.

I'd never felt so full.

But it wasn't the only new experience. Being with Preston had been lonely. During sex, we'd been two people playing roles, him only there for himself. My enjoyment wasn't a priority—only a bonus to him. I'd felt disconnected all the times we were the most physically connected.

But Greg was present in this moment with me.

Right as I reached the edge of him being too much to take inside, his body was snug against mine, and another tremor rippled along my muscles. He was buried deep, possessing me, and it felt amazing. Not only physically, either.

But just as soon as he'd given it to me, he began to take it away. His hips drew back, easing out and pulling the sensations with him, leaving me feeling empty. *No*, my mind and body screamed together. I clutched at the landscape of his chest, trying to get him to stay.

He pulled out completely, and panic swept me away like a rogue wave. "Again," I gasped.

The single word wracked his body with a visible shudder. He repeated my command, tinged with hope. "Again?"

"Oh, shit, Greg," I whined. "*Again.*"

EIGHT

UPON HEARING HIS NAME FROM MY LIPS, GREG'S FACE softened. He lowered until our lips touched and moved his mouth against mine, wanting that connection while he gave me the other I'd demanded.

"Oh," I moaned into his mouth as his hips flexed into me.

The first slide into my body had been amazing, but this second one put it to shame. Satisfaction fired all along my system, lighting me up with fireworks. He pulled his mouth away from mine, dragging it across my cheek, and groaned into the shell of my ear. The sound was the sexiest thing I'd ever heard.

His withdraw started sooner this time, and the same panic took over. He was still inside me when I cried out, "Again."

He grunted like I was killing him, but he loved it. "I shouldn't." It was a hollow statement, because he pushed inside me, and quicker this time too. "*We* shouldn't." His uneven breath fell in the crook of my neck as his body continued to move. "Doing this is wrong—"

I grasped his shoulders, like I could keep him right there. "It feels too good to be wrong."

Which should have proved that sleeping with him was, in fact, very wrong. Usually, the enjoyable things were bad. Like chocolate cake and buying expensive shoes you didn't need.

My confession drilled into him and flipped a switch. The muscles on his back tensed before he shifted, rising enough so he could stare down at me. His eyes were full of primal need. It was then he actually began to fuck me.

His first full thrust stole my breath. The second was hard enough it made my breasts bounce and drew his attention. He clamped his hands on them, holding firmly as he drove into me, his thumbs brushing over my peaked nipples.

I arched off the mattress, pushing myself into his hands, wriggling against his hips beating against mine. Gone was the unsure girl I'd been before. Beneath Greg, the sexual woman I'd always wanted to be came alive.

He looked stunning as the fading light from outside played across his chest, his expression intense and focused. I didn't bother holding back the whimpers and sounds of enjoyment, and he didn't either. He grunted and sighed as he rutted into me, both taking and giving pleasure.

"You're gorgeous," he uttered between hurried breaths. His gaze wandered appreciatively over my breasts and moved up to settle on my lips. "You're so fucking young and gorgeous."

The caress of his hands was madness. Fire licked at me with his touch, sensitizing my skin. And as his pace increased, so did the feeling of another orgasm. Was it possible? I'd never come from sex before, but Greg was obviously experienced. He'd mastered my body more in one short afternoon than Preston had done in three years.

He shifted so he was standing upright, locked a hand on each of my hips, and drove into me. The new angle threatened to make my eyes roll back in my head, and I gasped with satisfaction.

His lips turned up at the corner in an impish smile, and I could read the question reflected in his eyes. *"That's the spot, huh?"*

Moans drifted from me, too loud to contain, and the smile on his face faded somewhat. I was loud. Too loud. If someone decided to come up from the basement, they might hear us. He slowed his tempo, but I was greedy and frantic.

"I can be quiet," I said, "but, please don't stop."

He looked conflicted. "I love the little sounds you make, but—"

Only I wasn't making little sounds right now. He coursed a hand slowly up over the curve of my arm, along my shoulder, and up to cup the side of my face. It was sweet and sensual, and I turned into it, pressing my lips against the center of his palm in a kiss.

I'd done it without thought, but it sent an unintended signal to Greg. His hand molded to my face, covering my mouth. When he resumed his driving rhythm, I didn't mind the hand one bit. If anything, it only turned me on more.

"You want to know the first time I thought about you like this?" he asked quietly. His dick plunged and retreated endlessly, hitting a spot that made the rest of the world fade away. "When he took you to prom. The green dress you wore . . . You looked ten years older. After you left, I thought about all sorts of things. Bad things."

Pressure was building, bubbling under a lid, and dangerously close to release. I wanted to ask him about these thoughts, but his hand was over my lips, and I wasn't sure I'd be able to find my voice, either. My expression must have made it clear, because he kept going.

"I was jealous of him." Greg's eyes were hesitant. This was something he was nervous to reveal. "I was so fucking jealous. I knew after the dance was over, he was the one who got to kiss you. Touch you. Put his hands up your skirt and find out if you were wearing anything underneath it or not."

Whoa.

My moan bled through his fingers, and my head spun with even more lust.

"Were you?" His tone was playful and seductive.

I nodded underneath his hand. I'd worn a pair of black panties that were silk in the front and delicate lace in the back.

He strived to match the tone, but it faltered a little. He both did and didn't want to know. "Did he fuck you in that dress?"

I slowly shook my head, keeping my eyes glued to his. Preston and I had barely messed around that night. We'd gone to an afterparty at Colin's house, and Preston had so much to drink, he couldn't keep it up later when I attempted to go down on him. So, no. Preston hadn't fucked me in my prom dress.

"I would have." Greg's voice oozed. "I'd have bent you over a table, pulled up that skirt, and fucked you so hard, your legs would shake." His smile was sinister. "Just like they are right now, Cassidy."

Even muffled under his palm, my cry was loud and full of pleasure. I clenched around him, and he exhaled loudly, thick with enjoyment. I put one hand over his on my mouth, trying to silence myself, and wrapped the other hand around his wrist.

Each pump of his body into mine primed me for detonation, and as I closed in on my explosion, Greg must have sensed it. He pulled out abruptly, stepping away from the edge of the bed.

"Where—" I started, wanting to ask him where he was going, but he pointed to the center of the bed.

"On your hands and knees." He said it lightly, but it was a demand full of weight and urgency, and I found myself scrambling on top of the duvet. He climbed up behind me, steering my hips and positioning me how he wanted us to be.

The waiting for him to fill me again lasted a decade, and I sighed with relief when he was there, nudging his way between my legs. I swallowed thickly as he pushed all the way in. Holy hell, he felt even bigger this way. I stared down at my hands splayed open on the comforter and let him rock his hips into me.

Greg pushed my hair out of his way, so his hands could trace up and down my spine. I arched like a cat as he stroked me, never wanting this to stop. I could listen to his soft sighs of pleasure and the sharp slap of skin meeting skin forever.

But then his strong hand was on my shoulder, pulling me up off my hands, and my eyes went wide. A large mirror hung over the dresser on the other side of the room, and in it, I could see Greg's hands as they slid over my naked body. I watched as they caressed over my breasts, down the curve of my narrow waist, and onto the flare of my hips.

Over my shoulder, he watched us in the mirror too. I couldn't breathe, and I couldn't look away.

His thrusts were rigorous, pounding into my body, and when I threatened to fall, I latched a hand on the post to steady myself. It only made us look more erotic. My small, pink nipples jutted up and out, and at the crevice of my thighs, we could see the movement of his cock disappearing inside me.

I was slick between my legs, and faint sweat clung to my skin. It was the same for him. It beaded at his forehead and glossed his face. We looked so good together. I tightened my hold on the smooth post of dark wood, bracing myself so hard, my muscles strained.

My pulse thundered as he slipped one hand down, his fingertips searching my slit. He strummed there, making me gasp.

"Shit," I cried out, arching back so my head rested on his collarbone. Even with my head tipped back, I watched the mirror through my half-lidded eyes. How could I not? His powerful body behind mine, fucking me into oblivion, was a sight to behold. I'd never forget it as long as I lived.

"I love it," he murmured. "Seeing this and feeling you wrapped around me. Whatever happens, you were worth it."

NINE

I CLOSED MY EYES AS UNEXPECTED TEARS SPRANG INTO THEM.
How cruel was the world to us, to give Greg and me this perfect experience, and know we couldn't have it ever again? I
almost wished we hadn't acted on our desires. Now I'd always know what I was missing.

"I'm close," he said as a warning. "Are you close?"

Because my pleasure mattered to him, and my heart
twisted further. I didn't want to reach the finish because then
this would be over, but . . . "Yeah."

He double-downed his effort, determined to get me
there. His warm lips sucked on my neck as his fingers moved
furiously over my clit, and his pounding thrusts seemed to
go deeper.

"Oh," I cried. It rolled from me in unstoppable waves.
"Oh, oh, *oh!*"

"*Yes.*" His body hardened like stone, and then we both
broke apart, him only seconds behind me. Ecstasy ripped a
hole in my belly and poured hot pleasure in its place. I jerked
and contracted with each shock, and inside I felt the rhyth-
mic pulses of his climax.

Bliss sped through my veins, temporarily sweeping away
judgement, leaving only us in this moment together. He hung

onto me as I clung to the bedpost, both of our knees dug into the bed and our bodies shaking.

It seemed like as long as we remained like this, gravity couldn't touch us, and we lingered even as the orgasms faded to nothing. I turned my head toward his, and he slanted his lips over mine, kissing me with so much tenderness and care, it would have made me tremble if I wasn't already.

Eventually, we parted. I fell into a heap on the bed, endured another long, slow kiss from this impossibly beautiful man who could never be mine. He left me only to remove the condom, then returned to the bed, wrapping his arm around me like it was the most natural thing.

"This is weird, right?" I whispered. Cuddling. But I needed it.

"If it is, I don't care." He used a fingertip to trace my hairline, pushing a lock of hair back from my flushed face, giving me a serious look. "It's what I want to do."

God, he made me melt. I curled in closer, pressing my sweat-damp skin against his. When I was burrowed in his arms, one leg hooked over his, his fingers swept absentmindedly up and down my back, tracing faint patterns.

"Stay," he said.

A sliver of panic ran through me. "Overnight?" Because there was no way in a million years I could, no matter how much the idea excited me.

He skewed his face, maybe realizing how impractical the request was. "Just for a little while."

I took no convincing. I was tired, and warm, and happy right where I was. I let out a deep breath. "Yes."

His smile was wide and bright.

I blinked my blurry eyes and shifted before I realized where I was. Greg's arm was cast over my waist, holding me, even when we'd both fallen asleep. I couldn't tell what time it was. The sun was still up, at least enough to generate some light, but the room was dark and cave-like.

When I wiggled out from under his arm, Greg stirred, but didn't wake. He rolled onto his back and sighed, oblivious. I sat up and stared at the naked man, crossing my arms over my chest to hold in my warmth. I needed clothes.

More importantly, I needed to get out of this bed, out of this house, and down the street to my car. The dark clouds from before had moved in, and although it wasn't raining yet, it was going to start any minute. Thunder boomed and shook the pane of glass in the balcony door, like the universe was reminding me how to escape.

Except, I didn't want to.

It was impossible, but I forced myself to slip off the bed and slowly tug on my clothes, wondering the whole time what I was going to do. Should I wake him up? I glanced at the black clouds outside and back to the man on the bed. I didn't have time to enjoy how good he looked like that. He seemed younger when he slept, and he looked more handsome.

I was on borrowed time with the storm. I had to go.

Because not only would saying goodbye take too much time, I'd do anything to avoid it. I didn't want him to see me as I walked away and was left gutted. This afternoon might have been wrong, but it wasn't a mistake, and if he woke up with regret in his eyes, I couldn't bear to see it. It was better to slip away and not ruin what we had.

The door was silent as I pulled it open, and I watched through the glass as I closed it carefully behind me, making sure Greg didn't hear. I rationalized my escape as I hurried down the staircase. He worked crazy hours at the hospital. Didn't he deserve to get some sleep?

A fat raindrop landed on the part in my hair and rolled forward down my face as I scrambled along the wooded lawn. I wiped it away with a shaky hand. By the time my flip-flops hit the sidewalk, it was pouring. Cold sheets of rain soaked my tank top, my hair, and squished between my bare toes.

I was drenched when I crawled into the driver's seat of my car and shoved the keys in the ignition. Rain drilled against the windows, loud and angry. The car interior was muggy and confining, trapping me inside, where I couldn't run from my thoughts any longer.

Oh, my God.

What the hell had I just done?

TEN

MY BEST FRIEND LILITH WAS FIVE YEARS OLDER THAN I WAS.
She had sleek, iron-straight hair the color of caramel that
hung halfway down her back, and she stood almost six feet
tall when she was in heels, which she wore every chance she
got. She had to be the only woman on earth who slipped into
stilettos after a grueling day of work.

She couldn't wear them at the animal hospital.
Sometimes she had to chase an escaped bunny around the
exam room or needed good footing when an overly excited mastiff wanted to jump up and say hello. Her four-inch
heels weren't going to cut it against a dog that weighed more
than she did.

I'd become friends with the veterinary assistant on the
first day of my summer internship when we'd walked into an
exam room together, and the pet owner demanded we look
at her 'duck.'

"He refuses to swim," the woman whined.

Bless Lilith's heart—she gently let the owner know her
chicken, not duck, was in excellent health, and Lilith said it
in a way to minimize the woman's total embarrassment. It
wasn't until the owner was gone that we died with laughter.

"It's like she'd never seen a cock before," Lilith teased.

She always turned the conversation sexual, and I sort of loved that about her. It meant I could talk to her about sex stuff. She'd been on me all summer about the Preston situation, telling me every day to dump his selfish ass.

"I did it," I said this morning, using a flat mop to clean the exam room floor. "I called him, and we talked . . . I guess. He definitely got the message that we're over."

My friend grinned her approval. "Finally. How'd he take it?"

"He acted like it wasn't a big deal." I shrugged. "Like he thinks I'm going to come crawling back to him within a week."

"Please." She rolled her eyes as she flipped the sign on the door to let the rest of the staff know the room was clean and ready for use. "I can't wait for you to hook up with someone with actual dick game."

My hesitation was short, but just a fraction too long, and more than enough time for my new friend to catch on. Her pretty blue eyes widened.

"Cassidy," she accused.

I feigned innocence. "What?"

She hustled me across the hall and behind the stacks of prescription dog food, so we were out of earshot of anyone in the waiting area. Her voice fell to an urgent but excited hush. "Already?" Her smile was evil . . . and a little proud. "Who was he? Was it good? Shit, tell me everything."

It wasn't a trust issue that made me cautious. I knew Lilith would keep my secret. We'd had plenty of in-depth conversations after the animal hospital closed for the day, talking about boys and sex while we'd cleaned cages and done laundry. But this secret was huge, and worse—Lilith knew Dr. Lowe. After college, she'd moved into the converted pool house behind her parents' home, which was in the same wealthy neighborhood, just up the street from the Lowes.

"I'm waiting," she said playfully, although sort of serious.

I needed to tell someone. The amazing afternoon spent with Greg had planted feelings inside me that grew too big to contain. My voice dipped low, and she leaned over to hear me. "It was Preston's dad."

There was no reaction from her, other than a set of slow blinks, like she couldn't interpret the information.

"Did you just say what I think you did?" she whispered. "Dr. Lowe?"

I pressed my lips together and nodded.

An enormous, incredulous smile dawned on her face. "Holy Mother of God. How? Where? I have *all* the questions."

Too bad I didn't have good answers. I was still fuzzy on how it had happened. In fact, everything was fuzzy and complicated after Greg and I kissed the first time. "Uh," I said, searching for something to say. "I don't know. I gave him a hug goodbye, and it just turned into . . . more."

"Where was Preston?"

My face heated with shame. "That time? He'd left for work."

"*What?*" Her word was so sharp, surely someone in the waiting area heard her. She moved in until I was trapped in the corner. "How many times have you slept with him?"

"No, we didn't have sex the first time." It had been tame enough to be considered PG-13, although nothing about it felt tame. "Yesterday, Preston was still downstairs, playing video games with his friends, when Greg and I—"

"Greg," she repeated. "Holy fucking shit, Cassidy." She gazed at me in awe, as if I were a brand-new person, and then she grinned like a fool. "How was it?"

"It?" I played dumb.

She shot me a pointed look. "The sex."

Now my face burned a thousand degrees. "It was . . ." *Unbelievable. Magnificent.* "Um, great."

She gave a half-laugh, and her expression said she didn't believe me. "Just great?"

I scowled. "It was fucking amazing, okay? But . . . I can't believe I did that."

"Dumped your boyfriend and banged his dad right after? Yeah, me neither." Her amusement seemed to have no limits. "You're a bad girl, Cassidy. I never would have guessed."

ELEVEN

After I'd ransacked my room, the laundry, and my car, I sat on the edge of my bed and resigned myself to the fact my favorite hoodie, the Vanderbilt one I'd bought in the university store and had worn almost every night the first year of school, was gone. How the hell had I lost it?

My attention was normally great, but it'd been slipping since the afternoon I'd gone over to Preston's house to end things and wound up kissing his father. The last two days had been much worse. Since sleeping with Greg, he was all I could think about. Lilith wasn't helping. She'd insisted we get dinner together after work, mostly so I could tell her every detail.

Describing the memory to her made it more intense, but she'd been great about not judging me. A big part of that was probably her dislike for Preston.

I couldn't remember the last time I'd worn the hoodie. I hadn't been cold in weeks—all I needed to do was think about Greg, and problem solved. Heat flushed along my body, running down my center, leading straight between my legs—

Oh, no.

I groaned as I realized where my favorite sweatshirt was. I'd spilled a glass of water on my arm last time I'd worn it, and hung the black and gold hoodie up to dry on a hook on the back of the bathroom door.

Not my bathroom, but Preston's.

I could cut my losses, or reach out to my ex, but neither of those options excited me as much as the one that popped into my mind. I scooped up my phone, scrolled through my contacts to Dr. Lowe, and tapped out the message before I had time to think about what a terrible idea it was.

> Cassidy: Hey, it's Cassidy. Sorry to bother you, but I left my hoodie hanging on the door of Preston's bathroom. Can I come by to get it?

> Cassidy: Maybe some time when he's not there?

I threw the phone down like it was the devil. The feeling in the pit of my stomach was similar to the one I got when I'd called Preston for the first time, back when we were in high school, only this feeling now was more intense. My gut twisted in a knot. My request was dangerous, and it was hard to breathe while I waited for a response.

Time ticked by, one agonizing second after another.

Was he in surgery? Had he read the text and wasn't sure how to respond? Or was he upset I'd left without saying goodbye? I put my fingertips over my lips and frowned. I shouldn't have texted him.

I nearly leapt out of my skin when the phone chimed.

> Dr. Lowe: He's at work if you want to
> swing by now.

I read the text a million times, searching and hoping for hidden meaning, but it wasn't there. 'Swing by' implied quick—he wasn't asking me to stay. And why would he? I'd run away last time like a coward.

At least he didn't say he'd leave the door unlocked for me, because that would have been a clear sign he didn't want to see me.

I was such a jittery mess on the drive over, I didn't realize I hadn't turned on the radio until I entered Greg's subdivision. I'd driven most of the way there in silence, running different scenarios in my head of what was going to happen when I got to his house.

It was dusk when I parked in the driveway, and I followed the brick path up the front step, staring at the glowing button of the doorbell. It felt like the damn thing was mocking me. If I rang it, seeing Greg face to face would be unavoidable.

Wasn't that what I wanted?

What I *craved*?

I stabbed the button with a finger and listened to the dull chime ring out inside the house. The decorative glass insert of the front door was made of embossed panels, so I could only see a figure approach, but not his face.

The lock slid with a click, and the door swung open.

Greg wore jeans, a blue t-shirt that clung to his perfect form, and an unreadable expression. My heart tripped over itself at the sight of him. Memories of his hands on me, his body sliding inside mine, made my knees weak.

"Hey," I breathed.

"Hey." He pulled the door open wider and stepped back, ushering me in. I took two hesitant steps inside, and before I could say anything, he swung the door shut and moved toward the kitchen, abandoning me. "I brought your sweatshirt up for you. It's on the counter."

Oh.

I slinked after him, my head hung in shame. Sure enough, my hoodie sat folded neatly on the kitchen island, right in the same spot he'd leaned me over two days ago and put his hand down my shorts. I could still feel his fingers inside my panties, working to make me come.

He appeared unfazed by my arrival. He moved around to the other side of the island, putting a physical barrier between us, and set his hands on the polished countertop. His expression was still impossible to interpret. He didn't look mad, but he didn't look happy, either. If anything, he looked like he was trying very hard to hide whatever he was thinking, and it took all of his focus to be successful.

My gaze fell from him, down to the black sweatshirt waiting for me to collect it and go. "Are you mad at me?"

My voice had been small, but his was light. "For what? Leaving without saying goodbye the other day?"

His tone wasn't accusatory, but the words were. I pinched my face together with discomfort. "I'm sorry. It was about to start storming outside, and you looked so peaceful sleeping, I didn't want to wake you."

"I would have appreciated it," he said softly, "if you had."

My brain threatened to disconnect. It was such an adult thing to say, and he'd delivered it straightforward. I wasn't used to actually talking about stuff with guys, and it was yet another thing to make me feel inexperienced around him. Communication was foreign.

But if he wanted to be honest, I was willing to try the same. "I didn't wake you up because I was scared," I announced. "I didn't know how to say goodbye to you after we . . . and I didn't want to."

His posture straightened, and finally an emotion I could read splashed on his expression. Surprise.

"I'm sorry," I said again.

"When I woke up and you were gone, I didn't know what to think. I worried maybe you were freaking out."

Guilt coasted through me. I hadn't meant to hurt him. "No." I took a step closer, wanting him near. "That came later." I rounded the island, so it was no longer between us, and stared up at him. "I don't regret what happened. I mean, I know I should, but I just don't." I pressed my lips together and drew in a breath through my nose, struggling to find the courage to ask. "Do you?"

A crease developed on his forehead. He looked conflicted, and my heart sank to my toes. His hesitation was torture.

"No, I don't regret it," he said finally, "but that makes me the worst father in the world, right? A terrible person, at least."

"No—"

"Yes, it does. Especially when I want to do it again."

Anxiety released its hold on my shoulders, and I sagged against the counter. His eyes heated. The air between us shifted and stretched, growing from tension into something else, which tasted a lot like anticipation. I'd never been more aware of him, or the idea that we were alone in his house.

"But we can't do it again," I said, my words tight and unsteady.

Jesus, I couldn't believe I'd just said it. I hadn't meant it one bit—I'd issued this as a challenge. Would he pick up my wistful tone? Did he get what I was doing?

"No," he said, shifting on his feet so he was facing me. "Absolutely not." The corner of his sexy mouth curled up into a hint of a smile. "Hey, before I forget. As long as you're here, maybe we should go to my room and get you naked."

My mouth dropped open, and before I could say a word, his hands wrapped around my waist and hauled me against his chest. His mouth lowered to mine, and when our lips connected, I arched up into his kiss.

We moved together without breaking the contact, turning and stumbling into the side of the cabinets on our hurried quest toward his room, only stopping to chuckle at our clumsiness. His hands slid beneath the hem of my t-shirt and were warm on my back. The feel of his fingertips skimming up my bare skin was like nothing else. It sent hot shivers down my backbone.

"I thought I might not see you again," he mumbled against the side of my mouth.

"I'm sure we'd run into each other somewhere."

He stopped moving and locked his arms, caging me inside. "I meant like this. And I didn't like that idea. Actually, I fucking hated it."

Butterflies fluttered in my belly. "Really?" I whispered.

He was so sure, so confident. "I'm tired of telling myself I don't want this. Yeah, you're supposed to be off-limits, but that doesn't stop me from thinking about you all the damn time." His eyes sharpened, making it impossible to look away. "I can't stop thinking about the things I'd like to do to you, or things you'd do to me, or the way we looked together in my mirror."

"Oh," I sighed, and my eyes lidded with desire.

He dipped his head and traced a line up the curve of my neck with the tip of his tongue. Shit, I was going to burst into flames. I was drunk off him in seconds.

"Tell me," I asked eagerly, as he sucked on a sensitive spot below my ear, "what you want to do to me."

"You want to hear about my fantasies, Cassidy? Because there are a lot, and they are very, *very* bad."

Just like me.

I nearly said it out loud, but I'd turned to liquid under his mouth. I couldn't catch my breath as I swallowed a gulp, so I nodded enthusiastically. "Tell me. I bet I want to do them all."

He made a sound like I'd stroked a hand over his erection, even though I hadn't yet, and his face took a dark, sexual cast. It was primal and gorgeous.

Greg's mouth slammed into mine, his tongue pushing past my lips and invading. This kiss wasn't like the others. It was blistering, and punishing, and rewarding. He shoved a hand up my shirt and gripped my bra-covered breast, all while his mouth fucked mine.

We'd stopped in the living room, halfway to his bedroom, and we weren't going to make it. I wanted him here, and now, and he seemed to have the same desire. I fumbled my fingers over the snap of my shorts, my urgency making them almost useless—

A loud, mechanical rumble came from behind the door to the garage.

We froze, and the sensation was like a bucket of frigid water doused us. *Oh, no.* That sound only meant one thing.

Preston was home.

TWELVE

I WAS MOVING BEFORE I REALIZED IT. GREG HURRIED ME toward the kitchen, dragging me along on my sluggish, panicked legs. We had fifteen, maybe twenty seconds before Preston would come through the door to the garage. He'd know I was here, because my car was parked in the driveway. What the hell were we going to do?

I stared up at Greg, finding his face a calm, emotionless mask as he left me and scurried around to the other side of the island. "It's okay," he said quickly. "Let me do the talking when—"

No time. The door swung open, and Preston sauntered in. His gaze scanned the area in search of something, noticing his father on one side of the kitchen, and finally he found me. "Cassidy?" He looked confused. "What are you doing here?"

I opened my mouth to speak, but his father's deep voice rang out first. "She left her hoodie in your bathroom and asked if she could stop by to pick it up." Greg nodded toward the sweatshirt resting on the countertop as proof. "You're home early," he added.

Preston didn't notice the strain buried in his father's statement and shrugged. "The restaurant was dead, so they let me off." His attention returned to me. "Why didn't you text me?"

I blinked. Was he serious? Putting aside everything related to his dad and treating Preston solely as my ex, it was
weird as hell seeing him. What was I supposed to say? That
being in the same room with him made me uncomfortable,
and this was easier?

Better was the more appropriate word, because I'd come
over tonight with a bigger goal than just avoiding my ex or
retrieving my favorite hoodie. When I glanced at Greg, I tried
to tamp down my disappointment that we'd been interrupted.

Shit, what a selfish thing to be thinking about.

He must have thought I was looking to him for help, because he answered Preston for me. "I think Cassidy felt more
comfortable if you weren't here, since the break-up."

Preston went still. "The what?"

Breath halted painfully in my lungs.

Oh my God. He *still* didn't think we'd broken up? My
focus flitted from Preston to his father, and I could see the
muscles flexed tight along Greg's jaw. He looked hurt, and
maybe angry.

He thought I'd lied to him.

"We broke up." I said it too loudly because I was nervous,
but also because I needed to make sure both men heard me.
"Like, several times."

Preston unbuttoned the white dress shirt of his uniform,
shooting me a dubious look. "We had a fight. You were mad,
and I told you to call me when you were over it." He stripped
down to his white undershirt and tossed the uniform on the
counter like he'd just thrown down a gauntlet.

"No, that's not what happened. I told you we were over."

Preston's confidence cracked, and there was a glimmer of the boy I'd fallen in love with. He went grave. "You're breaking up with me?"

The temperature in the kitchen fell so rapidly, I thought about grabbing my hoodie and putting it on, but then worried I'd pull the hood closed around my face and try to disappear. Was I about to break up with him a third time, and with his dad watching?

I was barely able to push the word out. "Yes."

As his face twisted with pain, I felt the same twisting in my heart. Greg was rooted in place, even though his expression said he'd rather be anywhere else. Perhaps he thought if he stayed motionless, we'd forget he was there.

Not fucking likely.

"Why?" Preston demanded. I'd practiced the answer so many times, but now my mind went blank. "Is there someone else?" he continued.

I couldn't help how my eyes flicked to Greg's, but he wasn't looking at me. He stared at the counter, frowning. There was guilt there, which I understood. I felt it too. It was a thick, hard shell trapping everything in a confusing mess of emotions.

I ignored Preston's second question. "It's not working anymore."

"Yeah, I know these last few weeks haven't been the best, but I've—"

"It hasn't been working for a while," I said flatly. "Even when we were still in school."

He came closer and put his hand on the counter beside me, invading my space, and I sucked in a sharp breath. His proximity made me want to step back, but I also didn't want to appear weak. I needed to hold my ground and get through this.

"We're not the same people anymore," I said.

He scoffed. "That's not true."

"Yeah? If my grandmother had passed away last year, you would have gone with me to the funeral."

His posture went defensive. "I had to work. I told you."

"It's not just that. Before, you would have been there for me. But now you aren't." I got angry and hurt all over again at the memory. "We've barely seen each other this summer. I'm not your girlfriend. I'm an afterthought."

Preston's gaze hardened, and something like embarrassment colored his expression. He didn't turn or look away from me, but it was clear from his raised voice his question was directed at his father. "Is there some reason you're still here?"

Tension in the room bound me in place. It was uncomfortable for everyone, and worse when Preston pointed it out.

Greg straightened. "Don't take that tone with me. This is my house."

Annoyance flashed in his son's eyes. "Let's go downstairs and talk about this."

"No," I snapped, grabbing the hoodie and strangling it in my hands. "There's nothing to talk about. It's over, and I'm going. Goodbye, Preston." The fire in me waned a little as I turned to his father. "Thanks—" I nearly said his first name, but caught it just in time, "Dr. Lowe."

He looked torn about letting me go but nodded in acknowledgement.

I only made it a few steps toward the door before Preston was following me. "That's it?" He was hurting but masked it with anger. "You're gonna throw three years away because I couldn't go to one funeral with you? That's stupid."

Hot, angry tears stung my eyes, but I didn't stop moving. I needed to get out of this house and away from him before I said something I'd regret. He'd only heard what he wanted to, which meant he could shift the blame away from himself. Fine. As long as he was crystal clear we were done, he could think whatever he wanted.

"You know what?" he yelled at me as I fled out the front door. "Fuck you, Cassidy."

"*Preston*," I heard Greg snarl, but didn't look back at either one of them. I ran so fast down the pathway, one of my flip-flops caught an edge of brick and I nearly fell but managed to stay on my feet. I scrambled into my car, started it, and took off, needing to get down the road before the tears started streaming down my face.

My phone chimed with a text message as I raced home, but I didn't read it. I came in through the kitchen and went immediately up after waving hello to my mom. She was chatting on her phone, but waved back. I moved so rapidly, it didn't give her a chance to notice I'd been crying.

Tripod, our rescue black Labrador, bounded up the stairs beside me. You'd never guess from the way he moved, he was missing a leg. My mom may not have noticed my mood, but there was no getting it past my eagle-eyed dog.

Once I was upstairs in my room, sitting on the floor with my back against the bed, I drew my knees up to my chest and scanned my phone screen. Tripod sat beside me, nosing his way into my free hand as I tried to read.

Dr. Lowe: Are you okay?

I pulled my arms into my hoodie, shrugging it on as I wiped the dried tear tracks from my face with a sleeve, and thumbed out my response.

Cassidy: Yeah.

Three dots blinked across the screen, then disappeared. Like me, it seemed as if he wasn't sure what else to say.

Cassidy: How is he?

Dr. Lowe: Upset. I tried to talk to him, but he took off.

Alarm coasted through my system. Preston had stormed off? Before I could ask, more dots blinked on the screen.

Dr. Lowe: He's staying at Troy's tonight. Maybe he'll figure out he was an asshole and apologize to you.

That'd be nice, but I wasn't going to hold my breath.

> Cassidy: How are you? I'm sorry you
> had to watch that.

> Dr. Lowe: Don't worry about
> me, I'm fine.

I tipped my head back against the bed and closed my eyes, trying to clear my thoughts. What would have happened if Preston had come home five minutes later? He'd have caught me and Greg together. I pictured us with our pants down around our ankles, Greg fucking me from behind while he had me bent over the side of the couch.

The image gave me warm shivers.

Jesus, what was wrong with me? Preston was hurting, and all I could think about was his dad and how I wished we hadn't had to stop. I wanted desperately to hear all of Greg's dirty fantasies and see how many of them matched mine.

My phone chimed again, causing my eyes to pop open.

> Dr. Lowe: Do you want to talk about it?

Preston's angry *fuck you, Cassidy'* played in a loop in my mind, and I wanted it gone. I needed to think about something else. Anything else, before my hurt turned to rage. Three years together, and that was the last thing he said to me. *Fuck you, Cassidy.*

My gaze roamed over my bedroom and only made it worse. Memories of him were everywhere. It was amazing how much he'd been a part of my life in high school, and the room was like a freaking shrine to him. Even my bed was tainted with the memory of when I'd given him my virginity. I groaned and pushed to my feet, hoping I could outrun the angry feeling inching along my skin. Tripod lifted his head, set on high alert.

The picture of Preston and me at our senior prom was on my bookshelf, and I glared at the smiling version of us. I felt powerless against my memories and my anger. *Fuck me, Preston? No. Fuck you.*

I stared down at my phone and Greg's question if I wanted to talk about it. I was desperate to take some power back.

Cassidy: Yeah. Can I come back over?

THIRTEEN

I DIDN'T TAKE ANY CHANCES. I PARKED MY CAR IN THE driveway of the vacant house for sale, then hurried down the sidewalk and into the patch of trees bordering the Lowe property. Was it stupid to hide and sneak around like this? Yeah. But I was too focused right now on getting rid of Preston's voice in my head.

Greg must have seen me making my way up because the side door to his bedroom swung open and he welcomed me inside. His gaze drifted down to the tote bag clutched in my hands, and his eyebrows pulled together.

"Preston's stuff you're returning?" he asked.

I tossed the bag onto a side chair and shook my head. "I lied. I don't want to talk about it."

I closed the distance between us, gripped his face in my hands, and pulled his lips down to mine. The evening had been hard on my system. My arousal had been interrupted by anger, and the emotions swirled together, creating aggression I hadn't experienced before. But I liked the combination. I enjoyed the way it launched me into his arms.

Greg's reaction told me he did too.

His lips were pliant against mine, and I plunged my tongue into his mouth, eager to pick up where we'd left off. Just the connection to him was enough to quiet thoughts in my head. Maybe it was wrong to use him like that, but I couldn't quench the desire for him any other way.

Our kiss started with passion, but rather than explode, it slowed to a simmer. He eased me back and stared down into my eyes, contemplating whatever he wanted to say.

"You don't want to talk about it," he said softly, "but we should."

I sighed.

Fuck you, Cassidy.

I winced at the echo in my memory and tore my gaze away from Greg, staring over his shoulder to the bed, and beyond to the doorway to his bathroom. I knew I couldn't avoid it forever; I'd eventually deal with the Preston situation and whatever it was Greg and I were doing, but I didn't want to face it tonight.

"Fine." My shoulders slumped, and I acted every bit the sullen teenager I felt at that moment. "Can I have something to drink first?"

He straightened and nodded. "What do you want? I've got wine, beer—"

Breath cut off along with his words. He'd just remembered I wasn't old enough to legally drink. Yet, this was stupid. He knew college kids drank, and he let us do it at his house as long as we were responsible.

I wanted Greg to see me as an adult, even if I wasn't exactly acting like one. "Wine would be great," I said. "Thanks."

He hesitated and tried not to look as if he'd been backed into a corner. "Okay. I'll be right back."

Greg was barely through the door when I snatched up the tote bag and scrambled for the bathroom. Coming here had been crazy. Grabbing him and kissing him was crazier, but I was about to do something so insane, it was likely to blow up in my face. As I stripped off my t-shirt, I refused to look at myself in the large mirror over the double sinks. I was sure I'd look back on this moment with heaps of regret, but I pushed forward anyway.

My hands were unsteady as I undid the button of my shorts, and I fumbled along, hurrying to put the dress on. The thick fabric was the shade of evergreen trees, and I squirmed into the tight bodice. Thank God it still fit.

The back zipper gave a muted *vrrrp* as I tugged it up, being careful of the beading, and then I couldn't avoid it any longer. I lifted my head and stared at my reflection. My hair wasn't in too bad of shape. I'd pulled it up into a sleek pony-tail before coming here, but a few tendrils curled softly at the nape of my neck.

I'd put on makeup too, but I could have skipped the blush. My cheeks were flushed pink, and as I blinked at my wide-eyed image in the mirror, I saw how quickly my chest was rising and falling. Nerves swirled and rolled in my belly. Was I about to make a huge fool of myself?

Footsteps grew louder beyond the closed bathroom door, and Greg's voice was concerned. "Cassidy?"

"Just a second." Hopefully, he couldn't hear how breath-less I sounded.

Had I forgotten how heavy the dress was, or was it what I was about to do that weighed me down? I dug a hand into the plunging neckline and repositioned my boobs into the cups sewn in the dress. I didn't have much cleavage to work with, but I'd flaunt what I had.

I filled my lungs with a deep breath, grabbed the door-knob, and pulled the door open. The skirt of the dress was layers of chiffon and stayed quiet when I stepped into the room. In fact, everything was dead fucking silent when Greg's deep brown eyes turned toward me.

He didn't blink. He stood motionless, a glass of red wine in each hand. His gaze was locked on mine, but I somehow felt it all over my body. I sensed it etching over every spar-kling green bead that formed the intricate lace on the bodice, splitting into a deep V that showed more skin than I ever had in my life.

The prom dress had made my mother uneasy. She'd worried it was too mature. Too provocative and revealing, she'd said. But it was on clearance in my size, and after I'd tried it on, I hadn't wanted to take it off. Ever. My dress made me feel sexy and powerful.

Maybe too powerful right now. The way Greg was look-ing at me, I wondered if I might kill him. My mouth felt like it'd been filled with paste, and I licked my dry lips. "This dress—" I said, my voice wavering, "—is the one you said made you think bad things."

"Jesus, I remember." His eyes were so wide, it had to hurt.

He just stood there, not saying anything else, and the moment stretched between us until it grew uncomfortable. Oh, God, this train was steaming at eighty miles an hour to wreck over the side of Awkwardsville Cliff.

I clenched and unclenched my fists at my sides, hidden in the layers of my skirt, trying to quell the nervous scream in my mind. I focused on one of the wineglasses in his hand. "Is that, uh, for me?"

"It was," he said.

And finally, he moved, only it was to bring a wineglass to his lips and gulp the entire glass down in five loud swallows. If I wasn't so mortified with the situation, I might have been impressed. He deposited the now-empty glass on the dresser and switched the full one to his right hand.

"I'm sorry," I blurted. "This was so fucking stupid. I'll change."

It was as sharp as a scalpel. "No."

His eyes darkened and focused with intensity, and . . . shit, he almost looked mad at me, like wearing the prom dress pissed him off. I swallowed thickly.

"What was the plan?" He might have looked pissed, but his voice wasn't cold or angry.

"Plan?"

Greg stalked over. "Why are you wearing this dress?"

My gaze dropped to my bare feet. "Because of what you said."

"So, you wanted to give me bad thoughts?" He grasped my chin with his thumb and forefinger, forcing my attention up to his face. "Because it's fucking working."

Gone was the slow, smoldering tension between us. It broke into a million pieces when his mouth landed on mine. He took and consumed me with his kiss, owning me like I was a possession. It was punishing and dominating. He claimed me exactly like I wanted. I rose on my toes to get closer, only to find myself stumbling backward, blinking in surprise.

He'd pushed me away so he could sit on the edge of the bed, and his gaze trapped me in place. "Go on, then," he said. "Show me."

I tripped over the confusion in my head. "Show you—?"

"What you're wearing under your dress."

A sound burst from me. It was a mixture of surprise and satisfaction. This was what I wanted, but I was still anxious. Having distance between us was sexy, yet also unnerving. I moved backward until the dresser was at my back, giving me something to lean against for support. As I balled the skirt into my fists, I stared at the man across from me.

He took a sip of his wine, turning his head to the side so he could hold my gaze. Like he didn't want to break the connection with me, not even for a moment. I dragged the fabric up toward my hips, revealing inch after inch of my bare legs. His breathing ratcheted up as I cleared my knees. His Adam's apple bobbed in a swallow when I exposed my thighs.

He'd seen me naked before, but it didn't matter. It was all still *new*. A different kind of first.

The dresser creaked as I put more weight on it and lifted the skirt to show him the black satin panties. His eyes heated a thousand degrees, and I melted beneath them.

"Show me." His command was rushed and uneven. "Show me what you do when you're thinking about me."

My mouth fell open, and I clenched my fists on the fabric, tightening them into hard balls. What was he asking? He wanted to watch me?

"Put your hand between your legs."

I straightened, and embarrassment drove my gaze away from him. No one had seen me do that, and I couldn't with an audience. My skirt fell with a swish to brush my toes and cover my legs. "Uh . . ."

Greg stood, went to the nightstand, and dropped off his half-full glass of wine. As he moved back to his spot on the edge of the bed, he popped the button on his jeans and dropped his zipper. "This is what I did last time you had that dress on."

Oh my God.

I began to sweat as I watched him dig a hand in the front of his undone pants and begin to stroke himself.

"It's what I do any time I'm thinking about you, Cassidy."

He worked the jeans to sit low across his hips and pulled down the waistband of his boxer briefs. The slow, deliberate slide of his hard cock through his closed fist was sexy and hypnotic. I couldn't stop watching.

"Show me," he commanded again. "You put on that dress, so I'm not the only one with bad thoughts."

The wickedness of his order had me trembling against the dresser, and the brass pulls on the drawers rattled quietly. I stared at the glide of his hand over himself, each pass making him harder and bigger. A dull ache inside me burned, and I grew hot and slick between my legs.

The dress was supposed to make me feel powerful, yet I was powerless to stop the sigh from seeping from my lips, or the way my hands clawed at my skirt, hitching it upward.

Greg's face dripped with lust. His shoulders lifted in a deep breath as I buried my hand beneath my panties and stroked my sensitive skin. When I was alone, touching myself felt good, but it wasn't close to the same when he watched me do it. Didn't remotely compare. The sensation now was heightened and acute.

His lips moved, mouthing some sort of profanity, but the word wasn't audible. Or maybe I couldn't hear it over my own ragged breaths. The top edge of the dresser dug into my back. The beads scattered over my skirt bit into my palm where I held the gathered fabric up, out of the way so he could watch my fingers moving behind my satin underwear.

"Look at you." His voice was like velvet. "Teasing me like this. You're so bad." His fist stroked faster, pumping on his cock. "You know it, don't you?"

The answer didn't require thought. "Yes."

"You're a bad girl."

"*Yes*," I gasped. I was.

And I was eager to show him. I propelled myself forward, moving so fast, Greg didn't have time to react. I dropped to my knees in front of him, putting my hands on his thighs, and smoothed my palms up to join his hand pumping on himself.

There was a quick inhale of breath from him as I licked my lips and made it clear what I planned to do. I wasn't that experienced with sex, but I was familiar with giving a blow job. The action was easier to understand, and Lilith and I had talked about it recently. We were pretty sure you couldn't give a bad BJ unless you were trying to.

Greg moved his hand out of my way and slipped it gently onto the back of my neck. He didn't force me forward or down. It rested in the hair at the nape of my neck, and his warm fingers felt good. I closed my eyes, parted my lips, and lowered my mouth down over him.

"*Fuck.*"

That word was definitely audible. It resonated through my body.

He was soft, yet strong against my tongue. I moved cautiously, trying to take him deeper, but he was large and thick. So impossibly thick, and the warmth between my legs flared hotter. I'd wanted to go down on him, but as soon as I started, I longed for him to be moving inside me.

He wound his hand around my ponytail, subtly encouraging me to pick up the pace. His knees spread wider, but since his pants weren't down, his undone zipper scraped over my chin, and I pulled back.

Good lord, his eyes. They were dark and gorgeous.

FOURTEEN

G REG'S EXPRESSION WAS DETERMINED, BUT AS HE PEERED down at me, his face softened. He reached out with his other hand, grazing his fingertips over the line of my jaw. His thumb brushed over my kiss-swollen lips.

"Is this your fantasy, or mine?" he asked quietly.

I edged forward, setting my lips against his firm column of flesh. "It's *ours*," I whispered.

He groaned his satisfaction and grew louder as I took him in my mouth once more. Up and down I pumped on him, sliding his wet dick between my lips. I had to clamp a hand around the base of him to steady myself once his hips began to move and thrust toward me.

It was hard to breathe hunched over him, especially since I'd been out of breath before we'd even started, but I focused on my goal. If I could give him one-tenth of the pleasure he'd given me, it'd be worth it.

The connection between us had been tender, but as I spun my tongue over him, things began to shift. His short, shallow breaths were urgent, and tension coiled in his leg beneath my hand. Everything started to feel . . . needier. And darker.

And raw.

Had he reached a breaking point? Greg yanked me off him and hauled us both up to our feet. I was dizzy with the abrupt movement, and as I tried to get my bearings, I fell forward, bracing my hands on the bed. Wait, I hadn't fallen. He'd *pushed* me.

Greg's voice was deep and sexual. "I shouldn't have let you do that. You're such a bad girl."

Heat licked at my center, responding to his accusation. He was absolutely right. I was bad, and right now? I wanted to be very, *very* bad. When I tried to push off the bed, he set his hand in the center of my back and shoved, sending me face-down against the mattress.

"Say it," he commanded.

Every muscle in my body tightened with excitement, and I squeezed the words out. "I'm a bad girl."

"Yeah, you are." The back of my dress began to lift. Up the fabric dragged, leaving the backs of my thighs cool in the open air. "Making me want you, when I can't. When I shouldn't." He seemed to be grumbling to himself. "Making me feel guilty when I jerk off thinking about you."

I let out a gasp. I knew what that looked like because he'd shown me, and an incredibly sexy image splashed in my mind—Greg lying in bed, working himself over in a furious pace, thinking about me.

"But I can't stop," he continued. The dress was hiked up on my hips, exposing the intricate lace covering my ass. His strong hand fumbled over it, and then dipped down. It lingered between my legs, brushing a single knuckle over my aching center. I moved against it, rocking my hips to try to find relief. It was so sexy the way he just stood there, letting me undulate against his hand.

"What happens to bad girls, Cassidy?"

I froze. I hadn't realized we were playing a game, and now it was clear it was my turn. My move. I could answer any way I wanted. Tell him bad girls got sent home, or put in time-out . . . or fucked.

I balled the sheets into my fists, closed my eyes, and pressed my cheek to the bed. Hopefully he wanted the answer I was going to give.

"They get *punished*," I breathed.

It was immediate. There was a whoosh of air, and the smack of skin registered before the sensation of his spanking did. The sting radiated up my backside, rippling outward. I bit down on my bottom lip. No one had ever hit me before. Not Preston, not my mom, and certainly not the father I'd never met.

"You deserved that," Greg said in a seductive tone, "didn't you?"

"Yes," I panted.

It was like my body knew what to do, and I surrendered to it. I arched my back, jutting my ass up, wordlessly demanding more. I tugged at the sheets, clenching them to my face, and stifled the urge to beg for it.

His second strike had no warning and stole my breath. It hurt, but only for a moment, and then sweet relief washed over me. When he spanked me, it drove all the guilt away, and I craved the release from my emotions as badly as I did an orgasm.

Greg was breathing hard, and I pictured him looming behind me, my green dress billowed around my waist and my legs trembling against the bed.

"Do you need another?" His voice was uneven and hard to interpret. Was he nervous he'd gone too far, or desperate for more like I was?

I couldn't find words, so I bobbed my head vigorously. I pushed back toward him, eager to receive it. It didn't escape me how twisted our actions were, him spanking me like I was a disobedient child. Was I one, in Greg's eyes? Preston and I were the same age.

I didn't want to be thinking about my ex. Only the need that had me bursting at the seams. I swayed my hips, inviting Greg to lay his hand on my skin and make me burn. Only I had to wait a lifetime in agony before he delivered the blow.

Finally, it came. A whimper of pain escaped from me and was followed by a sob. "Again," I pleaded.

"This is . . . fucked up," he said, but then his palm seared across my ass with a loud slap. And another. My skin was hot and irritated under the lace panties, but it felt weirdly good and really fucking turned me on. I moaned my approval.

The spankings slowed yet grew more intense. In between the slaps, his hands smoothed over my heated skin, massaging and teasing. He raked his fingernails over the lace, and I wiggled against the sensation. It felt good, but also balanced on a knife's edge of being too much.

He tugged the waist of my panties up, forcing the fabric deep into my cleft and giving him more skin of my bare ass as a target. His spankings were sharp, but he struck me right in the center of my cheeks, and it didn't hurt now. At least, if it did, I was too far gone to care.

I groaned and rolled my hips, rising to meet his tempo, and I didn't recognize the throaty voice as my own. "Whose fantasy is this?"

He exhaled loudly. "Ours."

I moaned my agreement and pushed up to rest on my forearms, so I could straighten out my back. What would it feel like in this position?

There was the sound of rustling as he moved, but no slap came. His fingers dug into the sides of my panties, wrenched them down until they were stretched between my knees, and his breath rolled over the backs of my legs.

One deep, quick lick of his tongue made me jolt. "Oh!"

He did it again. A lightning-fast pass of his tongue over my clit and it detonated fireworks. I flinched at each staccato lick he gave me, and whimpers poured from my lips. It was too much and not enough. Teasing me to the point of being mean.

It was a new form of punishment, and my head spun. I loved it and hated it.

The spankings had built me into a frenzy, and all I needed now was one long push to make me fall over the edge. His tongue slashed at me while his palms ran up and down my legs, tracing every goosebump he'd created on me. I moved, gyrating against his face, but he kept perfect control and drew away when I tried to get what I needed.

I reached a hand back behind me and clenched a fistful of his hair, desperate. "Oh, please," I begged. "Make me feel good."

He went after me then like a man dying of hunger, and I cried out, my supporting arm giving way as pleasure rocketed through my center. My chest slammed against the bed as Greg braced my hips and closed his lips around my clit.

The explosion was instantaneous.

Our moans mixed together, although mine overpowered his. I quaked beneath his mouth, shuddering through the blistering orgasm and lingered in the fog of the pleasure, barely aware of anything happening around me.

Noises registered. A thud, the crinkle of foil ripping. Greg's t-shirt, still warm from his body, dropped onto the bed beside me. And then he was there, nudging. The tip of his hard dick pushed and intruded, one delicious inch at a time.

"Oh, Jesus. Oh, God," I babbled through my short gasps of breath. "Yes, that's it."

His sigh was heavy with satisfaction, and I felt it mirrored inside me. He slipped deeper as his hands grasped my waist and pulled me back onto him. All the way until his pelvis was pressed flat against my ass, and he was so hard inside me I couldn't see straight.

We stayed motionless, me bent over the bed and him standing behind, just breathing and enjoying the way it felt. Fuck, it felt so good. He throbbed inside me, and my body squeezed in reply. And even though we weren't moving, blood thundered through my veins. My pulse sped along, banging loudly in my ears.

I might die from this man. It was an impossibly dramatic thought, but it *felt* real. Greg's command over me was absolute, and I wondered . . . would I survive him?

There was only one way to know. I reached a hand back and put it on his hip, trying to send a signal I was ready. He grasped my elbow in one firm hand, and then the fingers of his other dug into my scalp, right at the base of my ponytail. He pulled me up off the bed, arching me like a bow and drawing his hips back slowly—

Only so he could slam into me, so deep and hard, it bordered on pain. Flashes of white danced in my vision, and I grunted, but I loved his rough thrust.

"You like that?" he asked darkly.

"Yeah."

He did it again.

And again. His hold on my hair began to ache, but I said nothing. As his tempo picked up, his grasp on my arm tightened, drawing me further back toward him so my spine was shaped like a U. He pounded into me, our bodies slapping together with a punishing, angry rhythm, and it was sexy. I listened to the sound of us fucking and grew wetter and hotter.

"Fuck, your pussy is insane."

I nearly came right then. No one had ever talked to me like that. If anyone else had said it, I would have shut down, but his dirty words and rough actions were the perfect combination of sin. I felt used, which was exactly what I needed. It was what I wanted from him.

He drove his cock into me, pushing me to the brink of what I could take, but never crossed over to being mean or cruel. He'd been having sex for at least twenty years, and he'd definitely learned a thing or two on how to do it.

My whimpers of enjoyment swelled and grew frantic. Tingles raced up and down my legs. Every inch of my skin felt alive. The slap of his body against mine hit all the right spots, inside and out. My mind focused in on a single need, the desperate release of tension.

"Oh," I gasped.

"Uh huh," he encouraged. "I'm gonna come. You're going to make me fucking come, Cassidy."

I went first, him only a few erratic thrusts after me. Sensations blasted up by spine and rippled across my skin, leaving me weak. Greg released me, and we collapsed forward, his heaving chest crushing mine to the sheets. His rasping breath filled my ear, stopping only for a moment while he pressed a seductive kiss to the side of my throat.

He came down off his high faster than I did. "I'll be right back." It sounded teasingly light from him, but I caught his meaning. "Don't go anywhere."

FIFTEEN

G REG'S COMMENT BROUGHT ON A FRESH WAVE OF GUILT. I shouldn't have abandoned him last time.

"I'm not going to make a run for it," I said, still struggling to catch my breath. "I can't move."

He gave half a laugh as he pulled up his pants, leaving them undone, and I watched him disappear through the doorway to his bathroom. He wasn't gone long, and as the first twinge of shame began to trickle into my mind, he reemerged—

Stark, fucking, naked.

My cheeks warmed at the image, and thoughts drained from my brain. He strolled across the room, coming to the bed, and helped me to stand on my wobbly legs. I turned clumsily to face him, not sure what to expect. Was this going to be awkward? Would he look at me with judgement after what we'd done, and how we'd done it?

No. His expression was soft and full of longing. As he kissed me, his hands smoothed over my curves, moving toward my back, almost as if searching for something. It was the zipper of my dress. He eased it down, and as the fabric began to peel from my body, his lips followed it.

My shoulders shuddered with pleasure. Greg worked deliberately to undress me, and I hadn't expected seduction after sex. It seemed unnecessary, but—oh God—it *felt* so incredibly necessary now. His featherlight kisses moving over my bare body was worship.

He eased the straps of the dress down my arms, pushed it to my waist, and trailed his lips over my breasts. He didn't linger there, though. He took a knee, and his deft hands worked the bunched dress over my hips, while his kisses marched over my belly. The dress fell into a fluffy pile at my ankles, pulling my underwear down with it.

On his knees in front of me, Greg worked his gaze up the length of my body, and I went from being worshipped to savored. The air around us was thick. Heavy with an invisible fog that stuck in my lungs. His stare was intense and amazing.

I didn't move until he rose to his feet and opened his arms, inviting me to step into them. I melted against him, greedy for his touch. We'd gone from soft kisses, to spanking, to brutal fucking, and now sensual cuddling? It should have felt strange, but it didn't. The way he swung from one extreme to the other was fascinating and perfect.

I lost myself in his deep kiss, where time suspended.

Somehow, we made our way onto the bed and squirmed beneath the covers, but he stayed upright, leaning his back against the tufted headboard. He probably worried if he got too comfortable, he'd fall asleep, and I'd bolt again. I wanted to show him that wasn't going to happen, so I tucked myself under his arm, putting my cheek to his bare chest.

He shifted to grab the glass of red wine off the nightstand, took a sip, and then settled in with me, glass still in hand. His face skewed with an expression that looked a lot like remorse.

"Your distraction worked like a charm, but we still need to talk," he said.

I plucked the glass from him, pressed it to my lips, and took a big swallow. I'd only had red wine twice before, and dear God, this was the worst of the three. I tried not to make a face as I politely handed it back. "Thanks." I struggled not to wipe the gross, buttery taste from my lips. "It's really good."

His knowing smile said he didn't believe me. But he turned serious as he set the wine down and focused on my eyes. "Are you okay?" Confidence fled from his voice. "I didn't mean to be like that."

All the hair pulling had made a mess of my ponytail, and I tucked a loose tendril behind my ear. "I'm fine."

The quiet in the room careened toward awkwardness.

"I'm fine," I said again, trying to convince him. "I, uh, liked the way you were. You couldn't tell?"

He appeared conflicted. "No, I could, it's just that was probably too much."

The single sip of his disgusting wine must have given me courage. "For who? You?" I straightened so I could stare directly at him. "Because it was great for me."

"Jesus." He cupped my face, and the corner of his mouth ticked up into a smile. "All right. Let's add it to the list of all the things we're not supposed to do, but do anyway."

I couldn't hold back my smile, even when I knew it was wrong.

I stared across his enormous bed to the wall beyond, where his undergrad degree from Vanderbilt was framed. Beside it hung an award he'd received from the hospital a few years ago. Maybe someday after I'd become a veterinarian, I'd hang my diplomas and awards on the wall like him. Like an adult.

Man, as if I needed another reminder of how different my life was from his.

The warmth from his touch went away when he took a deep breath, as if preparing for something serious.

"What are we doing?" he asked quietly.

I scowled. Like I had any clue. Plus, thinking about us together only brought on guilt.

"Okay." He said it like I'd given him an answer. "What do you want this to be?"

What I wanted wasn't possible. Greg would always be Preston's father and twenty years older than I was. "I don't know how to answer that."

"What we just did . . . you want to do it again?"

My pulse jumped. It was scary to confess, but I wasn't going to lie. "Yeah."

He tensed his shoulders, and visibly struggled to get his words out. "Me too," he admitted softly. "Which means we have to tell Preston."

"Oh my God, no." Had Greg lost his mind? Not in a million years was I going to do that.

"He's my son, Cassidy. When he was born, I put my needs before everyone else's and, shit, I was the worst father. Hell, I wasn't a father *at all*. But I got a second chance, and

I'm not going to blow it this time. It's taken years for him to forgive me."

"Uh—" I cut myself off just in time before saying it out loud. He thought Preston had forgiven him?

"What?" Greg's skeptical gaze drilled into me.

"Nothing."

I tried to act casual, but it was too late. He had latched onto my unspoken thought and wasn't about to drop it. I pulled away, hiking the sheets up tighter around my body, but he followed me, trapping me in place with a hand on my shoulder.

His tone was firm. "What were you going to say?"

I stared down at his hand, avoiding looking at him. "I'm not sure," I said reluctantly, "he's totally forgiven you yet."

Greg sucked in a sharp breath. For a long moment, it was the only painful sound in the room. I worked up the nerve to look him in the eye, and his expression was guarded. Maybe even defensive. It was striking how similar it was to Preston's earlier today.

Greg's hand slid away, and his voice turned dubious. "What makes you think that?"

I sighed. "He told me."

"When? A while ago—?"

"When school ended, and we were coming home."

I watched the balloon of hope deflate in his eyes, and he sagged back against the headboard, defeated.

For three years, I'd tried to get Preston to come around. His father hadn't been much older than he was now when Preston's parents had gotten pregnant. Just kids themselves.

I didn't know the details, and I'd only heard Preston's version of the story, but I was aware Greg had chosen medical school and a career over having a son.

Child support payments and birthday presents in the mail were all Preston had known of his father the first ten years of his life, and he'd told me again and again that wasn't something he was getting over any time soon.

"It's been getting better, though," I said. "You two are a lot closer now. Remember what it was like the first time I came over?"

Preston had only been living with his father a few weeks, and the tension between the two was palpable. Preston hadn't introduced me. I'd come in and barely gotten a look at Dr. Lowe before Preston was hurrying me down the stairs to the basement. It would be a month before I had my first conversation with his father.

Time wore away at them, softening the sharp edge of Preston's anger, but it hadn't dissolved completely. They'd done a good job at playing family long enough it was almost real.

"It's not going to change what I do," Greg said, running a hand down his long face. "I'm never going to give up trying to make it right with him. But, tell me honestly. Is it too late?"

I shook my head. "I don't think so. You just need more time with him."

God, the way he looked at me was heartbreaking, and my gut twisted. Yes, Greg had been an absent father at first, but he loved his son and was trying so hard now. That had to count for something. I mean, my father hadn't given a shit about me, ever. No child support payments or birthday presents in the mail. The only thing he'd given me was half my DNA, and sometimes I wanted to point out to Preston he hadn't gotten the shittiest deal in the dad department.

"But we can't tell him," I announced. "It'll destroy everything you worked so hard for. Burn every bridge you built."

"You don't know that."

"I know him," I clarified. "I know how he'll react." I could guarantee it wouldn't go well. Preston's *'fuck you, Cassidy'* would be amended to include a *'fuck you, Dad'* and maybe even a *'fuck you forever.'*

Greg frowned. "I'm not saying he'll be okay with it, but—"

"No," I said. "We can't tell him. And, yeah, I know it sounds like I'm trying to take the easy way out, but I'm not. He was my best friend, Greg. I know him better than anyone else, and believe me when I tell you, we can't do this. You'll lose him forever, and I'll be the reason."

His dark eyes clouded over with something I didn't understand. "You don't know everything about him."

Well, that was cryptic. "What?"

Greg's eyebrows pulled together, creating a crease of worry for a pregnant moment. "I just mean you can never know someone completely." He reached out and captured my face, cradling it in his hands. "He needs to know. He almost walked in on us this afternoon. What if he had?"

I sighed, and my heart gained five heavy pounds, sinking in my chest. "We don't even know what *this* is. How do we explain it to him?"

His expression shifted, and it was clear he knew I'd made a valid point. What if tonight was the last time we were together? I didn't see the upside in risking Greg's relationship with his son on something that might fade as quickly as I could stuff my prom dress back in the bag I'd brought over.

"So," he said, crossing his arms over his chest, "we lie to him."

A stone turned in my stomach and my voice was meek. "Until we can figure it out, I think we have to."

"Great." His tone was flat. "This is a great idea. If he finds out instead of hearing it from us, it'll be ten times worse."

"He's not going to find out." I heard the way the words sounded as they came from my mouth and cringed. Was I really pushing for this? Willing to sneak around behind the back of the guy who'd once meant so much to me? And I'd be doing it so I could continue having crazy-hot sex.

Jesus. I hadn't lied to Preston when I'd told him we weren't the same people we were before. I barely recognized myself anymore.

"We'll be careful," I said. "And we'll tell him, once the summer's over and he's done going through whatever phase he's going through right now."

I was sure we both had the same feeling of dread crawling through us, thinking about how terribly this could go wrong. I swallowed a lump and mustered up the courage to be vulnerable.

"We have three options. Tell him, keep it a secret, or stop. Just so you know, it doesn't matter how or what we tell him—he's going to think I left him for you."

And that betrayal would be too much. Preston wouldn't recover.

I gazed at the man sitting beside me. Greg's dark hair was ruffled, and his full lips turned down in a frown, but he was easily the most beautiful man I'd ever seen. His thick biceps were exaggerated, crossed over his powerful chest, and his smart eyes focused in on me.

Oh, option three wasn't an option at all.

"And I can't stay away," I admitted. "I don't want to stop. Do you?"

"No."

"So . . ."

The muscles along his jaw flexed and his eyes went narrow. He was in agreement, but not happy about it, and I understood. I wasn't thrilled about sneaking around either.

"Just until the end of summer." It was a statement, but he said it asking for validation.

I nodded. "Yeah."

He drew in a deep breath, pushed it out, and pulled me back against him. His lips brushed the edge of my hairline on my forehead. "This is a bad idea."

I set my palm flat against his chest. "We can add it to the list."

SIXTEEN

GREG BROUGHT ME A CAN OF DR. PEPPER WHEN HE GOT UP TO refill his wine, and I stared at the logo printed on the aluminum. Preston didn't like Dr. Pepper, and I'd never seen his father drink it either, which led me to believe the case always stocked in the garage was for me.

Greg hesitated before speaking. "Can I ask you something?"

No one ever said that unless something serious was about to come out, and I tried not to hold my breath. "Go for it."

"I've never heard you talk about your dad."

I blinked slowly. "Probably because there's nothing to say. I never met the guy."

"Is he still alive?"

I shrugged. "Maybe."

Greg looked like he just discovered he was standing barefoot surrounded by broken glass and wasn't sure which step to take next. All his options were going to be painful. "I'm sorry I brought it up. I didn't mean to make you uncomfortable. It's just, we've known each other a while, and I always wondered."

"My dad fled town as soon as he found out my mom was pregnant, and she hasn't heard from him since." My body went cool, matching my voice. "He didn't give a single thought to us, so I make sure to return the favor every chance I get."

I couldn't read what was going on behind his eyes, other than the panic swimming there. Was he thinking about what he'd done to Preston? It didn't compare. Greg hadn't been in much of Preston's early life, but he also didn't disappear. He hadn't walked away and left him without a father at all. Even scraps were better than nothing to a starving person.

I leaned over Greg, snatched the remote off the nightstand, and turned the TV on. It was super awkward, but anything was better than continuing the conversation, and my actions communicated it effectively.

The older movie on screen was low definition, and I'd turned it on somewhere in the middle of a scene where banquet tables with fine china were being flipped over and pushed to the side.

"The flowers are still standing," Greg said to himself quietly.

"What?"

On screen, a young Bill Murray shouted the same thing. More tables crashed to the side, and a green ghost floated around a crystal chandelier, dodging laser beams.

"That's my favorite line in *Ghostbusters*." Greg gestured to the TV. "When he pulls the tablecloth off and breaks everything on the table except the centerpiece."

I shrugged. "I never saw the old one."

It was like I'd just told him I didn't know who the president was. A personal affront. "How is that possible? Man, I loved this movie when I was a kid."

I watched the Ghostbusters come up with their game plan of trapping the green ghost. The special effects looked ancient. "How old is this thing?"

"I don't know . . . It came out in nineteen eighty-four, I think? I saw it in the theater with my parents." A weird look flitted over his face. Embarrassment? "I got freaked out," he said, "by the Stay Puft Marshmallow Man, and my mom had to take me out to the car. We missed the end of the movie."

A smile caught the edge of my lips. "I'm sorry, a marshmallow man? Those fluffy, white things?"

"Yeah, but he's, like, a hundred feet tall."

I chuckled. "Sounds terrifying."

"To a six-year-old, it was. He was running around crushing buildings." Greg settled in and got comfortable against the headboard. "Whatever, you'll see. We're watching the rest of this."

I raised an eyebrow. "Oh, are we?"

"This movie is a classic." He peered at me with scrutiny. "What else haven't you seen? *Caddyshack*? *Animal House? Ferris Bueller's Day Off*?"

I pressed my lips together. Did he realize those movies were already at least twenty years old by the time I was born?

"Jesus." He shook his head. "Okay, we start fixing this tonight."

So, we watched the rest of *Ghostbusters*, and I wasn't sure which I liked better—the ridiculous movie, or the way Greg watched me experience it. And when it was over, we talked. Like, an actual conversation about everything from my desire to go to veterinary school to his aggravation with a fellow surgeon whose phone chimed non-stop through procedures.

It was shocking how easy he was to talk to, and I tried not to make the comparison to the way things used to be between Preston and me.

"It's getting late," I mumbled while yawning.

The lights and TV were off, and the room was dark. Greg's hand twitched on my bare stomach, curling around my waist to hold me closer. "Mm-hmm. You should stay."

It warmed me that he offered, but . . . "I can't."

We both knew I couldn't. Besides my curfew, what if Preston came home early? I squeezed his arm to get him to release me, which he did. When I slid off the bed, he turned on a bedside lamp, and we both squinted at each other in the light.

He gazed at me while I pulled on my clothes, surveying me from the bed like I was the most beautiful thing he'd ever seen, and I went all wobbly.

"I'm not on-call next weekend, and Preston's heading to North Carolina on Thursday."

I'd forgotten about Preston's upcoming visit to his mom's for two weeks. It'd certainly make it easier to see Greg again, but exactly what was he suggesting? My hands slowed as I pushed my head into my shirt.

His voice was light. "In case you wanted to get cracking on the list of new classic movies you need to watch."

God, his smile was gorgeous. How could I say no? I hoped my smile back matched his. "Sure. I'd like that."

It was nearly one in the morning when I left his bed. I had to hurry to make it home before curfew. My mom was pretty lax about stuff—I could have texted her if I needed an extension, but it was already so late, and what kind of excuse would I give?

"Sorry, Mom. I'm hanging out in Dr. Lowe's bed and he just banged my brains out."

Yeah, that'd go over just great.

Lilith glanced around the bar area of the restaurant, then stared at me over the top of her half-empty pint of beer. "So . . . you're like, what? Dating Dr. Daddy now?"

"Uh, no. I don't think—" I couldn't 'date' Greg. First of all, where would we go? Nashville was a big city, but the suburb we lived in had a small-town feel. He ran into patients often whenever he and Preston went anywhere. "Honestly, I have no idea what we're doing."

"Other than boning each other."

I gave her a plain look, not rewarding her amusement. "Right. Just boning each other."

She took a long sip of her drink and chuckled to herself as she set it down on the tabletop. "I swear, Cassidy, this thing keeps getting better every time we talk. I can't wait until you're telling me you're going to be Preston's new stepmom."

My eyes went as wide as possible. "Oh my God, *stop.*"

Lilith pushed a section of her brown hair back over her shoulder and leaned in to get close. "I'm teasing. But, seriously, dude. He's hot *and* a doctor. Well done, you. You need to teach me your ways."

Me, teach her? Lilith was the sexually confident woman I wanted to be. "Yeah, right. And how many guys have I been with, again?"

"You mean, outside of the Lowe family?" She grinned.

"Ouch. That was savage."

"I know, I'm sorry. Couldn't resist." She propped her elbows on the round table and rested her chin on her hands. "Your number doesn't matter, because it's not a contest. Guys can fuck a bunch of different women and still be clueless about sex." She lifted her eyebrows. "Believe me."

"Well, Greg is—uh—not clueless."

Her smile was wide and genuine. "Glad to hear it. You deserve a good dose of vitamin D."

I laughed and shook my head. Her unabashed attitude still caught me off guard.

The crowd in the bar ignored us, and I'd forgotten they were there until a cheer went up over a baseball game on the televisions covering the back wall.

"Hey, you know who else is hot and probably gives good vitamin D?" Lilith said loudly, just as the hubbub died. "Clay Crandall."

The name didn't ring any bells. "And he is?"

"My new neighbor. I saw him moving in last week, and he's gorgeous. I went over to welcome him to the neighborhood right away—you know—because I'm friendly like that."

Her expression was devious, and I imagined her putting on her sexiest outfit before sprinting in her stilettos to his doorstep. "Not married, and no girlfriend—or boyfriend—in sight. He's some tech guy. I think he sells software? I can't remember. It was hard to hear over how fucking hot he was."

"I'm sure." My gaze dropped down to the black straw floating in my glass of Dr. Pepper. Sitting in the bar area, and my friend across from me drinking beer, intensified my feeling of being an older person trapped in a young body. Was I the only one in this restaurant who wasn't legally allowed to drink?

"God, I hope he never puts up curtains," Lilith said wistfully.

I smirked. "You pervert."

"Don't I know it."

Our server arrived, a scrawny guy with sideburns that were too long, carrying our dinners and aiming an enormous smile at Lilith. He was practically drooling in our food, but she didn't notice. Not the drool, or the guy producing it, either. Perhaps she was used to guys falling over themselves around her.

He dropped off my fajitas with a loud thud, and slowly slid her salad in front of her like he was presenting her his heart on a satin pillow. As she readied her fork, she gave him a quick, "thanks," and then dug in.

He slunk away, his shoulders slumped in defeat.

I'd only been friends with her for the summer, but if I knew one thing for certain, it was that Lilith would chase a bunny around an exam table all day, but she did not chase men. At least, not unless she absolutely *had* to have him.

"Dinner's on me tonight," she said as she crunched a crouton.

"You don't have to do that." The restaurant was just across the parking lot from the strip mall that held the vet clinic, and we always left our cars parked there after our day was over. I assumed she was going to order a second beer. "I don't mind driving you home tonight."

"I'm not buying you dinner for being my designated driver, I'm buying it to lessen the blow that I can't go to the *Joven* concert next weekend."

"What?" I froze mid-bite. We'd bought our tickets weeks ago, and I was dying to see them live.

"I screwed up. I thought my cousin's wedding was this weekend, but it's not, and my mom's being a jerk about me bailing. I can't get out of it." She gave me sad, puppy-dog eyes. "I'm really sorry. Do you want to try to sell our tickets? Or I can still pay for mine if you want to go with someone else."

I gazed at the sizzling skillet of fajitas in front of me. I was disappointed she couldn't go, but I still really wanted to. Did I know anyone else who liked *Joven*?

Oh.

I did. He'd caught me dancing in my swimsuit to their music once in his darkened garage. Plus, he wasn't on-call that weekend.

"Your face is weird," Lilith said abruptly, staring at me through the steam from my food. "What are you thinking about?"

"Doing something crazy," I said. "Like, maybe asking Greg if he wants to go."

Her eyes widened along with her smile. She liked this bad idea a lot. "Oh my God, do it."

SEVENTEEN

THE SUN WAS GLARING, AND MY PALMS WERE SWEATY AS I thumbed out the message on my phone.

Cassidy: Are you on your way?

The sidewalk outside the Bridgestone Arena was full of people streaming up the concrete steps into the main entrance. The crowd was jovial, and the fans were a wide range of ages. Occasionally, some guy would give me a second glance, as if wondering about the girl waiting in the shadow of the tall, silver building while constantly checking her phone.

My feet hurt, and I shifted uncomfortably on the heels I'd let Lilith talk me into wearing.

When I'd climbed into the Uber and headed for the concert, I'd felt awesome. My skinny black pants fit perfectly, and no tan lines were showing in my blue sleeveless top. My hair was cooperating too, letting me curl my brown locks into soft waves with volume, instead of the flat, stick-straight way I normally wore it. I'd watched YouTube tutorials on 'date night makeup' and followed painstakingly along, so I was confident my makeup didn't look like it'd been applied by a drunken clown.

But the Uber had dropped me off at the Nissan gate outside the arena more than thirty minutes ago, and I wasn't feeling awesome now. Greg and I were supposed to meet here at six thirty, and the opening act of the concert had started at seven. I'd hung out in a state of annoyance for the last ten minutes, but as the clock continued to tick along, my irritation turned.

I looked back at the texts I'd sent him over the last thirty-five minutes.

> Cassidy: I'm here!

> Cassidy: Nissan gate. Standing next to the Jack Daniel's sign.

> Cassidy: We said 6:30, right?

Something was wrong. Why wasn't he responding? He wasn't on-call with the hospital, so that couldn't be the problem.

A sensation of cold shivered through me, despite the July heat and humidity. Had he forgotten, or had he changed his mind? I abruptly felt like a fool, standing on the sidewalk in the most sexed-up outfit I owned, waiting for a man who clearly wasn't going to show.

How much longer should I wait, and . . . did I really want to go into the concert by myself, now that my evening had been ruined? I stared up at the series of doors, debating what to do. Lilith would say "fuck him," go inside, and have the time of her life. I wasn't angry at her, but mad at the situation. If she'd gone with me, I'd never have invited Greg and—

My phone vibrated.

Greg: I'm so, so sorry. Was on a post-
op phone call that would NOT end.
Ordering my Uber now.

He was still at home? It was all the way on the other side of town. I squeezed the phone so tightly in my hand, I worried I'd break it. If I was being reasonable, I knew it wasn't his fault, but it was hard to be reasonable when I was hot, had aching feet and a stomach that had been churning with anger for the last twenty minutes.

Greg: Where are you? Still
waiting outside?

I stabbed the screen with my fingers.

Cassidy: Yup.

Greg: Go on in, don't wait for me. I'll be
there in 15.

Cassidy: I have your ticket.

The dots blinked across the screen, then vanished, and finally . . .

Greg: Shit. You want to meet at the
lounge by the entrance? You won't
have to wait outside.

I glared up at the large windows opposite me, and my irritation burned hotter as I watched the people inside the air-conditioned building, laughing and sipping on drinks.

I didn't want to have to remind him, but he'd obviously forgotten.

> Cassidy: I'm not 21.

More blinking dots appeared and then disappeared, and I pictured him swearing to himself.

> Greg: Traffic's moving fast. I'll be there
> soon. Again, I'm sorry.

> Cassidy: K.

I wasn't sure what else to say. The situation sucked, but I should have expected it. Greg's job was demanding, and he'd spent more than a few dinners on the phone with patients or the hospital while Preston and I ate.

Scalpers tried to sell me tickets while I waited, anxiously watching the cars that pulled up with the Uber sticker in the window. Even though the concert had started a while ago, people were still arriving in droves, not interested in the warm-up acts.

A pack of guys, who looked only a few years older than me, meandered down the sidewalk, and their slow, steady approach put me on alert. A hyperaware sense of anxiety kicked in. I stared at the ground, not wanting to make eye contact. I'd been to enough parties at Vanderbilt to be wary of a group like this. Toxic masculinity mixed with pack mentality was a dangerous combination.

"Hey," a male voice said. I hoped it wasn't directed at me, and glanced at my phone, even though whatever was on screen wasn't registering.

"Hey," the guy said again, louder and closer. He had to be talking to me.

The pack had stopped moving, and the tallest one of the group was staring, an interested expression painted on his face. As he took me in, I had no choice but to evaluate him as well. He wore a gray t-shirt and ripped jeans, but they were the expensive kind where the rips were intentional. He was okay looking. His nose was a little long and his eyes matched his dull colored shirt, but my instincts were immediately to run.

"You out here waiting for me?" he said. The corners of his mouth turned up in a teasing smile.

"No, sorry."

I tried to look beyond him to reinforce my lack of interest, but he didn't move. He just stood there staring, and I reluctantly turned my attention back to him. His half smile had deepened into a wide grin.

"What's your name, gorgeous?"

I blinked. Did he *really* just say that? Even though it was technically a compliment, the way he'd delivered the cheesy line was anything but flattering, and I felt my expression sour. "My name is 'Not Interested.'"

His friends snickered, but the guy was unfazed. If anything, it seemed to egg him on. He stepped toward me, invading my space. He was close. Too close, and I backpedaled— only the wall was there, hot against my back.

His friends kept their distance. Most seemed uninterested in what was going on, but it was hard not to feel intimidated with the tall guy looming over me, and the way his smile reached his eyes, it was clear he knew it. He saw how nervous he made me and enjoyed it.

He was scary.

"Why not?" he asked, looking smug. "You got a boyfriend?"

I'd been raised by a strong, feminist mother, and since I was literally trapped, this guy had activated the part of me which was all teeth and claws. "Does that make a difference?" I snapped.

My question caught him off-guard, but he recovered and looked at me like I was being silly. His tone dripped with condescension. "Of course, it does."

"Why?" I lifted my chin and narrowed my gaze, giving him time to come up with an answer, but he stumbled. "Is it," I continued, "because that means I belong to someone else?"

Confusion threaded his eyebrows together. "Uh . . ."

"I already told you I wasn't interested, but, no. You won't respect that. You'll only step off when you think I'm another man's property." I straightened my shoulders and tried to stand as tall as possible, pretending I wasn't feeling threatened. "I'm not interested in you, or being anyone's property. Goodbye."

I heard one of his friends make a sound that was half-gasp, half-laugh, but I didn't take my attention off the guy peering down at me. He wasn't hiding his displeasure at being called out in front of his crew, and my stomach tangled into a knot. He looked pissed, and . . . shit, had I just poked a bear?

"Hey, is this guy bothering you?" a familiar voice said.

Relief swept through me as my gaze landed on Greg. He looked amazing in jeans and a black button-down shirt that fit him perfectly. But his attention wasn't on me. His intense, severe expression was directed at the guy in my face. The guy glanced at Greg, then back at me, and threw his hands up in the air as he moved backward.

"No, I was just trying to pay her a compliment. Tell your daughter to chill out, bro."

I cringed, but Greg didn't miss a beat.

"She's not my daughter, *bro*." His tone was dark. "You heard her. Get lost."

The guy scanned Greg with a skeptical look, then shook his head and gestured for his friends to follow him as he moved off. "Whatever."

As soon as the threat was gone, it flipped a switch in my body. I was supposed to be annoyed with Greg for making me wait, but the feeling had evaporated, and now I was just overwhelmingly happy to see him. His concerned eyes landed on mine. "You okay?"

I shrugged one shoulder, pretending it was no big deal, even though my heart was still pounding. "I'm fine."

His expression was fixed. "That was impressive."

"What?"

He shifted toward me, placing a hand on the small of my back and drawing me near. The warmth of his touch made the space between us feel intimate. Like it was just the two of us in the evening shadows.

His gaze captured me and refused to let go. "What you said to him. How you put that jerk in his place."

I couldn't think straight when he was this close and I could breathe in his cologne. "I'm not an object," I said and made a face. "I mean, I'm not going to be treated like one anymore."

The statement hung for a moment. He knew who I was talking about and nodded slowly in understanding. "Is it okay if I tell you that you look amazing, though? Because you do."

I softened. "Thank you. I'm glad you're here."

"Me too." His posture relaxed, and he motioned toward the entrance. "Ready?"

EIGHTEEN

THERE WEREN'T WORDS TO DESCRIBE HOW AWESOME *JOVEN* was live, but getting to see them with Greg beside me? That was magical.

During the slow acoustic part of their set, when the stage lighting was subdued, everyone turned on their flashlight apps on their phones and swayed to the rhythm. Like lighters, but it bathed the arena in silvery light. It was intimate and beautiful, and I snuck a glance at Greg.

The sharp lines of his face were exaggerated with shadows, but he was perfect like that, all handsome and carefree. We had to look like the strangest couple ever under the artificial haze, but I didn't feel strange beside him.

It just felt right.

And then *Joven* neared the end of the concert, and I loved how the bass reverberated through my body. I moved with the crowd as the music built. Hands were thrown in the air as people joined in, the music working everyone into a frenzy, especially the floor section where we stood. Even Greg was swept up in the energy.

As the band hit the climax, gold confetti burst from cannons, filling the air, and the crowd roared their approval. I screamed against the impossibly loud sound, grinning madly as I watched the confetti slowly flutter down, catching glints of light as it fell. My gaze snagged Greg's, and I found him wearing the same wide smile I had.

It was a perfect moment—one I knew I'd remember forever, no matter what happened to us. The way he looked back at me, it seemed as if he was thinking the same thing. It made my heart clog into my throat.

I didn't hear the crowd as they thundered and cried out at the end of the song. Everything faded from my ears as he set a hand on my cheek, tilted my head toward him, and sealed his mouth over mine.

No one would notice us in a sea of eighteen thousand people, especially when the strips of gold were still raining down, landing on our heads and shoulders. So, the kiss he gave me was safe, but—oh, it wasn't. His seductive, passionate kiss was incredibly dangerous. It left me feeling adrift and like he was the only thing I could cling to.

I told him I wasn't going to be anyone's possession, but maybe I'd been wrong. Because this kiss? It owned me.

"Stay with me tonight," he shouted in my ear, over the sound of fans screaming for an encore.

When I'd bought the tickets, the plan had been I'd crash at Lilith's place after the concert was over. I hadn't told my mom that had changed, so she wasn't expecting me until tomorrow morning. And although I hadn't gotten the invite from Greg until now, I'd prepared for it. I'd packed an overnight bag, tossed it in my passenger seat, and parked my car outside Lilith's house.

Just in case, she'd lectured me earlier today, *the opportunity presents itself.*

He peered at me with a hopeful expression, waiting on my answer, and when I nodded quickly, a thrill shot through me. I'd never really spent the night with a man. Sure, I'd slept over in Preston's room a few times in college, but it was on a futon, and his roommate was there. It wasn't the same. This was how adults did it, and I was eager for Greg to see me as an equal.

Our Uber driver was a nice guy, but so talkative, Greg and I could barely get two words in edge-wise once we crawled into the back seat. My phone vibrated in my purse, and I dug it out.

Greg: Want to go for a midnight swim?

I grinned and thumbed out a response. Meanwhile, the driver continued to tell us his thoughts about the Titans' chances in the upcoming football season.

Cassidy: What if I didn't pack
a swimsuit?

I stared at Greg across the darkened back seat, and his expression left me breathless. He looked wickedly sexy, even as his gaze dropped down to the glowing phone in his hands.

Greg: Did you?

Cassidy: Yeah.

Greg: Good. It'll be fun to take it off.

The anticipation was so hot, my face burned a thousand degrees.

I changed into my black string bikini in Greg's bathroom and twisted my hair up into a bun high on my head. He'd put on his trunks in his bedroom and then had gone to get us drinks, telling me through the door to meet him poolside when I was ready.

It was almost midnight, but still hot outside. The humidity was domineering, and the bugs in the woods beyond the fence were noisy, buzzing in cycles that ebbed and flowed. The exterior lights on the side of the house weren't on, but soft, yellowy light streamed down on the pool from the enormous windows overhead. And the deep end of the kidney-shaped pool glowed from the underwater lamp.

Two folded towels were stacked on the edge of one of the lounge chairs, and my gaze drifted across the stone patio until I found Greg, hunched over one of the skimmers, replacing the lid. As he straightened, I traced every sexy muscle on his strong back. They corded and flexed when he strolled to the table and retrieved two bottles of beer, each sleeved in a koozie with the hospital logo printed on the side.

He turned.

Jesus, it was unbearably hot the way he looked at me. His gaze started at my eyes and then poured down my body, lingering over my breasts, my waist, my thighs. When he reached my ankles, his gaze started back up, moving even slower. His Adam's apple bobbed with a hard swallow, and his expression oozed lust and sin.

It took every last bit of my strength to stop myself from yanking the beer bottles from his hands, tossing them to ground, and leaping on him. I'd wanted a lot of things in my life. Getting into a good school. Someday becoming a veterinarian. Maybe even a father who gave a fuck about me. But I'd never wanted anything as badly as I wanted Greg right now.

"I figured beer instead of wine." His smug smile was reflected in his voice. He held out one of the bottles, and I padded over, taking it from him. "Cheers," he said, clinking the necks of our bottles together. "Thanks for asking me to go with you. I'm sorry I was late."

I nodded. "I get it." He'd told me between acts at the concert that one of his patients had developed a nasty post-op infection, and the call had been a lengthy deliberation between doctors on how to handle it. It really put my annoyance at waiting for him in perspective. I took a long drink of my beer. "I mean, it was literal life and death, right?"

"Yeah, but—"

"Then I can wait. I'm not that important."

Greg froze mid-sip, and then lowered his bottle. "Don't say that. Of course, you're important."

I squirmed on the inside. "Yeah, I know. I just meant in your list of priorities at that moment."

"It couldn't be helped, but, Cassidy, you should know I was looking forward to tonight all week."

He looked so damn sincere, I momentarily worried my knees would give out. I sucked in a deep breath, but my voice went shallow, regardless. "Me too."

The beer was abruptly pulled from my hand, and he thumped both of our drinks down on the edge of the pool.

"What are you—" I started but couldn't finish as he scooped me up. He lifted me until I had no choice but to fold my legs around his waist and band my arms across his back. I held on tightly as he strode toward the steps of the pool and then descended into the water, one stair at a time.

Our mouths crashed against each other as the cool water lapped at our bodies. I floated weightlessly in his arms, lacing my fingers together behind his neck as he pulled us further along and the water reached our shoulders. Deeper we went in both the pool and our kiss. His lips pushed mine open, and he thrust his tongue inside, slicking his over mine.

The pool temperature was perfect. It controlled the fire between us, keeping it a simmering burn instead of letting it rage completely out of control. I ground my lower body against the bulge swelling beneath his dark blue trunks, and something inside him seemed to snap. He moved us so fast, it made a wake in the water, and before I could catch my breath, I was pressed against the cold, hard wall at the side of the pool.

He played with the strings holding my top in place, toying with me. A shudder shook my shoulders as he drew the pad of a finger down the line between my breasts and up the other side, tracing a V over my chest. My skin was hypersensitized to his touch.

It was so strange, and yet not at all, the way we could communicate without words.

Greg leaned forward, set his forehead against mine, and watched me intently as he tugged at the knot behind my neck. Tension went out of the strings. He caught one and used it to peel the wet cup away from my breast, exposing my already-erect nipple to the night air.

His arms wrapped behind my back, causing me to arch upward, and I stared at the stars in the sky above us as his mouth closed on my breast. He licked, and sucked, and bit softly at me, and I made all the quiet cries of pleasure he'd told me he loved hearing. I couldn't stop myself, even if I had wanted to. The empty ache between my legs was constant and throbbing.

The other half of my bikini top was shoved out of his way, and after he'd given that nipple the same amount of attention, the knot at my back was undone, and the wet swimsuit top splattered up onto the pool deck.

I hooked an arm around his neck to anchor myself to him, freeing me up to touch him. I massaged him through the thick fabric of his swim trunks, and our hands tangled as he undid the Velcro closure, allowing me total access. I wrapped my fingers around his firm, long cock and squeezed. The way his eyes hazed with pleasure made a smile creep across my lips. He was so handsome and distinguished normally, but seeing him coming apart was infinitely better.

I pumped my fist on him. Once, and again, going faster until the water between us sloshed noisily against the side of the pool. His skin was slippery in my palm, making it easier to pick up the pace. I studied him the same way he did me. I watched every labored breath he took. Each muscle that flexed along his jaw. How his lips parted to get more air.

Suddenly, he shifted his hips and broke my hold. His hands slid under my arms, and I yelped as he stood, lifted me up, and seated me on the edge of the pool, where I dripped and sputtered with surprise.

Greg's expression was dark and hungry. "Lie back."

Goosebumps lifted on my thighs at his urgent command, and I followed it instantly. The stone was warm on my back, but unforgiving, and I set my hands on my stomach, not sure what else to do with them.

He'd untied my bikini top slowly, but now he attacked the knots at my hips, yanking them open. I gasped as he jerked the fabric away, tossed it into a heap, and nuzzled his face between my legs. The rough, coarse ends of his beard brushed against my inner thighs. I clenched a hand on the back of his head, holding on as his tongue probed the most intimate part of me.

His kiss was electric. It jolted me with a shock, and I cried out on every long, deliberate lick he delivered. I moaned as he fluttered and massaged the tip of his tongue against my clit. Sparks shot across my skin, making me convulse. Greg wrapped a hand around each of my thighs and pushed them back toward me, opening me further to him.

The pleasure was intense. Like nothing I'd ever felt.

A breeze swept through the patio, and I shivered, but it was oddly good too. My nipples were pointed so sharply, they ached, but it was like he knew. One hand came off my thigh and reached up, roaming over my chest until he found the right spot to twist and pull that caused a dark groan of satisfaction to roll out of me.

I was quivering, beyond ready . . . not to mention, a little cold and uncomfortable on the stone. "I want you," I whined, lifting my head to stare at him.

His eyes flashed with cockiness. "You want me to . . ."

It was almost too much. My body responded to his confidence, clenching me like a vise. I had to squeeze the plea from my mouth. "Fuck me."

He slapped his palms loudly against the stone and vaulted up out of the pool, dripping on me as he pulled off his swimsuit and added it to the pile. His gaze swept appreciatively along the nude line of my body and then moved on to one of the lounge chairs, the one that lay flat. He flung a finger at it.

"There. Now."

It was like he could only think in basic words, and I understood why. He wanted to satisfy a raw, primal need. I wanted it too and scrambled to my feet. It was only once I took a knee on the cushion, turned, and lay down on my back that I realized what was about to happen.

Greg was going to fuck me in the exact same spot he'd watched me last month with his son.

NINETEEN

WHY DID THIS IDEA TURN ME ON SO BADLY?

As I got comfortable on the cushion, I watched Greg fling aside the top towel in the stack and snatch up the condom he'd brought out. Then he stalked toward me, his face serious, as he tore open the edge of the wrapper with his teeth and pulled the condom out. He came for me like a man on a mission.

His body was beautiful. Rivulets of water cascaded down his chest, slaloming between the defined ridges of muscles, and he glistened in the soft light coming from inside the house.

The chair beneath me groaned as he planted a knee between my legs and then finished rolling the condom down the length of himself. My breath caught in my lungs. Everything inside me was tight with anticipation and need. As he knelt between my knees, he cast his eyes downward, following the stroke of his own hand, readying himself.

"This is my fantasy," he said. He rubbed the tip of his cock on my slit, making me squirm and shift. I needed him inside me. Couldn't he see how desperate I was? His gaze moved along my body until it connected with mine. "My fantasy," he continued, "every day since I saw you out here with him."

My mouth dropped open in surprise then rounded into a silent moan as he pushed himself into me. It felt like he was everywhere. Inside my body, inside my mind, inside the deepest recesses I didn't allow myself to go. It couldn't be his fantasy—because it was *mine*. I tried to tell him, but his first thrust was so powerful, all I could do was grab the cushion beneath us and hang on.

"I was jealous. So unbelievably jealous." Greg widened his knees, which were tucked under my spread legs, and pumped his hips a second time. I recoiled with pleasure, and a victorious look lit up his eyes. "Watching him get to fuck you, when I wanted it to be me. I wanted it to be like this."

Oh. My. God.

I was a stick of dynamite, and his confession cut the fuse in half. One spark and I was done for.

He set his hands on my knees and slid his palms along my inner thighs, pressing me wide open to him. "I stood there watching, and I didn't know I was capable of being that jealous about anything until then. I wanted you so fucking bad, Cassidy."

I let go of the cushion and placed my palms against his damp chest, needing to touch him. I wanted more contact. Craved his mouth on me. He obliged my unspoken request and set his hands on the cushion on either side of my head, lowering his lips to mine. Our wet skin stuck to each other, and I moaned into his kiss as he eased faster, moving at a steady, seductive pace.

"What did you think," he said between hurried breaths, "when you caught me watching?"

His open mouth hovered, his lips brushing mine and threatening a kiss, but he was just far enough away, I'd have to commit to it. I undulated beneath him, and the way he teased the kiss was . . . sensual. But he acted as if I'd only get my reward when I'd earned it and told the truth.

"I wanted it to be you," I said in a blur. I hadn't even admitted it to myself, and now here I was, saying it out loud. "After I saw you—" How far should I go with this? Should I tell him all of it? "I closed my eyes and imagined I was with you."

"Oh, *fuck*," he said and descended upon me.

The intensity of our movements went wild. Finding out our dark appetites matched each other was liberating, and we reveled in it. His rhythm changed from seduction and passion, and crossed into a territory that was more primal.

The lounge chair squeaked and protested as he drove into me, but I moaned louder, needing to compete with the sound. I didn't want Greg's attention on anything other than me, not even for a second.

The question had lingered in the back of my mind for weeks, and I felt free enough to ask it. "How long did you stand there, watching?"

"Long enough to know I could do it better."

My eyes went wide. It was indecent, yet all the liquid in my body rushed to my center.

Greg's expression was pure dominance. "Am I right?"

"Yes," I said, gulping down a breath and nodding profusely.

"Good. I'm going to fuck you until all you remember is being with me on this chair."

"Oh, God," I gasped.

He made good on his threat. We fucked like nothing else mattered. Like animals programmed to do what instinct dictated . . . It was primordial. Basic.

And it was incredible.

I shook beneath him, trembling with satisfaction. His movement inside my body drowned out everything else. I didn't see the stars above, or feel the night breeze, or hear the crickets singing in the trees. There was only this stunning man over me, taking his pleasure and giving it right back.

Just as I began the climb toward orgasm, Greg retreated. He planted a foot on the ground beside the chair, so he was half standing and half kneeling, with one knee between my legs. Off came the condom with a quick jerk and it was flung to the ground.

I stared up at him over my heaving chest, stunned and not sure what was happening, but he dug a hand under my neck and lifted me up. He supported me like that, so I was sitting but leaned back in his hold, and then he seized my hand, guiding it to his dick.

He wanted me to jerk him off?

My face burned hot as I understood his intent. Once I began to move my fist, gliding back and forth on him, he reached down and plunged his middle finger all the way inside me.

His lips were at my forehead, and his warm breath rolled over my face. The faster I moved my fist, the faster his breathing went, along with the finger moving inside me.

His palm ground against my clit, and the climb toward my orgasm began again.

"Harder," he encouraged quietly.

I tightened my grip and watched a shudder glance through his shoulders. Blood whooshed through my system as my heart pounded, trying to keep up. God, it felt so good. I used my free hand to support myself, along with his palm behind my neck, and leaned back further, shifting the angle so he could drive deeper inside. All the way until he hit the spot that made my toes point with pleasure.

"Oh . . . *oh!*" I gasped.

A devious smile spread across Greg's face. "Yeah, that's it." He moved his hips in time with my hand sliding on him. "Just like that. Make me come all over you."

His words struck the match and held the fire to my fuse. I couldn't hold back even if I wanted to. Heat blasted through my core, and his sinful finger tapped the perfect place to make me detonate.

I groaned loudly as I came, sounding somewhat panicked because the sensation was *intense*. My body seized. I clamped down on the finger still inside me while my legs trembled uncontrollably, and my fist slowed to a halt. Moans streamed from my lips, broken only by desperate rasps for air.

I hadn't finished coming down before he grabbed my fist and encouraged me to pump once more. We made it three strokes before he exhaled sharply and jerked in my hand. I flinched as the warm, thick strands flicked onto my body, dousing my breasts and stomach. Wave after wave until he was spent, slowing our mutual grip to a stop, and the last drop dripped from him.

Holy shit.

I never understood it in porn. Until this moment, watching a guy come on a woman had done nothing for me. If anything, I found it degrading. A man marking his territory. But as I stared down at my spattered skin, I flooded with a different kind of satisfaction. I liked how Greg had marked me as his.

I liked it a whole fucking lot.

He eased me onto my back, and his expression lingered on his work. Was he admiring the way I looked? I bit down on my bottom lip.

"Stay right there," he whispered. "I'll be right back."

Where was he going? The thought hit me instantly. Was he going for his phone he'd left on the patio table, so he could take a picture? Every muscle in me clenched at the idea. It was foolish—dangerous to want him to do that, but I did. Another bad idea to add to our list.

But disappointment ripped through me as he grabbed a towel and unfolded it as he came toward me, his phone ignored. He stood beside the chair, readying to help me clean off, but hesitated once he looked at my face.

His voice was full of dread, like he thought he'd done something wrong. "What?"

"Nothing." I forced a laugh and reached for the towel. "It's stupid."

He drew away, pulling the towel with him and out of my grasp. His expression went skeptical. "What's stupid?"

I groaned inside my head. If Greg and I were going to keep our relationship on the down-low, I needed to get a lot better at being a decent actress. My tone was sheepish. "I thought you were going to grab your phone."

He didn't follow. "You thought I needed to call someone?"

"No," I squeaked out. Oh, God, I wilted with embarrassment. "You were staring at me like you liked the way I looked, and . . . You know." Although he clearly didn't. My voice was shallow. "Take a picture, it'll last longer."

He blinked away his confusion as he considered the statement. Then, his expression turned into something so lewd and exciting, it stole my breath. His bare feet slapped against the stone when he sped to the table, plucked up his phone, and hurried back to me.

The smart voice in the back of my mind announced its concern but was instantly overruled as Greg held up the phone and studied the screen. He was so focused, and I held perfectly still as he moved in and shifted to get exactly the right shot. When the flash went off, I jolted with unexpected satisfaction. I'd never taken sexy pics of myself, and certainly not with Preston. But the concept of this filthy picture in Greg's phone? It was so sexy.

And then he showed it to me.

I flushed hot all over at the image of myself sprawled out on the cushion, covered in the product of our dirty deed and wearing it proudly. My face wasn't in the shot, and I liked that. This night and this picture were a secret, just for us.

"Whoa," I said quietly.

He took the phone back and grinned as he locked the screen. "*Whoa* is right. That doesn't even do it justice." He set his phone down on the chair beside me, picked up the towel, and set about wiping me off. His hands moved slowly and sensually, and I sighed. When he was finished, he slipped in to lie beside me, although he took up the majority of the chair, and had to hang onto me to keep me from falling off.

I wasn't complaining.

It was a great excuse to wrap myself around him and press my cheek up against the warm skin of his chest. I didn't want this night to be over. I needed the universe to suspend time. Delay it enough so I could stay here under the night sky with him a little longer.

He traced the tip of his finger over my hairline, tucking a loose lock of my hair behind my ear. "We can't fall asleep out here," he said.

But his deep voice was soothing, and I snuggled closer. "Mm-hm."

"I'm serious. The mosquitos will eat us alive."

"I'm too comfortable. You're going to have to carry me."

I'd meant it as a joke, but he extricated himself from my hold, stood, and slipped his arms under my body.

"I was kidding!" I scrambled away from his hands and onto my feet. "Were you really going to carry me to bed?"

He reached a hand up and massaged the back of his neck, flashing a smirk. "I was going to attempt it. But I also did upper-body today at the gym, so I appreciate you making it easier on me. Just like I'm sure you appreciate me not dropping you while we're halfway up the stairs, because that was probably going to happen."

I laughed as I grabbed a clean towel and wrapped it around myself, covering up, and bent to rescue my bikini from the ground. He busied himself pulling on his damp swim trunks and then cleaned up around the pool, bringing me my nearly untouched beer. "Ready?"

I looked up at the glowing windows of the living room, and a thrill raced through me. I was excited to spend the night beside him in his house, in his bed. I tried to sound sultry and confident. "Yeah. Take me to bed."

It didn't have the desired effect, because he grinned widely. "Or lose you forever?"

Um . . . "What?"

His smile froze. "*Top Gun*? When Meg Ryan says, 'Take me to bed, or lose me forever.'"

I shook my head slowly.

"You haven't—" He visibly struggled to put his thoughts together into a sentence. All he could come up with was, "C'mon, seriously?"

I shrugged. "Sorry."

He feigned an exaggerated, disappointed sigh. "Okay, Cassidy. We're adding that to the list."

I laughed softly, but inside it brought on a fresh wave of heat. I liked adding to our other list better.

TWENTY

DURING THE NIGHT, GREG SELFISHLY STOLE ALL THE COVERS. I shouldn't have been surprised—Preston did it too. And then I mentally kicked myself for making the comparison. The Lowe men were similar, but certainly not the same, and once again, I repeated my mantra. I wouldn't make comparisons between them. It wasn't fair.

Beyond the windows, birds chirped and sang their persistent morning songs. As I stared at Greg's peaceful face resting against his pillow, the blanket twisted over his waist, I couldn't help but think a scary thought. Had he compared me to his past girlfriends?

Was that even what I was?

We hadn't defined this thing between us, and I was more comfortable that way right now. I'd just gotten out of a major relationship—my first love. I shouldn't rebound right into another. Plus, I'd go back to school in another month to start my sophomore year. He was forty years old with a demanding job. We couldn't date, even if he was interested in doing that.

Was he interested?

I sighed loudly and climbed out of the bed, needing to escape my thoughts. I dug into my overnight bag, tugged on a tank top and the boxer shorts I usually slept in, and scurried to the kitchen.

Coffee wasn't something I craved. I was a casual drinker, who preferred the chocolatey, pseudo-coffee drinks you could get at Starbucks. But Greg? He was hardcore. He needed his morning fix of caffeine like air. My gaze landed on the fancy, intimidating machine on the counter beside the stove.

I'd watched him fix his coffee enough times over the years, and I was smart. I could figure this out, couldn't I? I'd make him a mug, return to his bed, and wake him up. The coffee would make sure he had no reason to leave. Neither of us had to work today, and I pictured us staying in bed until lunchtime.

But the machine was evil.

It took me forever to figure out where to put the water in, and once I had, then I had to choose from the six silver buttons on the side with pictures that made no sense. I pulled up Google on my phone and typed in the brand of the coffee maker. There was a YouTube tutorial . . . only it was *seventeen* fucking minutes long.

"Come on, machine. Help a girl out," I grumbled.

"Good morning."

Greg's voice startled me, and I flinched, nearly dropping the phone. "Oh!" I spun to face him.

He was shirtless. He had on a pair of faded blue pants, tied at the waist, and they sat low across his hips. Hospital scrubs were supposed to be baggy and shapeless, but on him? Dear God, those pants were doing things to me. I tried not to stare at the defined, taut muscles of his lower abs or the way the dusting of hair there disappeared beneath the gathered waistband holding the pants in place.

All he needed was a stethoscope slung over his shoulders. Every dirty doctor fantasy flooded my brain in an instant, pushing out all other thoughts. If I pulled on the drawstring, undoing the knot, how fast could I get his pants down?

He padded on his bare feet toward me beside the machine, oblivious to how affected I was. He glanced at the water gauge, then picked up the pitcher to fill it again. "That's not going to make enough for both of us."

"I don't want any coffee." I was mesmerized by how comfortable and casual he seemed standing this close to me while we were both barely dressed.

His confusion only lasted a moment. "You were making it for me?"

I stood with my back against the counter and nodded.

His smile started in his eyes. "I guess I can't be mad at you for leaving my bed, then."

He leaned across me, trapping me in place as he grabbed one of the little cups of coffee grounds, put it in the machine, and pressed a button. The thing whirred to life, but the slow, methodical movements of the man towering over me already had my body raring to go. He was so close, and rather than move out of my space, he rested his hands on the counter on either side of me and stood only a breath away.

"What should we do," he asked in a low, wicked tone, "while we wait for the coffee to finish brewing?"

I had a million suggestions, every one of them bad—

A deep chime rang out from the front entryway, making my heart skip and Greg freeze. At the sound of his doorbell ringing, his accusatory gaze flew to the clock on the coffee maker. He was probably thinking the same thing I was. Who the hell was at his front door at eight in the morning on a Sunday?

He pulled his phone out, scrolled to an app, and gave an exasperated sigh. I leaned over to peer at the screen. The image was the front porch, and a blonde woman in her late forties or early fifties stood there, trying to peer through the beveled glass of the front door.

His voice was clipped. "Judy Maligner from next door. That woman cannot take a hint."

This was the divorcee who'd been trying to woo Greg with fresh lemonade and baked goods. I gazed at her for another moment. She was nice looking. She had on yoga pants and a sherbet-colored athletic top that was fitted and showed off how she kept herself in shape. Her short hair was styled, she was wearing a little makeup, and everything about her looked as if she were making an effort . . . all to appear effortlessly casual.

When her face turned down in an unflattering scowl, it suddenly made her seem much older.

Breath was tight in my lungs as we watched her on the screen. She shifted on her feet and examined through the dining room window, but unless she could see through walls, we were safe from her prying eyes.

Tension relaxed out of Greg's shoulders when Judy crossed her arms over her chest, pressed her lips together, and finally gave up. As she walked away, relief needled at me. The way Preston had described Ms. Maligner, it had given me a very different impression. I'd expected a frumpy older woman. One who was oblivious that Dr. Lowe was out of her league.

But was she out of his league?

Judy was pretty and slender. She had a job, owned a house, could order a beer at a bar. I wasn't stupid. I knew it made more sense for him to be with her than me, and suddenly I was grateful he'd brushed her off all those times.

"Did you ever go out with her?" I forced casualness into my words.

He put his phone away in his back pocket. "No."

"Okay." I bit down on the inside of my cheek, not sure why I'd even asked. It wasn't like I had any right to him before we slept together. Today was a different story. I'd spent the night and woken beside him in his bed. I wanted some kind of ownership.

Greg's dark eyes sharpened. "You're looking at me funny."

"Are you, I don't know . . ." I frowned. "We didn't talk about it. Are you seeing other people?"

He cocked his head to the side. "Besides you? No." A warm smile spread across his lips. "You?"

I choked on a laugh. "Um, no." Besides the fact I'd just ended things with his son, couldn't he tell I was too hung up on him? Greg dominated my thoughts, and every minute spent with him only twisted me up further.

"I'm only seeing you, Cassidy." He gripped my face in his hands, brushing his thumb over my cheekbone as he slowly lowered his mouth toward mine. "In fact, I'd like to see a lot more of you right now."

His lips were fire, but they were the slow, smoldering kind. His mouth was soft against mine, and my knees weakened as his tongue dipped past my lips. One of his hands smoothed down my neck, glided over my collarbone, and moved down further until his fingers inched beneath the neckline of my tank top.

My nipples snapped to points, tingling and eager for his attention. The strap was pushed over the curve of my shoulder and peeled down. I sighed and stretched into his touch, enjoying how his lips progressed down my neck, working toward his fingers massaging my breast.

A moan seeped from me, barely audible over the bubbling coffee machine, as he skimmed the sharp edge of his teeth across my pebbled nipple. *Christ, that felt good.* I wrapped my arms around his head, holding him to me, encouraging him to feast on my exposed flesh.

But a tingling, uncomfortable sensation flashed across the hairs on my arms and rocketed up my back. It was a warning of danger that my body sensed before the rest of me. A shadow fell on us, coming through the window over the sink, and drew his attention before mine.

He hardened into stone, and I glanced over my bare shoulder to see what he was looking at.

Oh. Shit.

TWENTY-ONE

THE HORROR I FELT WAS EXPRESSED PERFECTLY ON JUDY
Maligner's stunned face. What the hell was she doing in
Greg's side yard, staring at us through the window? And
how long had she been watching while I had a boob out and
Greg's mouth on me?

He grabbed my wrist and yanked me stumbling along
until we were out of her view, barely giving me a chance to
pull the strap up and cover myself.

"Did she see us?" I asked, which was pointless. Of course
she had, and his somber expression confirmed it. I tried to
bolt, not having any plan, but he trapped my waist in his
hands. His voice was soothing and calm. "Stay here. I'll throw
on a shirt and then . . . handle this."

I stared up at him. Even though he was looking down
at me, it was clear I wasn't really registering. I could see the
gears turning in his head, working. He was too focused on
damage control.

And that was exactly how I felt right now. I was doing
nothing to him but damage. I shook off his hold and strode
toward his room, needing to flee as if that would somehow
help our situation. "I should get dressed too."

He didn't argue. Instead, he followed me toward the
bedroom, but he moved much faster than I did and beat me

through the doorway. He snagged a t-shirt from a drawer, yanked it on, and gave me a serious look. "Stay put, okay?" he asked quietly. "I've got this."

My mouth dropped open to speak, but he turned and pulled the door nearly closed. His heavy footsteps grew quieter as he hurried toward the back-patio door in the kitchen.

I scrambled into the wrinkled clothes I'd packed for today and raked a hairbrush through my tangled hair, trying to make it look presentable. The only makeup on my face was whatever was left over from last night. God, I was the opposite of Judy in every way this morning.

A door closed, and two pairs of footsteps drifted in from the kitchen. I reached for the doorknob, but hesitated when I heard her voice, full of righteousness.

"Her car's in the driveway."

Greg's tone was pointed. "And?"

There came a sound like she was flustered. "Well, when no one answered the door, I thought she'd spent the night with Preston while you weren't home. I assumed you're a good father who doesn't allow that sort of thing."

"What 'sort of thing?'" Greg's words were sharp, and I pictured his expression matching his voice.

"You know what I mean. Letting your son's teenage girlfriend sleep over." She said the word *teenage* the same way I imagined prim and conservative Judy would say *atheist democrat*.

A long and very male sigh rang out. "First of all, Cassidy isn't Preston's girlfriend—"

"Well, I'd certainly hope not."

"And she's an adult. Second, how I raise my son isn't really your business. Did I ask you to come into my yard and look through my windows?"

The pitch and volume of her voice climbed. "I was doing you a favor! I thought you'd want to know how that *girl* spent the night, because it's so inappropriate." Judy drew in a deep breath. "Lordy, I had no idea just how inappropriate it really was."

"Judy—"

"She's a child. What are you doing with her?"

I slumped against the wall.

"That's definitely none of your business," he answered, maintaining an even keel, but I heard the edge beneath. He was close to losing his patience.

"This is why you're not interested?" she spat out. "I'm not young enough for you."

I sucked in a sharp breath.

"No," Greg snapped. "I'm not interested in you, because of *you*. I've tried to be polite, believe me, but that ended the second you decided to trespass on my lawn and invade my privacy. No more visits, Judy. Unless it's an emergency, you stay on your side of the property line. Understood?"

She gasped so loudly, I could practically see the indignation on her face. "You're unbelievable. Does Preston know what you're doing?"

His voice wasn't threatening, but it was plenty serious. "Come over here again and it'll be harassment."

"Oh, don't you worry. You won't be seeing me again." Footsteps moved at a clipped pace, then stopped abruptly.

"Her? Really, Greg? You're taking advantage of that girl and should be ashamed of yourself."

"I think we're done here, and I'd like you to leave."

The patio door slammed shut and was followed by a long, aching silence. I swallowed the lump in my throat, grabbed my overnight bag, and trudged toward the kitchen. I stopped just inside to spy him facing away from me, his hands spread on the counter and his head hung. He looked deep in thought.

I wanted to stay and yet needed to run. Anything to avoid the difficult stuff. My voice was a ghost. "I should go."

He straightened and turned, casting a glance at me over his shoulder, and just the profile of his torn expression made my heart hurt.

"How much of that did you hear?" he asked.

I tilted my head to the side and shrugged a shoulder. "You're not taking advantage of me," I said quietly.

He turned all the way to face me, crossed his arms over his chest, and leaned back against the counter, studying me. "Don't listen to her. She's just pissed, that's all."

Was he telling me, or himself? At least what he was saying made sense. She'd pursued him but been rejected. Maybe her anger had been a defense mechanism, but it was hard not to see a sliver of truth.

Greg looked resigned. "We need to tell Preston about us."

I sighed. "He's in North Carolina."

"I meant when he gets back."

Dread lined my stomach like lead, weighing me down. "I don't think it's a good idea."

He raised an eyebrow, signaling annoyance. "You think he should hear it from Judy instead?"

"Of course not." I scowled. "How's he going to hear it from her? You told her to stay away."

His irritation grew. "I did, but—"

"No. We talked about this." The anxiety left over from Judy's interruption lingered and churned, making me feel awful. "We said we'd tell him once we were ready."

His mood was worse than mine, and for the first time, he directed a gaze at me like I was an insolent little girl. "I know you don't want to, but we can't avoid this."

"I'm not ready."

He sighed. "You're acting like a child—"

The word died on his tongue, but it was too late. Anger and embarrassment welled inside me, rising like a bubbling caldron. "Oh, I'm a child now? I thought you told Judy I was an adult."

"I said you're *acting* like one. There's a difference."

I tightened my grip on my overnight bag. "I have to go."

He threw his hands up, then set them on his hips. "You know what? Fine. I think that's a good idea."

It wasn't what I expected. Wasn't he supposed to fight me on this? Tell me all the ways I was being wrong? Even though it was what I'd asked for, it felt like he was giving up, and suddenly it was the last thing I wanted.

His expression softened. "Last night was great, and I don't want to ruin that. She rattled us. Let's cool off for now, and we can talk later. Okay?"

Stunned wasn't a strong enough word for me. He was right. The unannounced guest had set me on edge, and getting some space and a clear head was the best idea. And he was right too about last night. I didn't want the confrontation with Judy to tarnish my time with him any more than she already had.

So, I nodded and agreed with an uneven voice. "Okay."

We'd said we were going to talk about it, but Greg didn't bring it up that evening when he texted to see how my day was. And he didn't mention it the next night, either. We pretended both the Judy and Preston issues didn't exist. Like they weren't looming over us, and we weren't on borrowed time.

Except Preston made that difficult. During my lunch break, my phone buzzed with a text message.

Preston: I miss you.

I clicked the button on the side of my phone to make the screen go black, wishing it'd take the message out of existence just as quickly. What did he mean, he missed me? I'd been around for months and he didn't care.

I groaned as I realized what was probably going on. He was lonely in North Carolina right now, away from his friends. It was the only reason he'd be thinking of me.

After a long day at the animal hospital, I passed on grabbing dinner with Lilith, needing to go home and take a shower. Not because I was feeling gross from work, but because standing in the tub under a stream of hot water was my safe space to release my emotions.

I loved my job. I wanted with all my heart to be a veterinarian. But some days were incredibly tough, and this morning I'd had to watch a family say goodbye to their beloved German shorthair pointer. I was almost as wrecked as they were but did my best to keep it together.

As the hot water beat down on me, it all came out in a cleansing cry.

And I felt better when my shower was over, but as I wrapped the towel around my body, there was still a craving for release itching inside me.

> Cassidy: Hey! What are you
> doing tonight?

I dried my hair while I eagerly waited for his response, and then got dressed in skinny jeans and the t-shirt I'd bought at the *Joven* concert.

> Greg: Rounds. One more patient and
> then I'm done.

My mind flashed back to him in the hospital scrubs, and my breath quickened.

> Cassidy: Are you wearing a white
> doctor's coat?

Greg: Yes. Why?

I mustered up the courage to type what I wanted.

Cassidy: I just wanted to picture my
fantasy right, Dr. Lowe.

Dots blinked across the screen, then disappeared. It twisted my nerves into a tight coil. Was he trying to find the right way to tell me my fantasy of him as my naughty doctor was wrong?

Greg: Come to the hospital.

"What?" I shrieked, alone in my room where thankfully no one could hear.

Greg: Park in the lot. We'll go back to
my place and you can see the doctor
coat in action.

The wave of lust was so strong, it nearly knocked me down. I latched a hand onto the counter to steady myself. As it slowly subsided, I considered the rest of his statement. If I left my car in the hospital parking lot, nosy Judy wouldn't be able to see that Greg had invited me over.

Cassidy: I'll be there in 20.

TWENTY-TWO

I RODE THE ENORMOUS HOSPITAL ELEVATOR TO THE FOURTH floor and crossed my arms over my chest as I stepped into the chilly hallway. It was hot and humid outside, but in the hospital, it was arctic.

The hallway was lined with windows, and the sun was sinking in the sky, glaring off windshields of cars in the parking lot below. Had Greg even seen the sun today? He'd been on call since four a.m.

It was quiet as I walked along the empty hallway. There was a space to my left with a few rows of chairs, but no one was seated there waiting. I pulled out my phone and stared at the text I'd received from him a few minutes ago.

> Greg: Go to the desk and tell the
> receptionist you're here to see me.

My heart tripped along at double-speed. The idea of role-playing as a patient of his? God, it turned me on. I was filled with anticipation for later tonight, excited to do this. But I also had anxiety about pretending now with strangers. Not just strangers, but his co-workers. It was dangerous, and maybe a little exciting too.

The desk was basically a wall with a sliding glass window, which was open, and when I approached, the woman seated behind it barely looked up.

"Hi. I'm here for Dr. Lowe," I said. Could she hear how unsteady my voice was?

If she did, she didn't seem to think anything of it. "Your name?"

"Cassidy Shepard."

She plucked a Post-It note off her desk with my name scribbled on it and nodded toward the waiting room chairs. "Have a seat. He'll be with you shortly."

I was tight and edgy as I slipped into one of the chairs and ran my sweaty palms along the side seams of my jeans. There was a clock on the far wall, and every loud tick from its second hand reverberated through my body. The wait was both uncomfortable and . . . *pleasurable.* My mind ran through different fantasies. How far would he let me go in the role play? Could I be the bold, naughty patient I wanted to be for him?

I practically yelped and leapt from the chair when the door swung open and Greg leaned out. "Cassidy? Come on back."

I didn't get a full look at him because he stood behind the door, holding it open for me. I shuffled along the carpet, and as soon as I stepped through the door into a new hallway, I was ushered to a room on my left.

There was a nice couch on one side, a coffee table with magazines, and two oversized chairs on the other. It was a nicer waiting room than where I'd just been, but much smaller. Only enough room for six people or so.

This had to be the place where doctors delivered their post-op summary to families. I turned to face him, and all the air whooshed from my lungs.

Greg was essentially wearing a suit. He wore black dress pants, a white collared shirt and a cobalt-colored tie. His suit-coat was fitted and white, and he completed the look with a turquoise stethoscope slung around his neck. My gaze traced the blue lettering over his right breast.

Gregory Lowe, MD

Trauma Surgery

It didn't matter that he had faint lines around his eyes hinting at his fatigue, or that his normally perfect hair looked disheveled, as if he'd run a hand through it one too many times. It didn't matter because he looked fucking perfect. My dirty doctor fantasy come to life.

And he gazed back at me like he wanted to eat me whole, which was more than fine with me. He sauntered over, and his confidence seemed to build with each step, widening his wicked smile.

His voice was deep and sinful. "What seems to be the problem?"

"Problem?" I whispered.

"You're flushed. Breathing hard." He seized my wrist, pressed his index finger to my pulse point, and peered down at his watch, counting the seconds. "Your pulse is elevated."

I had no idea my wrist was an erogenous zone, but in Greg's hands, every inch of my skin felt that way. I swallowed a breath. "I'm having a reaction to something."

God, his expression was corrupt and victorious as he walked me backward toward a wall. He feigned concern. "Any idea what's causing it?"

He wasn't playing fair, but I liked it. "No . . . *Doctor*."

The second the words left my mouth, we burst into flames. His lips slammed against mine at the same instant my back hit the wall. His hands were on my waist, then under my shirt, sliding over my belly and skimming upward. I clenched the lapels of his coat as our tongues tangled with each other, battling for control. He won, of course.

It made sense that our kiss was electric because I was a live wire tonight. His broad chest flattened against me, his hands molding to my bra-covered breasts while he pushed me against the wall. I tore my mouth from his and turned my head to the side so I could drag air into my lungs, and his hot, wet mouth latched onto the sensitive spot below my ear, biting and sucking until I let out a moan.

It was wild what we were doing, and how fast we attacked each other, but the *where* we were doing this was craziest part of it. He didn't seem to have any concerns though. "Undo your pants," he rasped into my ear. "I want to check and see how severe this reaction is."

"Oh my God," I gasped. Without thinking, my hands moved to follow his command. He pulled his lower body away from mine, just enough to allow me to do it. The snap of my jeans popped open, and I couldn't get my zipper down fast enough. *Should I be worried about someone catching us?*

I wasn't. I trusted him. Greg wouldn't put either of us in a position for that to happen, and his calm, focused expression reinforced it. He looked absolutely in control, both of me and the situation.

His dark eyes sharpened on mine, studying my response while he slid his hand down the front of my panties. My lips parted as his fingers found me hot and wet for him. What did I look like, clutching his arms right above his elbows as his fingers twitched on my swollen clit? I shuddered with pleasure. Had my pupils dilated? Could he tell my heart rate was racing through the roof?

His lips peeled back in a smug smile. "That is quite the reaction." Those skilled fingers stirred me further, and I tightened my grip on his arms, biting off a louder moan. Shit, his touch was magic. It lit me up. He could tell too, because his eyes burned with enjoyment. "And you're still not sure what's causing it?"

He liked this scene as much as I did. Maybe more. It gave him both power and the opportunity to fulfill my fantasy.

I couldn't answer his question. It was taking everything I had to stay quiet against the steady slide of his fingertips over my skin, each stroke bringing me closer to losing control.

"Hmm," he continued, leaning into me and murmuring it against my lips. "I have a diagnosis, but we'll have to delay treatment."

"Why?" I gasped. My greedy body moved against his hand. I was close. So fucking close.

"I need to administer it at my house." The kiss he gave me was erotic. "In my bed." His tongue slashed against mine. "Preferably with my mouth."

He showed me the way he planned to use it, fucking my mouth with his indecent kiss.

My bones went hollow, and for a split second I reverted to a spoiled child who didn't want delayed gratification. I had zero patience. I wanted the pleasure his hand had promised with every ministration, and I wanted it right goddamn now.

"Please," I pleaded. When his fingers began to retreat, I wrapped my hand around his wrist and stopped him. "Please," I whined again on a broken breath, grinding against his fingertips.

Conflict flashed in his eyes and then disappeared. "Soon, Cassidy. I don't want you to have to be quiet. I need to hear all those sexy sounds you make." He looked down at his hand still lodged in my panties and how I gyrated against it. "Although, I'm not going to lie, what you're doing right now is really fucking hot."

It was like he'd poured lava on my body. I sagged against the wall as he slowly dragged his hand out, caressing my skin as he went, and then attempted to do up my jeans. I shoved away from the wall and pushed his hands out of my way, because I could do them up much faster than he could.

"Okay, let's go," I said, my tone clipped and needy.

His grin was enormous.

Greg had pressed the keyring to his BMW into my hand and told me where he was parked in the doctors' lot, and said he'd meet me at the car in a few minutes.

The damp, aching throb between my legs was persistent. I was annoyed he'd left me right on the edge, but also liked it . . . a little. We both knew he could get me there, so when he'd made the decision not to, it was a way for him to flex his power. The more he did that, the further I fell under his spell.

The lights on the sleek black sedan flashed in the dusky, fading sunlight as I unlocked the doors, and I climbed inside the passenger seat. I'd ridden in his car a few times before, but never in the front seat, and I ran a hand over the smooth, premium leather. The car smelled like him.

I pictured him behind the wheel, day after day, driving this expensive car to the hospital and parking it in the doctors' lot beside the Audis and Range Rovers and Porsches. He worked so much, he barely had a life. All it consisted of was this car, his house . . . and his son.

Would there ever be space in there for me? And would Preston allow that?

I scowled at my thoughts. Why was I thinking about a future with Greg? I needed to be more like my friends and live in the present. Thinking only about today. I was turning twenty in a few weeks. I was still so young. No one expected me to make all the right decisions at this point in my life, or plan further out than the coming weekend.

A blur of white moving in the distance toward the car caught my attention. That coat. *Jesus.* My obsession with it wasn't healthy, and I felt feverish when Greg slipped into the driver's seat and stabbed a finger on the button to start the car's engine. While it roared to life, his gaze raked over me, and I melted against the seat.

"Drive fast," I whispered.

We didn't talk much on the short drive to his house, and the atmosphere in the car was taut with sex. I laced my fingers together and tucked my hands under my knee to keep myself from touching him. I didn't want to distract or slow him down, and I purposefully kept my eyes straight forward as we drove past Judy Maligner's house. I refused to see if she was standing by the window, watching Greg's every move.

My heart clogged my throat as the garage door rolled slowly up and Greg steered the car inside. His bedroom was only two doors away, and I clawed at my seatbelt, unfastening it in a hurry. He hadn't even shut the engine off—

His phone rang.

The dreaded hospital ringtone blasted through the car speakers, and I went wooden.

TWENTY-THREE

WAS GREG STILL ON-CALL? HE REACTED QUICKLY. OFF THE car went, disconnecting the Bluetooth, and he answered the phone directly.

"This is Dr. Lowe."

He didn't undo his seatbelt or get out of his seat as he listened. He barely moved at all, but the subtle way his posture stiffened told me everything I needed to know. We were heading back to the hospital, and I was going home.

The disappointment that ripped through me was *fierce.*

"Yeah," he said, glancing at his watch. "No, I'd like to. Thanks for the heads-up. Tell him I'm scrubbing in, but I'm on my way back. So, don't start without me, unless it can't wait." He hung up with a sigh and dropped his phone in his lap. "One of my patients is headed back to the OR."

"Oh."

He stared vacantly through the windshield into his garage. The long silence was unnerving.

"Don't we need to go?" I asked.

He turned in his seat to face me, and his expression was hard to read. "Maybe."

"Maybe?" I repeated. What kind of sense did that make?

"You could stay here. I don't think I'll be gone all night."

He looked tired, like it had been a never-ending day for him, but there was hope ringing his eyes. He wanted me to say yes to this.

If my only two options were going home or staying here to be with him later—well, my decision was easy.

I gulped down a breath. "Okay. What should I do while I wait?"

I expected him to give me a spiel about food in the fridge, or a "new classic" movie I needed to watch, but his gaze dropped down to the gear shift, and he seemed lost in thought. When his focus snapped back to mine, he didn't look tired anymore. He wasn't hopeful, or disappointed, or any of the emotions he'd had ten seconds ago.

Greg's expression was the same one from the private hospital room. Commanding and powerful. My mouth went dry, probably because all the moisture in my body headed to the center of my legs.

"I want you to take off your clothes, get into my bed, and make yourself come."

I gasped, but he wasn't finished.

"You," he said, "playing with yourself in my bed? *Fuck.*" He smoothed a hand down his leg, straightening the swell that threatened. "That's my fantasy. I want you rolling around in my sheets, making them smell like you. Make that whole room smell like sex by the time I get home."

My mouth hung open, and then I closed it with an audible snap. I wasn't sure what to say. My tongue was suddenly too big for my mouth. It wasn't initially one of my fantasies—not until he'd said it.

Now it was all I could think about.

His voice was deep in his throat. "Will you do that for me?"

"Yes," I whispered.

"Good." He was pleased with my immediate answer, and I was yanked into a hurried kiss. "I'll text you when I'm finished."

When he turned the car on, it spurred me into action. I opened my door and swung my legs out, climbing to my feet. My body was heavy and clumsy with lust, but I did my best to act natural. Still, I stood awkwardly in his garage as he pulled out, waved to me, and sped off. The garage door rumbled to life, jolting me out of my stupor.

I marched toward the door, climbed the step, and went inside.

In three years, it was the first time I'd been alone in the Lowe house. It was beyond strange and quiet as a museum, and since Preston hadn't been in the house for over a week, it barely looked like anyone lived here. Greg was so neat. Or maybe he wasn't home enough to make much of a mess.

Electricity crackled through my bloodstream. His request had charged everything with sex. Simply standing in the empty kitchen and gazing down the hallway toward his bedroom was a massive turn-on. The goal throbbed in my brain, and the same pulse was echoed between my legs.

There was an opened bottle of white wine in the fridge, and as I pulled a clean glass down from a cabinet, anticipation made my hand tremble. I poured myself a few swallows' worth, drew in a deep breath, and strolled toward the bedroom, ignoring Preston's graduation picture in the living room as I passed by.

I didn't turn on the bedroom light. I stood in the doorway, sipped the wine, and let my eyes adjust to the dark. Moonlight came through the windows, filtered by his wooden blinds, and cast strips of pale light over the bed. His room was so nice. Masculine and sexy. I sauntered toward the nightstand, put the glass down with a quiet thud, and set about following his first request.

Take off your clothes.

Was he thinking about me during his drive back to the hospital? Was he imagining my hands dragging my shirt slowly up over my head, letting my hair fall down my back as I dropped the shirt to the floor? I undressed slowly, a striptease for myself, but hoped he was picturing it.

Get into my bed.

Once I was naked, I folded down the comforter to the foot of the mattress, then slipped under the top sheet. The fabric was rich and soft, and it was as if every nerve ending in my body was alive. The brush of the sheets against my sensitized skin and hardened nipples made my breath quicken. Why the hell was this so sexy? All I was doing was climbing into bed, but it felt completely different than any other time I'd ever done it. As I lay back into his pillow, his scent was everywhere, and my eyes slammed shut, fighting against the sudden wave of longing I had for him.

Make yourself come.

I bit down on my bottom lip and shifted under the sheet, smoothing my hands over my breasts and working my way down. It was sensual and amazing. My own touch felt foreign and exciting. I was wet, and as I rolled two fingertips over myself, I gasped at the pleasure.

It'd take me no time to complete this task. All I had to do was picture him in that white coat and fantasize what the doctor was going to do to me when he got home. I squirmed, writhing in the sheets as I rubbed my clit, faster with each stuttered breath I took.

Should I slow down? Maybe it'd be better if he caught me like this when he came home. He'd yank me out of his bed, bend me over his knee, and pretend to show me what a bad girl I had been. I'd squeeze fistfuls of his expensive slacks in my hands while he spanked my bottom bright red.

I jerked my hand away from myself, stopping only moments from going over the edge. *That was close.* He didn't expect to be at the hospital all night, but it'd be a while before he'd be back, and I wanted to draw this out. I was supposed to make the whole room smell like sex, after all.

Fantasy after fantasy played through my mind, each one dirtier and darker than the last, and as I closed in on my orgasm, I stilled my hand just in time, edging myself. My body was primed, buzzing and clamoring for release, but I continued to tease until sweat dampened the roots of my hair at my temples and my heart beat like a furious drum.

I slid one finger inside where I was hot and wet, and sighed at the sensation. Then, I went for two, and imagined they were his fingers fucking me. It felt good, but not enough to make me come, and prolonged the session.

I tried my best to make it last, but when I couldn't hold back any longer, I frantically rubbed myself until a moan tore from my lungs and I arched up off the bed. Heat washed through me, scorching and searing, and I shuddered as the pleasure came, wave after wave.

It passed slowly, and I collapsed back on the mattress, drained. I was satisfied, but not satiated. The feeling was temporary—my self-induced orgasm was a Band-Aid, not a real fix.

Only Dr. Lowe could make it better.

I finished the wine and checked my phone, and although I'd taken my time, he'd probably be another hour. Which meant if I wanted to spend any time with him, I'd likely miss my curfew.

> Cassidy: I'm crashing at Lilith's
> tonight. Okay?

> Mom: That's fine. Thanks for
> letting me know.

Lying to my mom made me feel awful, but there wasn't an alternative. She was cool about a lot of things, but sleeping over at a guy's house wasn't one of them, and I couldn't imagine how she'd feel about me with Greg. The only true adult who knew about us was Judy, and that had gone over like a lead balloon.

My mom had met Greg a few times over the years. She was always friendly and polite, and had never said anything to me about it, but I had the strange feeling she didn't particularly like him. I'd caught her giving him side-eye more than once, and suspected she judged him for not being in Preston's life during the early years. She had baggage, and I got why she might have lumped him into the same category as my father.

I put the phone down on the nightstand and looked at the empty glass. The wine had been nice, and I could have another half glass before Greg got home. But I wasn't about to walk around his house naked. Lord knew Judy had seen plenty of me already.

His button-up shirts hung neatly in the walk-in closet off his bathroom, and I ran my hand along the sleeves absentmindedly. Would he mind if I wore one of them? He'd told me to take off my clothes, but he hadn't specifically told me to stay naked . . .

There was a simple white button-up shirt at the end that looked older and softer than the others. It probably wasn't in rotation anymore, and I took it off the hanger, slipping my arms into the sleeves. It was too big and yet just right. The shirttails ended at mid-thigh on me, and after I did up the bottom few buttons, I rolled the sleeves back onto my forearms.

Was it weird and narcissistic to think I looked good like this? I stared at my reflection in the bathroom mirror. My dark hair was tousled from my session in his bed, and my cheeks were stained pink from the wine and the intense heat simmering inside me. The shirt was thin, and if I stared hard enough, I could make out the faint dark circles of my nipples through the fabric. I oozed sex. It was fucking empowering.

I smiled to myself as I poured a new glass of wine and hoped I'd get a text from him soon. I went back to his bed, drank the wine, and scrolled through Instagram for a while.

It was either boredom or the environment, but I couldn't stay focused for long. The itch was back. The dark craving for Greg grew enormous in a small amount of time, and my mind went back to the fantasies from earlier.

He'd told me to make the sheets smell like me, and there was no way I was going to fail him. I pressed the luxurious fabric between my legs and touched myself, stirring my fingertips over the sheet until it was damp with my arousal. In my mind, what I was doing was fucking filthy, and undeniably hot.

Like last time, the fantasies escalated. I imagined him fucking me in every position, talking dirty the whole time as his body pounded into me. He'd make me beg for my orgasm. He'd shove his dick in my mouth and order me to swallow as he came down my throat. And he'd take pictures of all of it.

"Proof," he'd say, *"of what a bad little girl you are."*

I twisted in his bed, rolling and bucking at my own touch, fueled by images in my mind that were so bad, I should have felt shame for thinking them. I imagined Preston walking in on us, seeing his father's head buried in my pussy, teasing me with his skilled tongue. Preston would stand there, shock streaked over his face, unable to look away as he witnessed how much better his father was at giving me what I needed.

I was supposed to feel shame, but I didn't. I *couldn't.* Nestled in Greg's bed, I was impervious to guilt. I was safe here.

When the orgasm finally came, it wasn't as acute, but still strong. It flowed through my center and ebbed away, pleasure lingering for a long, suspended moment. I collapsed against the sheets, spent and struggling to catch my breath. Everything was warm and tingling in my body, and I relaxed, staring up through the darkness at the ceiling. I'd wanted to hold off until he was on his way home, but my dirty mind had been too powerful. Too needy.

I closed my eyes, resting for a moment. I'd need to. He'd be here soon, ready to turn my fantasies into reality.

TWENTY-FOUR

I STIRRED AWAKE, AND IT TOOK ME A MOMENT TO PLACE MY surroundings. It was brighter in the room than when I'd fallen asleep—the light was on in the bathroom and streamed softly across the bed.

I shifted, drawing up onto my elbows, and blinked quickly to adjust to the glow.

The stark white of Greg's coat stood out first, and my gaze traveled upward to meet his eyes. He stood with his arms crossed over his chest, leaning against the doorframe and a pensive look on his face.

I'd slept like the dead, and the corner of my mouth was wet. I quickly wiped the drool away with a hand, playing it off like it was a yawn and I wasn't embarrassed. "Hi. What time is it?"

"Quarter to three." His arms came down to hang awkwardly at his side. "I'm so sorry. I thought it was going to be quick. A few hours. But we had a hard time keeping him stable, and . . ." His gaze moved away from me, drifting to stare off at nothing.

I straightened and tried to steel my reaction. The hurt in Greg's eyes was unmistakable. Oh, God. He'd spent all night battling for his patient—

And he'd *lost*.

A hole opened in my chest, and I bit down on the inside of my cheek. I was dying to say something, to offer comfort somehow, but my brain failed me. I couldn't come up with a single sentence that wasn't trite or a tired platitude.

"How much trouble are you in?" he asked. "It's so late, your mom must be worried."

I shook my head. "I told her I was staying over at a friend's."

"Oh. Good." Relief spread across his expression. His voice was soft and light, masking his desperation. "Can you stay?"

Very little on earth could force me from this bed right now. "Yeah."

He drew in a deep breath and pushed it out, like he was cleansing his emotions. The wrinkles around his eyes were more pronounced now, and he looked exhausted as he moved toward me.

"How long have you been up?" I asked.

His warm fingertips caressed my cheek, moving to cup the side of my face and draw me into a kiss. "I don't know. Twenty-five hours, maybe?" His mouth tasted like coffee. Faint amusement darted through his weary eyes. "I thought I told you to get naked." He toyed with the collar of the shirt I was wearing. His shirt, technically. "But I like this."

I warmed, trying to match his mood shift. "You told me to take off my clothes . . . which I did."

I threaded my fingers through his hair and tried to pull him down to sit beside me on the bed, but he resisted. He captured my wrists in his hands and freed himself from my grasp, straightening and giving me a studious look.

"Are you still experiencing discomfort?"

Confusion flooded me. "What?"

"Your problem earlier." His expression hinted at the game. "Do you still have symptoms?"

My mouth rounded into an *"oh"* as I got it. Our scene from before, the fantasy I'd asked for. I softened. "Greg, you've got to be exhausted. We don't have to—"

A sad smile curled at the edge of his lips. "You're always thinking about other people and never yourself. That ends tonight. Cassidy, you want this, and I want to give it to you."

I frowned and opened my mouth to tell him he was being silly. It was three in the morning, but he cut me off.

"What if I tell you I need this?"

I inhaled sharply at his confession and understood instantly. Hadn't I texted him earlier tonight for a similar reason? To use my time with him to forget the heavy, emotionally draining day? I pushed my hair back, tucking it behind an ear, and struggled to refocus.

"Yes," I announced in an unsteady voice, "I have this ache that won't go away."

Gratefulness ringed his eyes, then vanished as he settled into his role. "Can you lie back? I'd like to take a look."

Just like that, the sexual charge between us was back. It snapped taut, making it hard to breathe. I leaned back into the pillow and let my hands fall to my sides, staring up at the gorgeous man looming over me. His scrutinizing, thoughtful gaze swept over me in the moments before he reached for the sheet and slowly peeled it out of his way. Down his attention went, taking in my bare legs, and then his attention returned upward, tracing the line of buttons on the oversized dress shirt covering me.

Perhaps his exam was clinical, but my skin burst into flames the second he touched me. His warm fingertips pressed gently to the lymph nodes in my neck, but his touch on my throat was sensual. He trailed his fingers down, gliding them to the hollow between my collarbones.

His hands on my body seemed to melt his exhaustion away and turned his voice into gravel. "Where does it ache?"

The muscles deep in my belly clenched. "Lower," I whispered.

As he eased back the sides of the open collar of my shirt, the steel of the stethoscope hanging around his shoulders glinted in the low light. I trapped my bottom lip between my teeth and tucked my fingertips beneath my thighs to keep my hands to myself. I wanted to snare his tie and haul him down to me, but I also didn't want this scene to end. It'd barely started, and I was already panting.

His dark eyes turned somehow darker as his fingers located the top button and pulled it free. "I'll have to undo this to continue the exam."

The white coat, matched with his soothing doctor's voice? I didn't stand a chance. I swallowed a ragged breath and hoped he didn't notice how furiously my chest was heaving. Although I was sure he did. It didn't seem like anything got by Dr. Lowe.

He shifted the open neckline to the side, just enough to expose my bare, extended nipple. He grazed over it with his knuckles before turning his palm over and gripping me.

"Here?" He looked so serious. So committed to his role. "Is this where it aches?"

I trembled under his watchful gaze, loving every second of this. I shook my head minutely. It drove him to the other side, and he repeated the action. The pad of one fingertip swirled a circle around my nipple, and then he pinched it between his thumb and the side of his hand. It was an electric shot straight to my clit, and I jolted.

"Lower," I gasped.

His half-smile was indecent. He liked what he was doing as much as I did.

He popped the buttons on the shirt one by one at a painstakingly slow tempo. I had my knees pressed together, squeezing against the anticipation of his hand running between my legs. My heart galloped and skipped along, making the blood rush loudly through my ears. God, I wanted him so badly, but the scary thing was I wanted to please him even more.

I shivered when Greg opened the shirt and exposed me completely. Goosebumps burst over my flesh, dotting my skin, and he coasted both palms over my trembling belly. His eyes were half-lidded and heavy with lust while they followed the path of his hands descent to my hips.

"Here?" His hands slid inward, his thumbs brushing lightly over my mound. "Or here?"

I arched upward. "Oh, God. There."

"Try to stay still." He was teasing and commanding in the same instant. His hands—his fucking hands—they moved so slow. One fraction of an inch at a time, until finally, he grazed my clit. A single stroke. That was all he gave.

"It hurts there?"

"Yes," I hissed. "Yes . . . *Dr. Lowe*."

He sucked in a sharp breath, and my head lolled to the side to take him in completely. He was standing at the edge of the bed, and I could see the swelling bulge in his dark slacks, well within striking distance for me. I reached out and ran my palm up his inseam, cupping him through his pants, only for him to swivel his hips away.

"That's not appropriate," he said, and sweet baby Jesus, I threatened to liquify under his intense, scolding stare. Nothing about this was appropriate, and I fucking reveled in our naughtiness.

Greg shifted on his feet, adjusting his stance so he could touch me with ease. He slipped his hand between my thighs and dragged it upward, all the way until the side of his index finger brushed against my throbbing center.

"Part your legs, please," he said.

My trembling legs fell open, giving him more room to explore. A moan ruptured from deep inside my chest, and he cocked one eyebrow, studying me. Without even trying, the throaty moan was just right. The sound I made was the same for pleasure or pain.

"On a scale of one to ten, how would you rate your discomfort?" As he asked it, the pads of his fingertips massaged my clit, and I clenched my teeth so hard, I wondered if I'd split my jaw.

"Eleven," I groaned.

"Well, that's definitely a problem." His gaze flowed down my bare body and zeroed in on his hand that stroked tiny circles where I was impossibly wet. When my hips flexed, rolling in time with his manipulations, he set the palm of his free hand flat on my belly and pressed down, pinning me to the mattress. "I can help alleviate your symptoms, but you have to hold still. Understood?"

I breathed out the words. "Yes, Dr. Lowe."

It was a million degrees in the room, and a bead of sweat trickled down my hairline. Staying motionless while I was essentially naked and he was fully clothed was a challenge, and it became a thousand percent worse as his hand increased both pressure and speed. I balled my fists into the open shirt at my sides, squeezing until my hands ached.

The sensation built with each stroke of his fingers, and I threatened to fly apart. It felt so good. Whimpers leaked from my mouth. I tried my hardest to stay still, but Greg obliterated that option when he sank his middle finger deep inside me, all the way to the last knuckle.

"Fuck," I whispered, bowing up off the bed.

Only for his strict hand on my belly to shove me back down. His gaze locked onto mine and his expression was firm. *"Quit squirming,"* his eyes said. But I couldn't help it. As he pumped his thick finger in and out of me, growing slicker with each decadent thrust, my hips undulated to match his movement. It was uncontrollable. My body was in command, and I was merely a slave to it. A passenger along for the crazed, exquisite ride.

And the view. God, he looked amazing. So professional in his fitted doctor's coat and tie. He looked like a man who'd finish surgery and then enjoy eighteen holes of golf. Instead, he'd come home to a naked nineteen-year-old girl waiting in his bed for him to fuck her senseless.

As long as I was disobeying him and not being a good 'patient,' I figured I'd cross the line completely. My hand shot out a second time and I skated my palm over the thick line of his erection, caressing and stroking the hard muscle beneath the fly of his pants.

His expression went razor-sharp, and it squeezed the air from my lungs. But instead of pulling away, his hand came off my stomach and ripped at his belt, trying to undo his pants one-handed. "You want to behave inappropriately? Let me give you a lesson in how it's done."

My pussy clenched down on his finger as he freed his hard dick from his pants, pushing the sides of his underwear down and out of our way. He had to hold his shirt and the end of his tie up, flattening it against his defined stomach with a hand. I barely got a chance to swallow a breath before the head of his cock was in my face, pressing against my mouth and demanding entrance.

He shivered as I parted my lips and welcomed him inside. A second finger from him pushed into me, stretching my body and moving at just the right speed to send quivers along my spine. The way his rough fingers fucked me mirrored the way he did it to my mouth. Our scene together was rapidly devolving, but I was swept up in the urgency. My fantasy wasn't breaking down—it was simply changing. Morphing into something unexpected and exciting.

I swirled my tongue over the hard column of flesh filling my mouth, using the tip to trace each protruding vein. He groaned in satisfaction, and heat swelled low in my back, rising upward as I neared an orgasm. His thumb flicked over my clit, strumming me as he jammed his fingers deep inside.

He could touch me a million times and I was sure I'd never get used to it. It'd always feel this amazing. It'd always cause my toes to curl and my heart to beat wildly.

Going down on him was like drowning, only in a way you enjoyed losing the battle. The struggle to breathe, the desperate movement to keep up. I wanted to push myself and see how much I could take. I opened the back of my throat and let him drive further—all the way until my eyes watered and a horrible choking sound ripped from the back of my throat.

Greg retreated in an instant, withdrawing completely. As he pulled away, I was left feeling impossibly empty, hanging right on the edge. My eyes went wide, and I reached for him, but his expression froze me in place.

He looked . . . unsure.

"Is everything okay?" My words were raspy, my throat raw.

A shift went through him, and the cool, confident doctor persona snapped back into place. "Can you turn over, please? Onto your stomach."

I really, *really* wanted to resume what we'd been doing just a second ago, but I was so close to coming and desperate for release, I was willing to do anything he asked. I turned onto my side, then rolled onto my stomach, pressing my breasts into the mattress. The pillow was cool against my cheek as I turned my head to peer up at him.

"That's good," he said. "Perfect."

He adjusted the waistband of his underwear, tucking himself away. His fly was yanked up, but the button at the top was left undone, and I frowned in my confusion. Were we taking a step backward? Had I done something wrong?

Greg's focus turned to his left. He leaned over, pulled open the drawer of his nightstand, and jammed a hand inside. Items rattled around, and then he dropped something onto the top of the nightstand with a crinkle of wrappers and a distinct thud. It was dim in the room, and before I could get a good look, he turned and blocked my view. He gripped the hem of the dress shirt I was wearing, drew it up, and cool air wafted over my newly-exposed ass.

Warm palms smoothed over my curves, sliding across my skin like it was made of silk. Any other time I would have found this sensual massage relaxing, but not now, not when my heart threatened to leap from my chest. My impatient body demanded satisfaction. I could barely tolerate it when he began to knead my cheeks, working his way down to my legs, rubbing the backs of my thighs.

"You're tense." His tone was reassuring. "Try to relax."

Was he kidding? I was tense because he'd left me in this worked up state half the damn night—

Thoughts scattered when his hand veered up between my legs, running through my cleft, and then continued its indecent path up, slipping shockingly between my cheeks.

Holy fuck.

TWENTY-FIVE

I JERKED AT HIS WICKED, DIRTY TOUCH, AND PUSHED UP ONTO my elbows. "Uh—"

At my startled reaction, his hands returned to their innocent holding pattern, caressing my body. He tried to conceal his embarrassment. "Pretend that never happened."

It was hard to slip in and out of the scene so abruptly. I didn't want him to be ashamed, and more importantly, "It's okay. You, um, just caught me by surprise."

It was one of those statements that came out before I really evaluated the thought. *Was* it okay? I'd never done that before. One night, first semester when I'd been hammered, Preston had tried anal. No discussion, no lube, or anything. We'd been having sex, and when he tried to put his dick in a new place, I'd given him a full five seconds to attempt it before realizing I couldn't deal. But hey, I'd given it the old college try.

Before Greg, Preston was pretty much all I knew in the bedroom. I hadn't believed oral sex could feel like it did now. I'd enjoyed sex with my boyfriend at the time, but I had no comparison. I hadn't known what I was missing. And I wasn't disgusted by the idea of anal stuff, or even outright opposed to trying it, but I was fairly confident I'd never enjoy it.

Was it possible with Greg I might?

His voice was so low, it was barely audible. "Yeah?"

His hands ventured once more, creeping closer to the new spot for us. He watched me intently, looking ready to retreat the moment a word came from me. But I pressed my lips together, curious. The fingers of his right hand trailed through my pussy, gathering up my arousal, and slowly spread it backward into my crevice.

My breath came out stuttered. His featherlight touch was unfamiliar. Naughty and corrupt.

But I . . . kind of liked it.

His left hand abandoned me so he could palm his straining cock through his pants for a moment, and then he scooped up the item he'd set on the nightstand. It was a small, clear bottle with a blue top. Fire blasted up my legs as I realized what it was.

The cap on the lube was flipped open. He tipped the bottle over and poured a small amount into his palm, then closed the cap with a sharp click, and dropped the bottle onto the bed beside me. He moved methodically, rubbing his hands together until his fingers glistened. All the while, the intense connection of our gaze never wavered.

The way he looked at me—it was consuming. He was powerfully sexual and commanding. I licked my dry lips and drew in a deep breath to steady myself.

Greg didn't waste any time. His fingertips started at the small of my back and inched down. His left palm cupped my ass cheek and peeled me open while the coated fingers of his right hand slid down, spreading the lube around. The sensation was unexpected.

In fact, it was stunning how good it felt.

He swirled over the taboo spot, each circle he drew was tighter than the last until the tip of his index finger was there, pushing gently to gain entrance. That . . . did not feel as good. It just felt weird, and I hesitated, tensing my shoulders.

His eyes were a deep brown ink, and his voice fell to a hush. "There are a lot of nerve endings here." His fingers resumed their swirling, proving his point. "Which means there can be a lot of pleasure. Trust me, Cassidy. I'm not going to do anything you don't want me to, and I promise I'm not going to hurt you."

I believed him, but a voice in the back of my mind said it was a promise he couldn't make. Not emotionally. I already thought about him too often. I cared about him too much. What was going to happen when the summer was over? If we kept this thing between us going, how would we ever explain it to Preston?

I pushed the thought away. I didn't want anyone else in the bedroom, even in my mind. It needed to be only Greg and me. "I trust you."

He didn't smile with his mouth, but warmth lit up in his eyes, and my shoulders relaxed, giving him a signal to try again.

This time, I held still as his finger prodded, moving over my slippery skin until it was right, fucking, *there*. I fisted the sheet beneath me as he pressed against the ring of muscles and slowly pushed past them.

I gasped at the sensation and clenched my jaw. It wasn't exactly comfortable. He'd said there'd be pleasure, but I wasn't feeling it yet. He hadn't gone far with the intrusion, but it was enough to stretch me and make me question if we should keep going.

"Try to relax," he whispered.

That was easy for him to say, but it only made me focus harder on what he was doing, and it was rapidly approaching unpleasant territory.

"Squeeze down on me."

My eyes went wide. "What?"

"As tight as you can go," he said. "Then, relax."

All the blood rushed to my face and I swallowed a lump in my throat but tried to do as told. I clenched, and when I released my muscles, he eased his finger deeper.

"There." He sounded pleased. "That's the feeling you want." His left hand curled down my ass cheek and dipped toward my pussy, teasing me while his sinful finger gained more ground.

I collapsed face first onto the bed and groaned it into the pillow. "Oh my God."

Because it felt wrong, but also oddly good. The filthy, nasty way he touched me turned me on, and—shit—his fingers playing with my clit made my vision blur. I tried to find the same sensation from before, pressing back against his finger, but as both of his hands began to move faster, control slipped from my grasp.

He was in charge. Playing me. Using me exactly how he wanted. Fucking me with a finger in my ass and a hand cupping my pussy, working me over into a frenzy. I was practically humping the bed, rocking my hips back and forth to get the contact I desired. It was so incredibly erotic. I moaned as he pushed deeper, sliding a little further with each pass.

"How does that feel?" he asked.

Strange.

Good.

Different.

Words jumbled in my brain. I grunted an unintelligible sentence that thankfully was muffled by the pillow. I squirmed under his control. I clawed at the sheets, gripping and releasing, struggling to find something else, but it was mindless.

I'd been right, Greg could make me like it. I was so close to orgasm, I needed to come and was frantic to get there. But he slowed me down considerably when a second finger worked to join the first. It took my body time to grow used to it, and then I was right back on the edge.

"I'm going to—" I warned.

This time when he withdrew, I lifted my head and groaned my frustration loudly, more than a little annoyed. He'd denied me so many times already. Was that on purpose? Was he trying to bring out the selfish side of me?

"Where are you going?" I demanded.

He left me on the bed and stormed into the bathroom, not answering me. I heard the faucet run, followed by the sound of soap pumped from a dispenser. "Take off your shirt," he said, raising his voice over the running water.

He reappeared in the doorway moments later, a towel in his hands, and as soon as he was done using it to dry his hands, he dropped it to floor, forgotten. He stalked back to the side of the bed. His demanding posture and urgent move-ment told me he wasn't playing around anymore. I pulled one side of the shirt off and then the other, while he picked up the strip of condoms and tore one package open.

The air in the room thickened until it was like breath-ing in a sauna. I felt lightheaded. Anxious, yet excited to try something new, with a partner who cared about what I want-ed. Maybe even more than his own desires.

Greg climbed onto the bed, straddling the backs of my thighs as he dug his cock out of his pants and put the condom on. My breasts were flattened under the weight of my body, and I shifted to make myself more comfortable.

Damp hands caressed up the length of my spine, send-ing tiny bursts of fireworks across my skin. I arched into his touch, practically purring like a cat. His tie tickled me when he leaned over, putting his chest against my back, and he tangled a hand in my hair. He used his hold to turn me into his kiss.

"Stop me," he uttered.

It wasn't a challenge. The soft way he'd said it was a check-in. He wanted to make sure I was okay with going further. I sipped air through my lips and let his hot mouth glance over the shell of my ear.

"Is this your fantasy?" I asked.

"Yes." His hard cock rested where my cheeks split, and he moved his hips subtly, sliding it back and forth in the val-ley. "Fuck," he said, "I might just come from the idea of it."

The undone buckle from his belt was cold against my hip, but everywhere else I was warm and shaky. His lazy, teasing thrusts made me insane. They whispered all sorts of naughty things, telling me how badly I wanted to have him. It didn't matter where. I trusted him to make it good. My pleasure seemed to be his top priority.

He supported himself on his hands on the outsides of my shoulders and lifted as I rose onto my elbow. I curled a hand behind his neck, keeping him from going too far.

I blurted it out before I lost my courage. "I want to try it."

A shudder rolled through the body pressed to me, and he made a cut-off sound of surprise, as if too excited to hold it back. I loved that I could do that to him. Having that kind of impact made me feel powerful and confident—something I'd never had before when it came to sex.

Greg fumbled a hand on the bed beside us, fishing for the bottle of lube, and once it was located, he sat back on his heels. Cold, thick liquid dripped where we'd need it, oozing down in an enjoyable slide.

He leaned forward again, resting his left hand right beside my elbow, and his clothes brushed against my back. I imagined what we looked like, him in his serious doctor's attire and me pinned beneath him, stark fucking naked. Every muscle in me squeezed tight with anticipation as I felt the tip of his cock gliding back and forth over my asshole, teasing what was about to happen. God, he was thick. I scrunched my eyes closed, mentally preparing myself.

"Relax," he breathed. He dropped a line of soft kisses on the curve of my shoulder, trailing up my neck.

He pressed against me, increasing the pressure as he tried to get inside, and then abruptly—

"Oh!" I gasped.

The burning sensation was a lot. Almost overwhelming, but I blew out a long, slow breath, trying to even myself out. He'd stopped the moment I'd made a sound and held absolutely still. I shoved my face against the pillow, but couldn't breathe, and when I turned my head to gain air, his hand was right there, splayed out on the mattress beside me.

"Slow," I ordered in a hollow voice, but the command must have rung as loud as thunder in his ears because he did exactly as I said. He slipped a fraction of an inch further along.

I wasn't in control of myself. I let my body take over, and as he eased deeper, I sank the edge of my teeth into the knuckle of his index finger. Anything to distract from the strange, powerful sensation that was so confusing, I had no idea if I liked it.

If my soft bite was hurting him, Greg didn't let on. His tentative, gentle movements caused my brain to fracture into pieces. And as his impossibly slow tempo went along, the sensation began to shift. I relaxed, loosening up to his invasion, and with that . . . I got a hint of the pleasure he'd told me about.

It shouldn't have felt good, yet it did. He made soft sounds of enjoyment. Tiny sighs and groans of satisfaction, and I quivered in response. It was so sexy. I unclamped my jaw, releasing my hold on his finger, and the bite I'd given him morphed into a kiss. It was my wordless signal I was comfortable, which he seemed to read loud and clear.

He lifted the finger and slipped it into my mouth, allowing me to suck on it.

I nearly came from his simple action. He matched the sluggish pace of his body moving inside me with the pulse of his finger pushing in and out of my mouth. I sucked hard, hollowing out my cheeks, and simulated going down on him.

"Fuck," he moaned. His lips landed on the nape of my neck, ghosting damp kisses. "Oh, *fuck*, you feel so good."

Heat flashed through me as a jolt of electric current. I was doing it. Letting Greg have me in a way no one else had. The connection between us grew stronger and more intense with every breath we took together.

"How did you do it?" he asked and continued before I could question him. "How'd you get yourself off tonight?" His right hand slid between me and the sheets beneath my stomach, coursing further down until his searching fingertips found my aching pussy and stirred. "Like this?"

The buzz he created in my body was so loud, it was deafening. A moan poured from my mouth, and his cock, lodged deep within me, throbbed with my sound of approval. He rubbed faster, generating more friction.

Tension coiled in my belly. My breath came faster and faster, so hard I could barely keep up. My heart pounded in overdrive. I was going to fly apart—his swirling hand was the devil. I couldn't resist, even if I tried.

"Jesus, Cassidy." The long strokes he gave began to pick up in pace. "You make me feel like I'm twenty goddamn years old." His finger withdrew from my mouth, and he pushed my hair back over my shoulder, out of his way. The scruff of his short beard chafed against my neck. "I can't get enough of you. Tell me what you thought about."

"You," I said. "Fucking me."

His tone had a hint of teasing and a lot of smugness. "That's all?"

My defenses were down, and I wasn't worried about judgment, and still my face heated. "The first time, yeah."

"And the second?"

I rolled my hips, moving with his fingers. His touch was enough of a distraction, I didn't hold back the truth. "That Preston walked in on us."

Greg tensed, and just the hesitation in his body was enough to make me want to die of shame. Why the hell had I admitted it? Worse, why the hell had my twisted mind thought it up in the first place?

But the fingers touching my clit flexed and resumed their task, and I bit down on my bottom lip. He began to move again, only this time his slow, deep thrusts felt darker. Dirtier, more carnal. His voice was gravel. "Yeah? What did he do?"

"He . . . watched."

His cock jerked, and a grunt came from Greg. It sounded like my statement had turned him on. I should have guessed it would. We seemed so evenly matched in the bedroom. My fantasies were his too. He lowered down until his firm chest pressed against my back. "What'd he see?"

God, that question was corrupt, right along with my answer. "He saw your head between my legs. Going down on me until I begged you to fuck me. And when you did, he watched you do what he never could."

Greg froze a second time, only this wasn't in hesitation. From the pulsing motion of his cock, I could tell this was caution. He'd gotten extremely close to losing it. His fingers worked furiously between my legs, urgent. "Shit, I need you to come. Are you close?"

I swallowed a huge gulp of air, nodded, and my vision narrowed. My legs shook uncontrollably as he pistoned his body over mine, sawing his thick, hard dick in and out of my ass. Never in a million years did I think I'd end up here. Not even my fantasies tonight included this, but . . . dear God. I latched a hand around his supporting wrist and clung to him, panic welling up from within.

I was going to come, but worried it was going to be on a whole different level than I'd had before. It was inevitable, this new experience, yet I was a little terrified of what was going to happen. He'd delayed the orgasm so long. Would I scream? Would I do something embarrassing?

I jammed my hand in between my body and the bed, fumbling toward his expert fingers to slow him down and control the pace, but I was much too late. My climax hit me like a gunshot and ricocheted through my body, burning a thousand degrees. A desperate cry burst from my lips as pleasure flooded my core. It was followed by spiderwebbing tendrils of satisfaction, sweeping along my limbs as I convulsed beneath the crush of his strong body.

"Yes," he murmured. "*Yes.*"

And then the muscles in his chest went rigid. His body locked up for a half-second and began to shudder in mindless jerks. I could feel every throb of him as he spurted his orgasm, wave after wave. It was intense and overwhelming.

I went hazy in the aftermath.

Everything was tingly numb as he slowly retreated, dropped a kiss on the sensitive spot right below my ear, and climbed off the bed. I vaguely acknowledged him in the bathroom, moving around and running the tap. The bathroom light was clicked off, plunging the room into darkness. When he came back to me, he was warm and naked, and pulled my leaden body into his arms.

His kisses were deep, slow, and passionate. It was like he wanted to learn the taste of me, and I squeezed my eyes closed tight—strange tears threatened to fall, but I successfully held them back.

"Are you okay?" he whispered.

"Yeah." I ran my fingers over his chest, wondering what was going on in the heart beneath my fingertips. Was he okay? After I'd confessed such sinful things? He seemed to be, but nerves fluttered in my ribcage anyway.

It was quiet and peaceful between us for so long, I was sure he'd dozed off, but then he let out a deep breath.

"Tonight in the operating room," he started. His embrace tightened, like he feared I might pull away. "I've lost patients before. It's always rough, but this one was . . . really hard."

"I'm sorry," I whispered. It didn't even compare, but I'd had a rough day too, and it felt good to be able to be there for each other.

He used his fingers to stroke lines up and down my arm. "I'm glad you texted me."

"I wanted to see you."

"I wanted that too." In the darkness, I could see the displeased look cross his expression, but it seemed self-directed. He tried again. "What I meant to say is, I'm really glad you're here, Cassidy."

My chest swelled and tightened, and I pressed my palm flat over his heart. I wasn't invisible—he made it sound like my presence was *everything*. It was something I hadn't had in a long time, was desperate to hear, and it meant even more coming from him.

I'd been nothing but honest tonight, yet this was truer than anything else I'd said to him. "Me too."

TWENTY-SIX

EVERYTHING CHANGED AFTER THAT NIGHT.

I hadn't allowed myself to think about a future with Dr. Gregory Lowe, but that restriction vanished as the sun rose the following morning. We had everything working against us. His schedule, the age difference, and the Preston situation. Despite it all, I wanted to try, and he seemed to as well.

We saw each other as much as we could during the final week while Preston was out of town. Greg inflicted his "new classics" movies on me while I tried to teach him how to use Snapchat. He told me the filters were stupid, so I put flowers in his hair and showed him how gorgeous he looked. He'd ripped the phone out of my hands, threw it onto his bed, then tossed me down beside it, his hands going for the button of my shorts and an evil grin on his face.

On Thursday evening, he texted me he was leaving the hospital and invited me over for a late dinner. I quickly replied.

Cassidy: See you soon.

I was halfway out the door, my purse slung over my shoulder, when my mom's voice rang out from the kitchen.

"Where are you going?" she asked lightly. "Preston's?"

I skidded to a stop. It wasn't until that moment I realized I hadn't told her we'd broken up.

My mom was a genuinely busy person. When I was in high school, she'd been crazy active in volunteering. PTA vice-president. Music boosters. Senior class trip chaperone. She didn't do it to invade my life, and hadn't either. She just liked being involved and couldn't sit still. Even during the weekends when she was home from her demanding IT job, my mom was *go-go-go* with her nine million hobbies.

The latest one was her garden in the back yard. She was growing everything from vegetables to roses, and determined to make it all the best it could possibly be. She was out there from sunup to sundown, digging and planting and fertilizing and watering.

It meant I rarely saw her this summer.

I closed the door and pivoted on my heel to face her. She wore an old marching band t-shirt from my sophomore year, cotton shorts, and a baseball hat to shield her eyes from the sun. She stood at the fridge filling her water bottle. Even in worn-out clothes and no makeup on, she looked good. Young and pretty, with sharp eyes and mouth that was quick to smile.

The easiest, fastest way to get out the door was to say *yes*. It wasn't a lie technically. I mean, I *was* going to Preston's.

My mom and I were close-ish. In high school, I'd felt like I could tell her anything, but the year away at college had changed us a little. After eighteen years of it just being the two of us, I thought we both liked the privacy. We got to be women on our own.

"Uh." Guilt coated my insides. It tasted like a lie as I said it. "Preston's. Yeah."

The water dispenser dripped, and my mother wiped her hand on the side of her shirt. "Oh, I saw Dr. Lowe yesterday."

My breath caught. "What?"

"I took my car into the dealership. Turns out I had a nail in the back tire, and he was there, waiting on an oil change."

"Yeah?" Could she hear how I forced casualness into my voice? "Did you say hi?"

"Yeah." Her tone was matter-of-fact, but then her eyebrows pulled together. "Well, sort of. He was on the phone at first." She screwed the cap shut on her water bottle. "I wasn't trying to eavesdrop, but I heard him asking for restaurant recommendations to take his girlfriend, so I told him about that seafood one we went to last month. That place was great."

My heart slammed to a stop. "Girlfriend?"

She must not have heard me squeak out the word. "He gave me the strangest look." Her blue eyes abruptly zeroed in, and I used every ounce of acting strength I possessed to look indifferent, even as I cracked into a million pieces inside. Somehow, my mom didn't seem to notice. "If anything," she continued, "he was kind of rude."

It hurt to speak, and I didn't know what to say anyway, so I just stared at her.

"Frankly, I'm surprised he has time to date." The change in my mom's expression wasn't subtle. The corners of her mouth ticked downward as she soured. "I hope it doesn't bother Preston."

"What?" I didn't understand what she meant, but also the world was starting to turn upside-down. Greg had a girlfriend. How was it even possible? When was he squeezing in time to see this other woman?

My mom shrugged. "You said you hardly ever see Dr. Lowe. Now it sounds like Preston has to share his father's limited time with someone else."

And in my mother's eyes, Greg still had a lot to make up for.

I blinked, readjusted the purse on my shoulder, and stalled to give my brain time to come back up to speed. "I didn't know he had a girlfriend." All I could think about was getting answers from him. "But I've gotta go."

"Okay." My mom brightened. "Have fun."

As I opened the door and trudged through it, the voice in my mind whispered back it was highly doubtful.

During the drive over, I attempted to organize my thoughts on what I should say. Should I mention the meeting with my mom and see if he'd come out with it? Or did I go in, guns blazing and full of wrath? That was a tall order. Sure, I was angry. It was inside me somewhere, but it was buried under two tons of hurt and disappointment.

I nearly slammed on the brakes when I pulled up to the vacant house down the street from Greg's. The 'for sale' sign on a white post flapped in the breeze, and a large red sticker cut a diagonal across it, boasting it was now sold. Which meant I couldn't hide my car in its secluded driveway anymore. I had no choice but to park in Greg's, where I knew Judy would see it.

Fucking great.

I parked, went inside without announcing myself, and found Greg in the kitchen. He took one look at me, and concern swept through his expression. He'd been setting the table, but hesitated. "What's wrong?"

I slapped my purse down on the island and gave him a hard look. "You ran into my mother yesterday."

"Oh. Yeah, I did." He abandoned his task and strode toward me. When I took a step back, his concern grew ten-fold.

"She said you were rude to her."

"If I was, I'm sorry. She completely caught me off guard. As soon as I got off the phone, she was right there, and I didn't know what to say. I don't think she realized she was giving me a restaurant recommendation on where to take you to dinner."

"What?" Circuits crossed in my brain and fried out. "She told me you have a girlfriend."

It was his turn to look confused. "Isn't that . . . you?"

Me? His question physically knocked me back. I was thrilled and scared at the same time. Putting a label on us meant it was serious, and I wanted that, but I also didn't want the consequences that came with it.

My reaction didn't go over all that well with him, and his expression went plain. "I'm forty years old." He sighed. "Honestly, I don't have time for games. I like you, and you like me, and we've been doing . . . whatever it is we've been doing for over a month now." He put his hands on his hips, showing off his perfect frame and his toned arms. "Even though I know it's complicated, I'd like to keep doing it. Don't you?"

I did, but I was scared. Preston was the only real boy-friend I'd had. Was I ready for another relationship so soon? And with my ex's dad?

Greg's posture softened. "Talk to me."

"I do, but . . ." My gaze dropped to his feet as I finally gave up fighting what I knew was unavoidable. My voice was small. "We have to tell Preston."

When he moved, Greg's shadow joined mine on the tile floor. "We do." His hand covered mine resting on the coun-tertop, and he used it to slowly lead me into his embrace. I could sense his gaze on me, and it forced my attention back up to him. "I thought I was going to have to fight you on this." His dark, deep eyes studied me, gauging my feelings. "I was thinking I'll do it next weekend. You'll both be heading back to school, so it will give him some space right after."

It made sense. It'd probably be easier for Preston to get through his feelings if he didn't have to see his dad every day, or at least live under the same roof.

"Shouldn't I be the one to tell him?" He was my ex, and until recently, had been my best friend.

Greg shook his head. "I need to do it. He's going to be . . . upset."

"Do you want me there when you—"

"No. I'd like to explain it to him alone. That way he can focus on me instead of you."

I tugged my eyebrows together and pressed my lips into a line. He wanted to spare me from Preston's anger and take the blame, but that wasn't fair. We hadn't planned on getting involved, Greg and I had just . . . happened. I didn't like him having to do this on his own, but he was older and wiser, not to mention Preston's dad. Their relationship was the most important thing in Greg's life. I had to trust him to know what was right.

"You're sure?" I asked reluctantly.

"Yes."

"Okay," I said. "I don't like it, but if you think that's best—okay."

He gave a slight smile. "Good. I'll feel better when it's done. No more hiding."

I shot him a funny look. "Who's hiding? You told someone you have a girlfriend. Who were you talking to?"

"Chief of surgery. I was asking him to clear my calendar for Wednesday."

My breath caught, but I hoped he didn't notice. Did he know? "What's Wednesday?"

His expression was coy, and good lord, he was sexy as sin like that. "Someone's birthday." He dropped a quick kiss on my lips. "I should tell you, twenty is the worst birthday."

I was stunned. Preston was terrible at dates and usually forgot. Even when he remembered, it felt like a last-minute scramble. He wasn't one to look ahead in his calendar. But Greg? He probably had alerts programmed into his phone, and the idea that one of them included me made my heart flutter.

"Do you have plans?" he asked.

I draped my arms over his shoulders and pulled him close. "I do now."

TWENTY-SEVEN

GREG DIDN'T TAKE ME TO THE RESTAURANT MY MOTHER HAD suggested, thankfully. We went to a fancy chef's table place in Music Row, where the entire dining room consisted of long tables arranged in a square around the open kitchen. Diners sat on the outside, watching the show as the two chefs prepared the different courses and plated them to look like art.

The food was amazing, but the company at my side was even better. Greg wore a charcoal gray suit without a tie, and a white dress shirt with the top few buttons undone. He looked every bit the part of confident, rich doctor during the drive over in his BMW, his expensive wristwatch gleaming in the early evening sun.

I smoothed my palms down the floral dress I'd borrowed from Lilith, that was just a little too sexy and formal to call a sundress. The spaghetti strap top was simple black, cinched at the waist, but gave way to a flowing skirt patterned with cream-colored flowers. She'd also lent me a pair of gorgeous black heels, where the straps crisscrossed around my ankles and made me feel like a bombshell.

That was, until I was seated beside him in the car, heading toward dinner. My forty-year-old boyfriend was undeniably sexy, so what the hell was he doing with a barely twenty-year-old girl? I loved that he wanted to take me out, but

I dreaded it at the same time. What kind of looks were we going to get from everyone at the restaurant?

Huh.

No one batted an eye at us.

Maybe my makeup and sexy dress gave me enough of an edge to look older. I had a fake ID in my purse I'd gone back and forth on bringing. Preston and I, along with a group of our friends, had bought them last semester from a shady website which I was certain was a scam, but a month later a package from China arrived at Preston's dorm. An innocuous teddy bear with six expert fake IDs stuffed inside.

I didn't get carded at dinner. Greg ordered a bottle of white wine and the server brought two glasses. As I sat at the table, a glass of sauvignon blanc in hand, watching the sizzling skillets and impressive knife skills on display, I felt like an imposter. I was a child pretending to be an adult, but as long as I faked it convincingly, no one but Greg would know.

His hand rested in my lap, and I was worried I was going to vibrate out of my seat. He was so comfortable with this. With being with me. I loved every freaking minute of it and did my best to look like I belonged with him. When it was just the two of us, I did, but out in public? That was going to take some getting used to.

Course after course was served, and although I wasn't usually an adventurous eater, I ate every drop on the odd-shaped bowls and square plates, maybe even the garnish I wasn't supposed to. Wine buzzed through my system, mixing with the powerful effect of his touch on my leg.

"How is he?" I finally asked, after the last course had been served. We'd avoided talking about Preston all evening, but I couldn't put it off forever. He'd come back from North Carolina on Sunday, and tonight was the first time I was seeing Greg since his son had returned.

Greg's expression shuttered. "He's fine."

The mood between us shifted faster than a rabbit bolting from a cage, and I struggled with how to get it back on track. "Uh, good. How were your rounds this morning?"

"I asked him to stay at a friend's place tonight," he announced quickly.

"Oh." I hesitated. "Why?"

The hand on me moved. It slipped beneath the hem of the dress, so his palm brushed against the top of my thigh, and the bare skin contact sent a tinge of pleasure zipping to my center.

"Because," Greg's eyes darkened a shade, "I have something to give you."

"What is it?"

"A surprise."

I inhaled deeply, and anticipation thickened my blood. Whatever Greg had planned, he didn't want Preston around for it, and I tried to curb my enthusiasm. It was a lost cause, though. It'd been five days since I'd seen my boyfriend, and my fantasies and my own hand only got me so far. I leaned over, mustered the most seductive voice I had, and whispered in his ear.

"I can't wait."

By the time Greg parked in the garage, my slight buzz from the wine had disappeared, and that was disappointing on multiple fronts. Walking in the ankle-breaking shoes was easier when I was distracted and not concerned about looking foolish.

Preston's Jeep wasn't in the garage, and Greg's shoulders relaxed a degree. The tension I didn't realize I was holding left my body too. He shut off the car, climbed from the seat, and hurried around the back end of the car to open the door for me. I took his offered hand and let him help me to my feet, where I teetered on the shoes.

"Thank you for dinner," I said.

He stood so close, I breathed in his cologne, and tried not to swoon at the scent. His arm slipped around my waist. "You're welcome. Let's go inside so you can open your birthday present."

He led me up the step into the house, but instead of taking me to the bedroom, I clip-clopped on my heels into the living room, where he sat me down on the couch. I gazed up at him, puzzled, but he just smiled and bent at the waist. He captured my face in his hands.

"This gift is kind of selfish, I'm sorry." He caressed his lips over mine, moving too quickly to call it much of a kiss.

"What?"

"Hold on, you'll see." He released his hold and stood. "I'll be right back."

I watched him disappear down the hallway to his bedroom, and then I swallowed dryly. What was he about to give me?

When Greg reemerged, he was carrying a pale pink box tucked under an arm, and he wore an expression that was an even mixture of excitement and something that looked suspiciously like anxiety. He sank down beside me on the couch and gently set the apparel-sized box in my lap.

"Happy birthday, Cassidy."

I cast my gaze down, and all the sound in the room faded out.

The pink box had a black satin ribbon banded around one corner and tied in a bow in the other, and the words *Agent Provocateur* were scrawled in fancy script across the top.

"I hope it all fits." His voice was uncharacteristically tight, and then dropped low. "It does in my fantasy."

With nervous, excited fingers, I slipped the ribbon off a corner, opened the lid, and pulled the tissue paper back.

It was a bra, garter, and panty set of dusty pink tulle trimmed with black lace, and two stockings of luxurious black silk. I ran my fingers over the delicate lingerie, then slowly held the bra up to look at it closer.

"Do you like it?" he asked softly.

"It's beautiful." But the price tag dangling from the back was outrageous. "Greg, I can't—"

"Oh, yes, you can. I told you this gift was selfish. It's more for me than you." His eyes gleamed with mischief. "I'll send it back if it doesn't fit, but there's only one way to find out."

I grasped the sides of the box, not sure what to do. I hadn't seen the bill tonight at dinner, but it had to be a small fortune, and now this . . . I didn't want a sugar daddy.

He must have sensed how uneasy all of this made me. He set a hand on my wrist. "There's more that goes with that."

"More?" I didn't know how to feel about what he'd already given me. I mean, I liked it, but was I supposed to? Shouldn't I feel uncomfortable about it? My mother had raised me to be polite and reject gifts that were too extravagant.

He smirked, and it looked utterly indecent. "You'll like it, but you have to put that on to find out what it is."

I swallowed a heavy breath while my gaze traced the intricate lace. I wanted this sexy lingerie and was excited to see how it would look on my body. Even if I demanded he return it, I was pretty sure I wouldn't let go of the box when he tried to take it from me. But my curiosity was even greater. What else did he have planned?

"Trust me." His words were laced with enough persuasion, my decision was made.

"Where should I change?" I stood, clutching the box in my hands, my palms clammy. I assumed he didn't want me to do it in front of him—he'd want the big reveal.

"My bedroom." His grin was enormous, lighting up his handsome face. "Come back out here when you're ready."

I carried my gift into his room, set it on the bed, and quietly shut the door. My heart pounded loudly in my ears as

I eyed the box, and my face flushed hot, but I went to it, gripping the sides of my skirt in my hands to take off my dress. When it was done, I laid it gently on the bed, then undid the hooks of my strapless bra.

Every piece of the expensive lingerie he'd given me fit, but it took me a while to put it on. I moved painfully slowly, terrified of getting a run in the black stockings. I'd also never worn a garter belt before, and it took me a minute to figure out how to catch the top of my stocking in the clasp and lock it into place.

As I tugged the panties up over my thighs, a soft knock came from the bedroom door. "How we doing in there?"

I could picture the smile on his lips as Greg stood on the other side of the door.

"Good, but I need another minute," I said. "So many straps," I muttered under my breath.

When I had it all on, I stepped into the shoes Lilith had lent me, doing the delicate buckles around my ankles, then strutted into the bathroom where a full-length mirror hung on his closet door.

Jesus.

The pale pink mesh of the bra, panties, and garter belt matched my skin tone. It was see-through, so the coins of my darker nipples were faintly visible. In contrast, the black lace trim drew lines on my body, crisscrossing below my waist and leading down into the straps that held the black tops of my stockings up.

I peered at the girl in the mirror and barely recognized her. I wanted to be the brunette sex kitten who was staring back at me. Her legs looked long and beautiful wrapped in black silk and ended in those fuck-me stilettos. She wasn't a teenager, she was in her twenties now, and she was about to walk out of this room, greet her boyfriend, and thank him properly for the evening.

It was darker in the living room than when I'd left it. He'd turned off the lights, but more than a dozen candles flickered around the room, from the side tables, the bookcases, and the fireplace mantel. They cast a warm glow in the space, and wavering shadows up onto the walls.

His sharp intake of breath pulled my attention away from the room and set it firmly on him. He was still wearing his fitted gray suit and was just as breathtaking to me as I seemed to be to him. My heart fumbled along in my chest as his gaze raked over me, taking in every inch of lace and tulle adorning my curves. His lips parted, like he was going to say something, but he only drew in another breath. His expression dripped with unabashed lust.

Finally, his broad shoulders straightened inside his suit coat, and Greg appeared to recover, although his voice was breathless. "You look fucking amazing."

"Thank you." I smiled. It was powerful when you felt good about how you looked. Almost like a drug, and hearing him confirm that magnified the effect. I couldn't wait to have my hands on him. "What's the other part of—"

It was then that I noticed it. In the low candlelight, I hadn't realized there was a new addition in the room. One of the wooden, armless kitchen chairs had been brought in and placed on the rug in the center of the room. It was only a chair, but in my gut, I knew it was *more*, and anticipation wound tighter around me.

"Do you like it," he said, "when I tell you what to do?" He took one confident step toward me, then another. "Is it one of your fantasies?"

Oh, lord. My blood sizzled. "Yes," I gasped.

His pleased expression made my knees go weak. "I figured it was, because it's mine too."

"What's the chair for?"

He didn't take his gaze off me as he made his steady approach. He seemed to gain authority as he closed in. "That's not important right now. Everything fits, right?"

My throat welled shut as he stood over me, his attention trapping me in place. I nodded slowly, transfixed by how dazzling his eyes were. Flecks of caramel mixed with rich mocha.

"Good. Turn around," he commanded. "And hold still."

TWENTY-EIGHT

I TURNED IN PLACE ON MY QUIVERING LEGS, EAGER TO FOLLOW
Greg's orders without knowing what they were about. There
was rustling from behind me, and then his cool fingertips
found the clasp of my bra—not to undo it, but to grasp the
sales tag.

A *snip* rang out.

I held absolutely still as he methodically cut off the tags.
When it was done, he set them and the pair of scissors on the
bookshelf, ran his fingertips up the length of my spine, and
leaned in until his chin rested on my shoulder.

"You're going to be a good little girl and do everything I
tell you to, aren't you?"

Fire raced through my bloodstream. My eyes slammed
shut, and I shivered at his delicious voice. "Yes, doctor."

The heat of his body abruptly vanished, forcing my eyes
open. I had my hands pressed to my thighs, willing myself to
stay still and wait for his instruction, but the desire to chase
after him was strong.

The chair that didn't belong in this room creaked quietly as he sat in it. He settled for a moment before he spoke.
"Come here."

I went as fast as the heels on the rug would allow, but as
soon as I was beside him, Greg's hands ensnared my waist

and positioned me before him. He walked me backward, taking me in once more with a sweeping, appreciative gaze. As soon as he had me placed how he wanted, he released me, sat back in the chair, and gripped the sides of the seat beneath him.

"I'm not going to touch you." He declared it loudly, his voice ringing in the cavernous space, traveling up to the balcony of the second floor.

Anxiety ratcheted inside me. "What?"

"I've spent the last year wanting you, but I wasn't able to touch. Tonight, you're going to see what that's like." His gaze drilled deep down into me. "You're going to watch what you do to me."

"I don't understand," I sputtered, shifting on my heels as I stood before him, only an arm's length away.

"You know how many times I imagined you coming to me? How badly I wanted you to seduce me?" He rolled his shoulders back in the chair and widened his legs, getting comfortable in his seat. "That's my ultimate fantasy, Cassidy."

Oh. My. God. My chest tightened. "You want me to seduce you?"

The smile that curled across his lips was like the devil's, and it was fucking hot.

But panic bubbled inside me. I didn't know the first thing about seducing someone. He'd always been the one to initiate and take the lead. I floundered instantly, not sure what to do.

He'd asked me to trust him, so I should have known. Sitting motionless on the chair, his hands curled around the seat, he was still in power. He still held absolute control over me.

"I can see your nipples through that bra," he said. "Are you turned on?"

How could I not be? It was a rhetorical question, but I dragged in a breath. "Yes."

"Do you want me to touch them? Do they ache?"

"Yes," I said through tight teeth.

"Then, use me."

My hands hung listlessly at my sides, but I tensed them into fists as I struggled to keep up. "Use you?"

"You want my mouth on them?" He looked sinister and sexy in the flickering candlelight. "Come and show me what you want."

In a snap, I understood.

He'd guide me through the scene when I needed it.

I stalked toward him, channeling the sex kitten from the mirror, and leaned over the chair, shoving my bra-clad breasts in his face. I snaked my hands around his head, pulling his mouth from one nipple to the other as he licked and suckled through the mesh, teasing me until the cups were damp.

A moan wrung from my lips as he nipped at me. Just the edge of teeth through the fabric was white-hot, and a sharp crack of pleasure whipped through my body. As I stood over him, letting his mouth rove over my sensitive skin, I felt powerful. He wasn't just giving me pleasure—I was taking it.

It got to be too much. I longed for his hands on me, and drew back, panting heavily. Maybe the cool air would help me get control of myself.

"I can see everything in those panties." His gaze was fixed at the seam of my legs. "I see how wet that pretty pussy is."

An unstoppable groan burst from my lungs. His dirty mouth did things to me. There was no defense against it.

"Do you need my mouth there, Cassidy?"

I gulped and nodded. Everything was spiraling out of control. He wasn't moving an inch but flexed his power over me all the same.

"Take those panties off," he ordered.

My body moved on its own, no approval from my mind. I slipped my fingers beneath the band of fabric covering my hips and began to drag the panties down.

His voice was firm, but not harsh. "Slow."

I complied, keeping my hooded gaze locked on his as I bent at the waist, pushed the underwear to my ankles, and stepped out of it. Although I wasn't cold, goosebumps blossomed on my skin. Power stirred between us, swirling like the eye of a hurricane.

Greg's tongue darted out to wet his lips as he stared at my naked flesh, eyeing me like the perfect cut of meat. Anyone else, it might have felt lewd, but not him. His unadulterated desire was a powerful aphrodisiac.

Since I understood the game now, I went in for the kill. I closed the space between us, threaded a hand through his thick hair, and lifted my leg, pulling his lips to where my body was hot and slick. His eyes went wide and then closed, happy to fulfill my request.

I hooked one leg over his shoulder.

My knee threatened to buckle at the first swipe of his tongue, and the grunt he gave was erotic. I held my tenuous balance as he stroked and massaged my clit with his velvet tongue, giving me the most intimate of kisses. The scene played out before me. His head was right beside the black band at the top of my thigh-high stocking, his mouth moving over my bare, pink skin.

I don't know how long I stayed like that, rocking against his face while he fucked me with his tongue, only that it was impossible to hold the position for long. My supporting foot ached in the shoe and wobbled in the stiletto. I dropped down, sliding until I was seated in his lap, and crushed my mouth to his, wet with the taste of me.

"Dr. Lowe," I murmured between kisses, trailing more along his strong jaw, and buried my mouth into the side of his neck. "I want you." I said it the exact same way I'd have told him I needed him, but I was desperate to be a good girl and play my role of seductress.

"Take off your bra," he said between two labored breaths. "Slow. Like I'd do it."

I lengthened my spine, sitting upright on him, and twisted my hands behind my back, searching for the clasp. As I undid the two hooks, he watched me with a heavy stare. He was so close, his warm, hard breath washed over my skin, teasing. Was this the only touch I was going to get from him tonight?

The bra slid away from my body, releasing my breasts, and I dropped it delicately on the floor. It cost more than my last paycheck, after all. Greg tipped his forehead toward me, letting it rest against my collarbone, and I arched instinctively into him. The whiskers of his beard pressed in the valley between my breasts, and—good God—it felt so good when I moved, rubbing my heavy, tingling skin against his face.

He sighed, and the beautiful sound reverberated through my core. "Fuck," he said, long and low.

Between my parted legs, I felt the swell of his hardening dick, and I swiveled on him, grinding against what I wanted inside me. The chair beneath us creaked, but not from my movement—it was his tight grip on the wood.

I couldn't stop the smile that spread across my face. "You want to touch me?"

"I shouldn't."

I got the impression his strained tone wasn't acting. He wanted to stay in his role, but his own rule was hard for him to follow.

"Please?" I whisper-moaned, shifting on him again.

He groaned, and then his body solidified. "No. On your knees."

I exhaled loudly, punched with a new wave of lust. His order injected me with desire. I slid down out of his lap like he'd poured me off him and buried my knees into the plush rug. I stroked my hands over the smooth wool covering his thighs spread on either side of my shoulders and blinked my sultry eyes up at him.

Greg's expression was turmoil. He was fighting a battle between breaking his rule and staying in the scene, and at that moment, I didn't care which he chose. There was no wrong answer. Not as long as we were together.

His posture stiffened, and he settled back into his role. "Undo my pants. Let's see how well you can say *please* again with me in your mouth."

I clasped the end of his belt and worked it free from the buckle, then focused my hurried, graceless fingers on the hook and zipper of his fly. His legs corded with tension as I tugged on the pants and underwear, him shifting just enough for me to work the clothes over his knees and down to his ankles, my kneeling legs tucked beneath.

His jaw set when my hands found him, hard and ready. I licked my parched lips, preparing to take him in my mouth, and as I slid down around his cock, his eyes closed, his head tipping back toward the ceiling.

Who knew there was so much pleasure in doing this? It had never been a chore, but before Greg, I'd rarely enjoyed going down on a guy. As his deep sighs and satisfied moans filled the room, it stoked the fire burning inside me, hotter each second. I tightened my legs, squeezing and clenching my muscles internally that gave me a hit of self-pleasure.

His hips flexed, pumping ever so subtly up into my greedy mouth, when I clasped a hand at the base of him. I worked my hand in time with my mouth, sliding over the slick, saliva-coated column of flesh that was hard and etched with a vein.

"Do you want to fuck me?" he asked through gritted teeth.

"*Please*," I mumbled, my mouth full of him. The word was garbled, but my eager tone had to make it sound like confirmation.

"There's a condom in my pants pocket."

I fished inside the left one, came up empty, then found the coin-shaped packet in his right. When I held it up to him—

"Open it. Put it on me."

I'd never done that before, but I trusted him to tell me if I screwed it up. I tore the corner of the foil open with trembling hands, pulled the condom out, and set off to accomplish my task.

A quiet hiss, full of enjoyment, came from him as I rolled the latex down. When it was done, I sat back on my heels, my hands resting on the garter straps on my thighs, and waited impatiently for my next set of instructions. He stroked himself, one quick pass to ensure he was covered, and his hand pushing down the condom was strangely mesmerizing.

Greg's expression was a bunch of emotions at once. Longing. Desire. Domination. But his tone was absolute. "Come here."

TWENTY-NINE

I PUT MY HANDS ON GREG'S KNEES, PUSHING UP TO STAND. HE was seated in the chair as I towered over him, but there was no doubt who was in charge. His gaze shifted to his lap, then drifted back up to meet my eyes, wordlessly ordering me to climb onto him.

My chest was tight. My heart rate kicked into high gear.

"Slowly," he reminded as I draped a leg over his lap, straddling him. He wasn't touching me, but was I allowed to touch him? I reached behind his head, gripping the chair back as I used my other hand to position him right at my entrance. I teased the tip of his cock against my damp skin, rolling the head of him over my swollen clit.

I wasn't in command, but I felt so fucking powerful like this.

His eyes darkened until they were black holes. Did he know I was completely under his spell? I could show him. I began to lower down, one crucial inch at a time. I balanced on the balls of my feet, my thighs quaking as I slid onto him.

Our pleasure-soaked moans mingled together.

As I impaled myself all the way down to his base, I furiously gripped the back of the chair with both hands, my forearms pressed to his suit-covered chest. I gasped at the sensation of him inside me. Hard, and throbbing, and statue still.

"That's it," he murmured. "Slow."

It was in direct conflict with the voice in my head that demanded fast and brutal. I was shaking with need. It pounded incessantly through my body. The primal urge to find satisfaction was almost overpowering.

When I was fully seated on him, we both drew in a deep breath. I stared at him, desperate for his next command.

"Can you come like this?" I couldn't tell if he said it out loud, or if it was a seductive voice I dreamed up. "From just the feel of me inside you?"

I let out a shuddering breath. It felt like heaven. Was it enough to get me there?

The ghost of a smirk played over Greg's lips. "I could. You feel how hard I am?"

I bit my bottom lip and nodded. He jerked inside me, and my body answered back, clenching on him.

"Yes." He brought his lips toward mine, lingering only a breath away. "Just like that." When I tried to close the gap between us, he turned his head away. "Could you come like this, without even moving? When I'm so deep inside you?"

The whine that escaped my lips sounded dire. As hot as the idea was, I didn't want that. I craved passionate, exhausting fucking, the kind where our sweaty skin stuck together and I had to hold back screams.

But Greg just sat there, his hands tucked beneath him, gazing at me expectantly. Waiting for me to take the lead. Another cry burst from my lips, a wordless plea.

"No?" he asked. "Then, fuck me. Touch yourself how you'd want me to do it."

I leaned forward, pushing my heels into the rug, lifted off him, then drove my body down. One powerful thrust, and I was addicted. I repeated the action, again and again, ramming myself down on him. My thighs burned with the exertion. My hands ached from their clench on the chair back. Sweat dampened the temples of my hair as I rode him, my breasts bouncing with the force of it.

"That's right." His voice dripped with encouragement. "That's it. Use my cock to get yourself off."

It was like I was on auto-pilot. Or maybe Greg was in the captain's seat, driving me toward the finish line. I took one hand off the chair and wrapped it around my breast, squeezing like I wished he'd do if he were touching me. I smoothed it down, panting and gasping, moans rolling from my throat as my palm coursed down my ribcage, diving toward the spot where our bodies were joined.

I was lightheaded from how hard I was breathing and the effort to maintain my punishing rhythm. The outsides of my vision went blurry, so there was only him. Only this man who saw me, dirty fantasies and all, and was more than happy to give me what I wanted.

His gaze followed the descent of my hand, and he muttered a soundless word that looked like *fuck* as I pressed two fingers to my clit. They were my fingertips, but I pretended they were his. I moved them, drawing a slow circle around the bundle of nerves that made me flinch with acute pleasure.

"Faster," he demanded.

I wasn't sure if he meant the tempo I was riding him at, or the way I moved my hand to touch myself, but instead of asking, I just increased both. My hand on the back of the chair slipped. It came down to clench a fistful of his suit lapel. His expression was . . . intense. There was no other way to describe it. Determination twisted on his face and burned in his eyes.

Gravity sucked me down into him. Each pump of my body on his ratcheted me deeper, like a slingshot being pulled back, primed for release. The warning sirens of an orgasm triggered in my system. I was close. So fucking close, all it would take was one stroke of his fingers anywhere on my skin.

My moans and whimpers swelled as the heat inside my core surged. I writhed on him, casting my head back as I jerked his face into me, yanking on his suitcoat. I crushed his head to my heaving chest, undulating like a girl possessed, and shivered as his mouth locked around one of my nipples.

"Oh, God, yes," I cried.

The stream of words came from him rapid-fire. "That's it, fuck me."

His hands suddenly moved. One gripped my thigh, and the other slid onto the small of my back. His palm and fingers pressed into me so hard, my bare skin dented around it. He pushed and pulled, urging me to ride him faster.

"Come on me." His words were law—no alternative. And as the orgasm dug its hooks in, pulling me upward, he sensed it. "Fucking *yes*."

I gasped for air but couldn't find any. My hand stilled, pressing down on my clit, futilely trying to restrict the ecstasy that ripped through my body. It was a tornado. Uncontrollable and unpredictable. I convulsed as it spiraled outward, and Greg's hands flew to my waist, holding me from bucking off him.

It lasted forever. The sensation washed from head to toe and back again, finally diminishing until I regained control of myself. I was shaky all over. At some point I'd lunged for him, and now I was a quivering mess in Greg's arms, my forehead pressed into the crook of his neck.

His hands caressed my back, tracing each bump of my spine. I closed my eyes, nestled into him, and savored the moment. It was quiet, other than his rapid breathing.

"That was intense," I whispered.

He shifted, nuzzling his mouth toward me until our lips met. The kiss started slow, but didn't stay that way for long. It exploded as his tongue pushed past my lips and filled my mouth. He commanded me with words and without. With his possession and when he wasn't even touching me.

As he rose to stand, carrying me up with him, I felt the opposite. Like I was falling for him, too hard and much too fast. Greg's feet shuffled two steps across the rug, hindered by the pants at his ankles, and then we were both falling—him laying me down on the nearby couch. He draped me over the armrest, so my back was arched and followed the curve, and my hair fell, the tips brushing the floor below.

He hadn't allowed himself to touch before, but now Greg made up for lost time. He climbed onto the couch, kneeling on the seat cushions as he drove his cock back into me, and his hands went everywhere. They glided over my stocking-covered legs. Smoothed over my garter straps. Coursed up my stomach and seized my breasts.

I swallowed one giant breath after another as he beat his hips into me, so deep it was almost too much. But even the uncomfortable sensation had a depraved and decadent edge that I loved. I had to reach behind me and grip the armrest to hold on, so his vicious thrusts didn't send me over the side.

He was close. I could tell by the way his brow furrowed and the muscles in his chest tightened. His moans changed in pitch and grew urgent. Chaotic. I wanted him to lose control like I had. I wrapped my hands around his head as he latched his mouth onto my breast, his tongue slashing at the sharp point of my nipple.

God, it felt incredible. So good, I wondered if I'd come again. His relentless mouth roamed from one breast to another, working me into a frenzy. I arched further, bending backward uncomfortably on the couch arm, slamming my eyes shut as pleasure built behind a dam—one he knew exactly how to tear down and unleash everything.

Pressure mounted at the base of my spine, and my grip on the upholstery went white-knuckle. "Oh," I gasped. "Oh my God." I was seconds away from the dam breaking, and I wanted my lips on his as it happened. I opened my eyes—

Only to see Preston standing in the entryway, horror etched on every inch of his shocked face.

THIRTY

I SLAPPED MY PALMS ON GREG'S SHOULDERS AND TRIED TO push him off me.

"Oh my God," I said again, only this time it was with shame and not enjoyment. As I scrambled backward and snaked my hands over my body to cover my bare breasts, he lifted his head, discovered what caused my panic, and turned to stone.

"Shit!" Greg spat out. He leapt off the couch and jerked his pants up, covering himself.

"What. The. *Fuck?*" Anger tensed Preston's shoulders as he glared at his father.

Greg shrugged out of his suitcoat in an instant and draped it over me. I was beyond grateful and pressed the satiny lining of the coat to my naked skin, rising off the couch to stand beside him. My mind flooded with too many thoughts at once. What was Preston doing here? How had we not heard him come in? And how long had he been standing there, watching us?

In my fantasy, him catching us was erotic, but reality was icy cold and the furthest thing from sexy.

"What are you doing here?" Greg asked. It was confused, desperate, and maybe a little accusatory.

Whatever shock and hurt Preston had was pushed out of the way to make room for seething fury. "I forgot my bag. I thought I could sneak downstairs and get it without bothering you. I wasn't aware you were going to be out in the living room, *fucking my girlfriend on the couch.*"

I sucked in a breath and choked back the urge to remind him we weren't a couple anymore. He was angry enough, I didn't need to provoke him further. At least this explained why we hadn't heard the garage door. I'd been too lost in my surprise to realize how strange it was Preston had come through the front door. He'd probably been hoping to get in and out of the house quietly and without disturbing his dad's date.

But Greg felt compelled to correct him. "Ex-girlfriend. You two were broken up before Cassidy and I got together."

The statement seemed to knock Preston sideways. His eyes went enormous, then narrowed down to slits. "Together?"

Greg shifted, moving subtly in front of me like a shield. "We were going to tell you."

Preston sneered. "I should have known. I should have fucking expected it. You don't care about me, *Greg.*"

It'd taken him more than a year of living with his father before he'd come around to calling him Dad, and the step backward now was painful. The name was sharp and cutting. Greg reacted as if he'd been shoved, and Preston looked pleased the verbal blow had landed.

"You do whatever the fuck you want," he continued. He stood taller, full of righteousness. "Always have, and always will."

I pressed my hand harder to my chest, holding the coat in place, but more to try to stop the pain in my heart. Whether or not he was right, or whether it was fair, he'd probably always feel that way, no matter what his father did to try to make up for it.

Greg's tone was defensive. "That's not true."

"You're so goddamn selfish."

"I used to be, yeah," Greg said. "I screwed up with you and your mom. There's not a day that goes by where I don't wish I could change what I did."

As far as I knew, they'd never talked about it, and I held my breath, wanting to fade into the background.

Preston's expression turned sour. "Bullshit, and I don't want to hear it."

"Yeah? Too fucking bad, because you're going to. Cassidy and I didn't plan on this happening, it just . . . did. You've got to understand, we didn't do this to intentionally hurt you."

It was painful to watch the two most important men in my life fighting, and know I was the cause. All of Greg's hard work to make it right with his son, all undone in the blink of an eye. I dropped my gaze down to my feet as I struggled to rein in my emotions.

"I'm sorry you found out like this." Greg's voice brimmed with remorse. "Preston, I care about you so much—"

His son's humorless laugh cut through the room. "Yeah, if that were true, you wouldn't have fucked her." It was like I wasn't there, wasn't in the room. All of his focus was locked onto his father. "You *knew* how much she meant to me."

"Do I?" Greg's posture changed abruptly, shifting from defense to offense. "If she meant so much, then why the hell did I find you and that naked girl in the hot tub the week after you came home from school?"

Both men were acutely aware of my presence when I gasped.

That was the only sound for a long moment. Time seemed to stand still, other than the dancing shadows on the walls from the candlelight. My body went numb, my mind empty. A survival instinct kicked in, refusing to accept the statement so I could spare myself the pain.

My voice was a ghost. "What?"

The week after you came home from school. Which meant not only had Preston cheated on me, but Greg knew about it . . . and he hadn't told me.

I didn't know where to focus or what to do. Sensation slowly returned to my body as awareness sank in, but I felt out of sorts. Like all my organs had turned upside-down.

Preston's gaze hesitantly floated my direction. At least it was nice to see a different emotion splashed on his face instead of anger. He didn't seem as tall or indignant when he looked guilty as sin. His words were hollow. "It was one time. I made a mistake."

I couldn't be here. I had to flee before I broke into a million pieces. The betrayal from the Lowe men was too much. I couldn't deal. I tottered backward on the heels, needing immediate distance. How the fuck was I going to get to my clothes in Greg's room? It was a million miles away, and even though they'd both seen me naked, now they felt like—

Strangers.

The hurt painted on my face made Preston angry all over again, but not with me. No, he blamed his father for revealing the stunning information. He shot daggers at Greg, like it was all his father's fault and not his own.

Classic fucking Preston.

He didn't care about me or my feelings—only that his father had gotten him in trouble. Meanwhile, Greg was the opposite. Concern streaked his expression as he reached out for me.

I stared at his hand, unwilling to move toward it or away. How could he keep this enormous secret from me?

"Seriously?" Preston snapped, staring incredulously at his father's outstretched hand. Maybe it looked like Greg had chosen me over his own son, and Preston wasn't about to have it. He made a noise of frustration and took off, his heavy feet pounding on the hardwood as he stomped to the top of the stairs and went down them.

"Preston." Greg took a step toward his son, stopped, and cast a glance at me over his shoulder. "Don't go, Cassidy. Please? Will you wait for me in my room?"

I couldn't force an answer from my lungs, but he must have thought I'd agreed because he nodded and hurried toward the stairs.

One slow step at a time, I lumbered my way into Greg's bedroom and dropped his gray suitcoat onto the bed. Only I'd done it mindlessly, too close to the edge, and it slipped off, spilling onto the floor in a heap. I couldn't find the strength to care about fixing it.

The straps holding the shoes to my ankles were undone, followed by the garters. I peeled the thigh-high stockings down my legs one at a time, all while trying not to think about what had just happened. The swing from guilt, to anger, to hurt was a rollercoaster I'd been locked into, even as I'd begged to get off.

I dressed slowly. Gone was the feeling of being a bombshell or a sex kitten. I was a stupid twenty-year-old girl. A naïve and trusting fool. How long should I wait here in this empty bedroom for Greg to return?

The garter belt and stockings were tossed into the open pink box. I'd left the bra and panties out in the living room, so they were lost to me now. I sat on the edge of the bed, wondering if I sat still enough, I'd turn to unfeeling stone.

I didn't know and didn't care to know the details about what Preston had done with someone else. If it was true and it had been one time and a mistake as he'd said, it didn't matter. I'd done everything to try to hold onto him. Given him everything. Even as his girlfriend, I still wasn't his top choice.

It was impossible, sitting alone in the dark bedroom, to not feel worthless.

"Cassidy."

Greg's deep voice snapped me from my thoughts. I focused my gaze on him as he stood before me, and my heart sank further in my chest. The lines around his eyes were deeper. He combed a hand through his unruly hair and had a hard time meeting my gaze.

I already knew what was about to happen, but I fought against it. I pushed to my feet and crossed my arms over my chest to prevent myself from touching him. If I grabbed him, it'd only be harder to let go.

He said nothing. He shoulders rose and fell with deep breaths, like breathing was difficult for him.

I couldn't wait another second. "Well?"

"He told me I was going to have to make a choice." Finally, he dragged his gaze up and connected it to mine. His eyes were full of sadness.

"Him or me," I whispered.

Preston was forcing his father to choose which relationship to end, and I couldn't see any outcome where I would win. Even if Greg chose me for some insane reason, I knew I couldn't allow it. My bottom lip quivered, but I refused to let any other emotion show.

Greg wasn't going to pick me. No matter how shitty and immature Preston was acting, of course he'd win. Greg would sacrifice me for a chance with his son every time, and in my rational mind, I understood that.

But my heart? That was a different story.

Greg wasn't fairing much better than I was. "He says he'll quit school and move back in with his mom if we keep seeing each other."

The first stage of grief—denial—washed through me. "He'll get past it." The words tasted bitter coming out of my mouth. "Like you said, he never cared about me."

"That's not what I said."

I shifted on my bare feet and gave him a hard look. "He didn't care enough to stay faithful. And not enough to tell me the truth, either." Stage two—anger—came on strong, and power filled my voice. My eyes burned with hot tears. "Why didn't you tell me?"

"I tried." His voice lacked his usual confidence. "I warned you that you could do better."

His answer only made me madder. "Not good enough."

Greg's lips pushed into a resigned frown. "Remind me what your reasons were for not telling Preston about the first time we kissed."

I froze. I'd told him nothing good could come from him knowing. It'd only cause him pain. "That was different," I said quickly. It was unconvincing, even to me.

"The day I caught him, I hated him a little. I wanted you so badly, but you were with him . . . and then he ran around on you. It was cruel to both of us."

"And yet, you didn't say a word." More than a month after he'd caught Preston, I'd still been his girlfriend, oblivious.

Frustration tightened Greg's posture. "What was I supposed to say? There was no upside to telling you."

There wasn't. He'd applied the same rules to me I'd used for Preston, giving me a taste of my own medicine, and God—I *hated* it.

"I get why you're upset, but I was in an impossible situation," he said. "I still am. I don't like what he's done, or this ultimatum he's given me, but the fact is he's still my son."

"I know." My voice was as broken as I was inside. "Maybe he'll change his mind."

I don't know why I said it, because I didn't believe it. Preston was outstanding at holding grudges. Panic poured into my stomach. It weighed me down and pulled me away, even when I wanted to stay put. I sensed the end coming like an out-of-control train approaching but fought to hold my ground.

The tense silence in the room grew thick and stifling.

Finally, Greg let out a long breath. "I don't know what to do."

I clenched my teeth together until muscles along my jaw ached. Was he saying this for my benefit? "Please," I bit off. "We both know what has to happen."

He frowned. And then he had the nerve to look confused.

My emotions were a mess and untrustworthy, but a tiny part of me wondered if this was an act. He was much too smart to not see the obvious answer, and yet it became increasingly clear I was going to have to say it out loud. Like he was forcing me to make this decision and be the one to end it. I sucked in a deep breath to muster up the courage. "We can't see each other anymore."

He blinked and delivered the statement the same way I imagined he told families how their loved ones were gone. Utterly emotionless. "All right."

I thought I'd braced myself, but his quick acceptance stung so much worse than I was ready for. I pressed a hand to my stomach, keeping myself from doubling over.

"Well," I snapped, "you could at least pretend that wasn't easy."

Heartbreak flashed through Greg's dark eyes. "It wasn't. It *isn't*. I care about you so much and I—"

I shook my head. "Yeah? Did you even fight him?" I already knew the answer was no, because in his quest to win his son's forgiveness, he had been a pushover. "Or did Preston immediately get his way, just like he always does with you?"

It wasn't a nice thing to say, but I wasn't feeling nice at that moment, and it was true. Greg knew it too, but his posture went stiff. "I know you're upset," he said flatly. "Believe me when I tell you this is the last thing I want, but I don't have a choice."

But he did, and my anger spilled over, running past the point of control. It brewed into a storm and my whole body began to shake. "Right. Because you made me make it for you."

A whiny, patronizing voice whispered in my head. "*Poor Cassidy Shepard. Her dad walks out, mom's too busy, her boyfriend strays—even the new one won't stick around.*"

I let out a desperate cry, choking off a sob. "God, just once, I wish I could be someone's first choice."

He opened his mouth to say something, but . . . didn't. He didn't argue my accusation or defend what he'd done. There was no fight in him for me. No struggle over losing what we'd had, and suddenly I felt like there was nothing left between us.

Greg must have seen the realization flit through me, because he reached out, attempting to hold me.

"Don't!" I blurted, stumbling backward. The memory of the last time we'd tried to say goodbye seared unwelcomed through my mind.

My refusal wounded him, but he nodded slowly, dropping his arms to hang at his sides. "I'll drive you home."

"No." I didn't want to be around him another second. I could barely look at him. Preston looked a lot like his father, and in my stress, it was becoming increasingly difficult to keep my anger compartmentalized. It bled from one Lowe to the other. "I'll walk to Lilith's."

He sighed. "I can drive you."

"No." I was firm this time. "We can't see each other anymore, and I'd like to start right now."

I pushed past him, snatched the pair of heels up off the carpet, and strode on my bare feet into the kitchen, where I grabbed my purse. He followed me, making some statements about it being late and dark out, but I ignored him. I went back through the living room and into the entryway, propelling myself forward.

It will be easier, I told myself, *when you are out of this house. Away from him. Outside, where you can breathe again.*

"You know I don't want this," he said when I opened the front door and stood at the threshold.

I gave him a cool look. "I guess the only one who gets what they want is the spoiled boy downstairs."

"I'm sorry," Greg said when I stepped onto the front porch and walked out into the night, my bare feet moving across the concrete walkway.

I didn't respond. Didn't say goodbye, or even acknowledge him.

Maybe he was sorry. Maybe one day he'd think he'd made a mistake. A new one he'd been forced into to try to undo the one he'd made with Preston years ago. But that didn't make any of this easier.

I walked away from the Lowe house for the last time, alone and crying under the moonless sky.

THIRTY-ONE

LILITH TOLD ME IT WOULD GET EASIER, BUT IT DIDN'T. At least, not the following week. After the break-up with Preston, it hadn't been that hard to quit him cold turkey. But Greg? I couldn't stop thinking about him, wondering what he was doing, and if he was missing me. Was he doing anything to try to change his son's mind?

And if he was able to get Preston to budge, what then? We felt . . . over. Greg and I hadn't spoken since that night. He'd sent me one text a little after I'd left his house.

> Greg: Did you make it to your friend's?
> Are you okay?

When my phone had chimed, I was sitting cross-legged on the floor, my back against Lilith's couch and my grimy feet tucked under me.

> Cassidy: Yes.

> Cassidy: You were right. My 20th
> birthday was the worst.

I regretted sending it later, after I'd calmed down. I hadn't meant to be mean. Preston had put Greg in an impossible situation, and he'd had to bear most of the anger I should have directed at Preston.

My mother picked up on my sullen mood, and I finally told her Preston and I had broken up. I didn't tell her when it had happened—I let her assume it was recent and the reason I was mopey.

I counted down the days until I'd be back at school, in a new environment where I hoped I'd be magically free from my thoughts about the surgeon with dark eyes and great hands.

I only had three more days to go when the universe decided to be downright vicious. I'd just downed two ibuprofens for my killer headache when my mom asked me to go to the store. We needed fixings for dinner, she'd said.

I was shopping in the bread aisle when I saw him.

Greg stood in the bustling produce area hovered over tomatoes, a plastic bag held in one hand as he examined the bin. Nearby, a woman clearly wanted to get to the onions, which he was blocking, but she hesitated in asking him to move. Too polite or shy, or maybe too taken with him. His long fingers selected the tomato he was looking for, slipped it into the bag, and then he turned.

My stomach hurt, seeing him again.

He noticed the woman waiting, said something, and pushed his cart quickly out of her way. As he tossed what seemed to be an apology to her, he gave a sheepish smile. Just that flash of a smile lit up his face.

The pain in my belly was a band, low and tight across my hips.

Had he sensed my gaze on him?

Greg's head lifted, and his attention turned my way. And as he recognized me, standing wooden with a package of hamburger buns in my hands, his posture went alert. I had to move. Warning signs flashed in my body, telling me to get the fuck out of there before I broke down. No one wanted a blubbering twenty-year-old girl in the bread aisle, trying to hide sobs between loaves and baguettes.

My stomach churned the whole time I stood in the checkout lane. I was sweaty and nauseated, anxious to be done and back home. But when I returned, the feeling didn't subside, not even after dinner. I cursed myself for letting the near run-in get to me like this.

It was stupid. My overreaction, my feelings. I hadn't even been in love with Greg. Why was I acting like I had?

"I don't feel well," I said to my mom soon after we'd finished the dishes. "I'm going to bed."

She looked concerned. "You need anything?"

Just to stop thinking about him. "No, I'm fine. Goodnight."

I plodded up the stairs, changed into my pajamas, and curled up under the covers, closing my eyes and hoping to shut off my feelings for a few hours.

I awoke chilled, but also covered with a thin layer of sweat.

My room was dark, and the alarm clock on my side table said it was a little after two in the morning. The dull ache in my stomach had graduated into full-out pain. Burning, centered pain.

I rolled over onto my other side, willing it to go away, but it only seemed to intensify as I tried to go back to sleep. It got to the point where I started to wonder if something was wrong. Why did it hurt so much?

Thirty more minutes was all I could take before I dragged myself from the bed down to my mom's room, my phone clutched in a hand. She'd always been a deep sleeper and put her phone on 'Do Not Disturb' after eleven. Texting her from my bed wouldn't do any good.

She was snoring quietly, lying sprawled out in the center of her queen-sized bed. "Mom," I said. "Mom, wake up."

She jerked from sleep, blinked her disoriented eyes at me, then launched upright. "What's wrong?"

"My stomach hurts." I had to band my arms across it. "It hurts really bad."

I was seated in the passenger seat of her car in less than five minutes. Her face was completely white as she raced toward the emergency room. I'd been a lucky kid. No broken bones, no major health scares, so we were both in foreign, scary territory. I tried not to think about what was wrong, because my mind immediately went to terrible scenarios and made my anxiety worse.

We'd barely taken our seats in the waiting area before they called us back into a room. People said the emergency room was slow, but it seemed to move at lightning speed for me. The nurse, a woman who looked like she'd seen it all— and probably multiple times—came into the room and took my vitals.

"What do you think's wrong?" my mom asked.

"I'm not the doctor," the nurse said automatically.

My mom wasn't deterred. "Right, but what do you suspect?"

The woman swiped a thermometer across my forehead as I shivered. The "bed" in the room was more like a table with a bend in it, and really uncomfortable. I wanted to curl up into a ball and couldn't, so instead I gripped one of the metal side arms.

"Is there a chance you could be pregnant?" she asked.

My heart stopped at the same instant my gaze flew to my mother. She knew I was sexually active and had actively encouraged safe sex. But she believed that was happening with Preston, and if I was somehow pregnant? It wouldn't be by him.

"I'm good about taking my pill," I said quickly. "And using condoms."

"Temp is one-oh-one," she commented, although I wasn't sure to whom. "My guess would be appendicitis."

The seasoned nurse was absolutely right—a CT scan confirmed it. By four a.m. I'd been admitted, taken to a room on the third floor, and antibiotics started through my IV. The pain medication they gave me helped, but it also made me shake worse than before.

While we waited for my doctor to come in and talk about the next steps, my mom, wearing the clothes she'd haphazardly thrown on hours ago, dozed upright in a chair beside my bed. I eyed her with a bit of jealousy. I was exhausted, but too miserable and freaked out to sleep. I was hooked up to machines that clicked and hummed, and the room never got quite dark, even with the lights off. Sounds from the hall were steady as well. Heavy beds rolling by. Shoes squeaking on the polished floor.

"Twenty-year-old female. Acute appendicitis," a female voice said just on the other side of my door. "We've got you scheduled for OR two at five-twenty."

A set of footsteps faded at the same moment a short knock rang out, and the heavy wooden door to my room pushed open without waiting for my reply. My mother stirred and straightened in her chair, perking up as the doctor entered. He made it two steps into the room before he looked at me.

All the air whooshed from my lungs.

Greg froze, disbelief streaked on his face.

THIRTY-TWO

GREG'S STUNNED GAZE WENT FROM ME, TO MY MOTHER, THEN on to the whiteboard beside my hospital bed that listed my stats. As if he needed to see all of it before it really settled in.

"Dr. Lowe," my mother said, and for the first time in her life, she looked pleased to see him.

He paced quickly to my bedside. His worried expression was so brutal, I twisted away.

"No," I said feebly.

He didn't seem to hear me. "How's your pain?"

Bad, I wanted to say. *Terrible ever since you made me leave you.* Instead I curled up into myself, keeping a lid on my mouth and my emotions.

"She's been better the last hour," my mother answered, rising from the chair and moving to stand next to the bedrail on the side opposite him.

"Good. That's good." He shifted back into doctor mode, his focus still on me. "We'll get you feeling a lot better once we've taken your appendix out."

Then he launched into a whole thing about what the appendix was, why it was going bad, and how it would be removed. His practiced speech about using a tiny telescopic camera and small cuts and scars barely registered. My mother listened dutifully, nodding along and asking questions. I just stared at the two lumps of my feet under the heavy blanket covering my lower body. Was it the drugs they had me on, his presence, or the combination of the two that made it difficult to focus?

"Cassidy." My name was a soft command in his voice. "Do you have any questions?"

I rolled my gaze to him. He had one of those fitted hats on to keep his hair back, the same blue as the hospital scrubs he wore. No white coat, thank God. Even dressed down in shapeless clothes, he was still masculine and sexy.

When I didn't say anything, he set a palm on my bedrail, bringing him closer. A gesture that probably meant nothing to my mom but felt weirdly intimate to me. I peered at his fingers, tracing each one with my gaze.

In less than an hour, that hand was going to hold a scalpel and cut me open.

"I don't want you to do the surgery," I said.

His grip tightened in reaction. "I know it's scary, but your appendix has to come out. There's no other way to treat—"

"No." He'd misunderstood me. "I don't want *you* to do the surgery."

He released his hold on the rail and straightened. "What? Why?"

My mother looked just as surprised. "Oh, honey. It might feel strange because he's Preston's father, but he's a doctor. Don't worry about him seeing your body."

What the hell? My cheeks warmed with embarrassment. She thought I was freaking out about my ex-boyfriend's dad seeing me naked. That wasn't high on my list of concerns. "It's not that."

"Okay. Then—?" she asked.

Greg stood with his hands resting on his hips. He appeared casual at first glance, but I saw the tension in his forearms and the way his shoulders were higher than normal.

"Mom, can you give us a minute? I need to talk to Greg alone."

I realized my slip too late. I'd never called him by his first name, and her gaze narrowed on him. Her tone was cool. "Greg?"

When she held her ground, I said it with force. "Please?"

I couldn't focus on the fact that she was unhappy right now. We didn't have time. I was beyond exhausted, uncomfortable, anxious, and I couldn't find a better way to ask her to leave. I also didn't want to dance around the conversation I needed to have with him.

My mother examined Greg with new suspicion. "Fine. I'll be right outside when you're done."

The door had just clicked shut when he spoke again. "Tell me why you don't want me to do the surgery."

I stared up into his brown eyes, and my voice went shallow. "Because I don't want it to be the last time you put your hands on my body."

He sucked in a deep breath, and his expression turned to defeat. He couldn't argue and tell me it wouldn't be. Neither of us knew what the future held.

I crossed my arms over my chest, which probably made me look like a pouting teenager, but the pain in my belly was growing, and I needed to hold myself together long enough until he was gone from the room. "I want someone else."

Beneath the pain I inflicted, his jaw set. "This isn't a teaching hospital. I'm the trauma surgeon on-call." He took in a breath. "I could opt out of this, but it might be hours of scrambling before we find someone else available. And also, Cassidy? I'm the *best*. You think I'm going to let someone else do this? Not a chance."

I was annoyed that the weak part of me faltered at his bravado. Of course, the cocky surgeon wanted me under his knife. It was the only way to ensure I got the best possible care. But it also felt like control, and this was one time I didn't want to be under it.

Irritation simmered below my surface, threatening to erupt. "I said no. I don't want your scars on me for the rest of my life."

"Jesus Christ." He ripped his gaze away from me and glared at the wall. "I know you're unhappy, but this isn't the time to start acting like a child." I gasped, wounded by his child comment, but he wasn't finished. "This is serious. Do you understand that? The recovery for laparoscopy is two weeks. Four incisions, most about half an inch long. If you wait and your appendix ruptures? Everything changes."

He set his hands wide on my bedrail, leaned over, and hung his head. "I'd have to open your abdomen and re-move all the toxic bacteria inside from the rupture. That scar would be eight, maybe nine inches, and your recovery would be measured in months. *Months*, Cassidy." He lifted his head and gave me a piercing stare. "You don't get to pick your doctor then, because at that point, it's a race to the OR to save your life."

Tears welled in my eyes, but I blinked them back.

He took a hand off the bed, scooped it behind my neck, and brought our faces together, his warm forehead pressed to mine. "I don't want your life in my hands. Don't make me do that kind of surgery."

He didn't want my life in his hands, but in that moment, I realized it was already too late for my heart. I closed my eyes and unleashed a tear, which he used his thumb to brush away.

"I understand," his voice fell to a hush, "I'm not your first choice. I wasn't for a long time. But today, I'm your only choice."

The realization hit me with a physical impact, and I jolted in Greg's hold. He'd hinted more than once he'd had feelings for me while I was with Preston. In fact, he'd told me, but I'd brushed the statements off.

Had he felt like he was my second choice this whole time? Because he wasn't.

"I . . ." I started, speaking before I had my thoughts.

What difference did it make now, laying all the cards on the table? We'd kept our relationship a secret, and it hurt Preston, and Greg had kept Preston's betrayal from me. How could the truth be any more painful?

"I think I might be in love with you," I whispered.

He sighed and closed his eyes. His expression was unreadable, and his silence was fucking terrifying.

"Forget I said it." I shifted out of his hold and sat back in the bed. "It's the drugs you've got me on."

A slow, sad smile warmed his lips. It spread and spread, until he was grinning, and I'd never seen him look more beautiful.

"I made a promise to him," he said, "but I fucking swear, today won't be the last time I touch you." He seemed reluctant to put distance between us, but stood. "You have to trust me. Okay?"

I swallowed a breath and brushed a lock of hair back, out of my eyes. "Okay."

"Good." Relief swept through him so hard, he looked ten pounds lighter. "Then I'll see you in recovery."

THIRTY-THREE

THE LAST DAY AND A HALF HAD BEEN AN ORDEAL FOR MY MOM and me, but she'd been much stronger than I had. She didn't leave my side, choosing to sleep on the cramped window bench in my hospital room last night. Now it was time for breakfast, and I'd pretty much thrown her out of the room, urging her to get a decent cup of coffee or a meal she wouldn't have to eat out of a Styrofoam container.

God. I'd spent the summer wanting to be an independent adult, not realizing how nice it was to have my mom around—not until I'd needed her.

The surgery had gone well, or so I'd been told. In recovery, I'd been out of it from the sedation and didn't remember a thing. My mom said Dr. Lowe came by to check on me soon after I'd woken up, but she hadn't said anything else, even when I pressed her on it.

And I hadn't seen him since.

I shifted in the bed against the pillow propping me up. My incisions were in my belly, but my back hurt no matter what position I was in. The hospital was nice, yet everything about the room was uncomfortable, and I turned my gaze toward the window and the sunlight outside. The morning nurse said I'd probably be discharged this afternoon, and I was desperate to be home and in my own bed.

There was a knock on the door, jolting me. I expected it to fly open—none of the busy hospital staff waited for a patient to invite them in. The knock seemed more of a courtesy announcement. But whoever had tapped on my door, they lingered outside, waiting.

"Come in," I called.

The oversized door was pushed open, but the boy remained in the hallway, staring into my room with disbelief.

I couldn't believe who I was seeing either. "Preston?"

He moved hesitantly inside, shutting the door behind him, and then glanced around the room, checking to see if there was anyone else. Satisfied we were alone, he set his focus on me.

What the hell was he was he doing here?

His expression was full of worry, almost like seeing me in a hospital bed, an IV hanging at my side, had him rattled. I found his presence right now unbearable. My tone was so harsh, it even surprised me. "What do you want?"

Preston jammed his hands in the pockets of his jeans and drew in a deep breath. "Hey. How're you feeling?"

I was tired of sugarcoating things and no longer cared about how the truth was going to make him feel. "I'm feeling like you're the last person I want to see right now."

He nodded. "Yeah, I figured." His face was grim, his posture tense. "Greg told me what happened. I was worried about you."

So, he was back to calling him Greg. I hurt for his father, and it made me angry. I gave my ex-boyfriend a flat look.

"You didn't care about me when we were together. It's a little weird to start now."

He had the nerve to look wounded. "Don't say that. Cassidy, you know you—"

I lifted a hand, cutting him off, because I had no patience left. "Why are you here?"

He was restless, unable to stay in one place or hold my gaze. He paced a circuit from one end of the room to the other. "What he said, about the girl in the hot tub? I fucked up. I'm sorry, okay?"

I wanted to believe what I was hearing, but my skeptical side didn't trust it. "You came . . . to apologize?"

He stopped pacing. "Yeah."

"Why?"

My simple question derailed him completely, judging by his stunned look. "What?"

"Why?" I repeated. "Why do you feel the need to apologize?"

He looked at me like I was losing my mind. "You don't think I did anything wrong?"

I gave a tight, humorless laugh, but pain flashed through my incisions. "No, I do. What I mean is, coming here and saying this isn't exactly fun for you. You could get away with not doing it. So, why are you?" Like most people, Preston would avoid responsibility if given the opportunity. "No one's making you apologize."

The moment my off-handed statement registered, his gaze drifted to the door, and my stomach flipped over.

"Oh," I said quietly. There were a half-dozen reasons he could have given on why he'd come. He could have said he felt bad. That he hadn't meant to hurt me. But, no. I suspected Preston was here only because his father was on the other side of the door and had put him up to this.

Which made any apology he gave me empty and worthless.

"I screwed up, and I'm sorry." Preston's voice might have been sincere, but I couldn't tell. He didn't give me much of a chance anyway, because he scowled. "But don't think that makes what you did with my dad okay. Because it's not."

I was so tired, and for once, shouldn't I get to be selfish? This conversation wasn't going to do anything but make me feel worse, so I wasn't going to have it.

"Can you just go?" I turned away from him, blinking away tears I refused to cry.

Silence dragged, but finally he sighed his frustration. "I told him this was stupid."

His footsteps rang out as he marched to the door and yanked it open. I didn't want to look out into the hallway and find Greg waiting there, but my heart had a different plan. It wasn't about to give up the chance to see him again.

Greg wore the white doctor's coat. He had on black pants, a white dress shirt, and a black tie with small dots decorating the silk. The sides of his coat were pushed back so he could rest his hands on his hips, and he peered over Preston's head to find me in the bed.

My watery eyes were all he needed to see. He set his jaw and glared at Preston. "No, not good enough. Try again."

His son went stiff. "I held up my end of the deal. I said I was sorry."

"Looks like you need to tell her again."

"You know," Preston snapped, "you can't actually make someone forgive you."

"Oh, believe me, I'm *aware*." Greg's voice was heavy with meaning. "I'm not giving up, and you don't get to either."

His arms came down to hang at his sides, and his posture straightened. In fact, his whole demeanor shifted. His determined, focused look locked onto his son. "Preston." His voice was full of gravity. "I'm sorry I made the wrong choice when I was young and stupid, and I'm sorry I was a selfish, shitty father to you. I can't change what I did, but I wish I could." He softened, everything from his stance to his tone. "You want to be selfish and shitty to me? I get it. I haven't earned your forgiveness, so all I can do is keep trying."

Preston took a step backward and looked off-kilter. He wasn't expecting his father to make such an overture—in front of me, no less—and wasn't sure how to defend himself against it. He stared at his father with pure disbelief.

Greg's voice firmed up. "You haven't earned her forgiveness either. What about that?" He said it as a challenge. "I think the least you could do is not give up."

Preston looked at his dad like he was a ghost, and the words came from him in a blur. "I'm not dealing with this right now."

He puffed up his chest and strode from the room, not caring who was standing in the way as he went. The side of his shoulder clipped his dad, forcing Greg out of the doorway. Disappointment clung to his expression as he watched his son go.

Was Preston ever going to accept his dad's apology? Or had I screwed that up, driving a permanent wedge between the Lowe men?

I felt a hundred emotions at once. Part of me was shamefully excited to see Greg again, but the crushing longing for him was there too, reminding me I didn't have him anymore.

"I'm sorry about him," he said. His shoulders rose as he drew in a breath. "And I'm sorry about a lot of things. That I couldn't choose us. That I made you end things. I was weak, and couldn't bring myself to do it."

There hadn't been any fight in him when we'd broken up, I'd thought.

But . . . had I been wrong?

He'd gotten Preston to come to the hospital and attempt to apologize, so maybe he was fighting for us, just in a different way. Did he have a plan? He was smart and calculating, and right now I could practically see the wheels turning in his head.

I stared at him in the doorway, beautifully backlit by the bright hallway, and ached for him to come inside the room. I was desperate for him to storm over to my bedside, scoop me up in his arms, and set his mouth on mine, like he couldn't tolerate another moment without kissing me.

But Greg and I both knew wishing for things didn't make them happen.

His words were hushed, only for me. "I miss you."

The pain I felt wasn't where his scalpel had cut me open. It was buried deeper inside. "I miss you too."

He took one hesitant step across the threshold of my room. "I'm working on it. On him."

I swallowed a breath. He'd said he wasn't giving up, and the way he looked at me now, I knew he meant on everything. This man was driven, and he wasn't going to quit when facing an obstacle.

My pulse leaped with hope.

When his phone chimed, disappointment created a deep crease in Greg's forehead. He glanced at the screen, then back to me. "It's the second time they've paged me."

I nodded and pulled the blanket tighter around my waist, mustering the bravest face I could, hoping he'd understand my meaning. "Okay. Go do what you need to."

Polly, our one-eyed cat, didn't care for Tripod. In fact, she was old and ornery, and didn't like anyone except my mom and me. It was late afternoon as my mom helped me into my bed, and both the dog and cat paced my room like two boxers preparing to go at each other.

But they weren't interested in fighting, only in staking their spot beside me. As soon as I was settled, propped up on some pillows, Polly leapt up on the bed. She curled into a tight ball beside my hip. Her ears went back when the dog also jumped on board. He wasn't small or graceful, and I grimaced as the bed rocked.

"Tripod, no!" My mom clapped her hands to try to shoo the dog off, but Tripod flattened himself against me, his head in my lap. He gave my mom the deepest puppy dog eyes he possessed, and she sighed. He was stubborn and spoiled, and when it came to my mom, he always got his way.

"He's fine," I said.

I would have laughed, but my incisions were tender. I'd discovered coughing, sneezing, and laughter were things to avoid right now. I put my hand on his head, and his tail thumped hard against the mattress. Polly's ears went back again, perturbed, but she didn't abandon her spot.

"You need anything else?" my mom asked.

"No." I lifted the TV remote in one hand and my phone in the other. "I'm all set." I gave her a grateful smile. "Thank you. I feel like we were there forever. I hope your garden's okay." She hadn't even mentioned it while we were cooped up in the hospital.

She laughed and waved a hand, brushing off my comment. "They're plants. I'm sure they're fine."

"But thanks for staying with me."

She gave me a weird smile, like I was being silly. "That's what mothers do." She faked seriousness. "But, honey, do that to me again and you'll be in big trouble."

"Yes, ma'am. I promise, no more appendicitis for me."

Her gaze dropped to my wrist. "Want me to cut the bracelets off?"

"Oh." I eyed the plastic hospital ID bracelets clasped to my right wrist. My name, date of birth, and Dr. Lowe were printed on it. A small part of me didn't want to take it off yet, but then I thought I was being ridiculous. "Yes, please."

She left and returned with a pair of scissors, and I held still while she cut the bands off.

"I'm in love with Dr. Lowe," I said abruptly.

My mom paused, arched one eyebrow, and set the bands on my nightstand. "Oh, Cassidy, I know. I figured that out watching you two in recovery."

Oh no.

I sank back against my pillows as dread filled my chest. Had I told him I loved him, again, this time while she was in the room? And had he stayed silent a second time? "What did I do?"

"You looked at him."

I blinked. "That's it?"

"You looked at him the same way I used to look at your father." Her expression was flat. "Men like him are a lot of heartache."

I pulled my face into a scowl. "He's not like my father."

Once again, I got the look like I was being silly. Or maybe naïve. "He's certainly old enough to be, isn't he? Plus, a man who walks out on his son only cares about himself."

"He was young and made a mistake, but I can tell you, Preston's the most important person in his life now."

Her expression was pure skepticism. "I find that hard to believe."

"He'd do anything for his son, and that included giving me up."

She sighed, then ran a hand over Tripod's back, making the dog's tail thump noisily on the bed. "I don't know how to feel about that man anymore. He broke my baby girl's heart, but also saved her life." When she stopped petting him, Tripod nuzzled her hand on the bed, and she resumed. "He looked at you the same way, you know. He came right into that recovery room, took your hand, and held it the entire time he told me how the surgery went."

I took in a breath, and as my lungs expanded, there was the dull pain reminding me not to do that. I tried to picture the moment. Greg standing over my hospital bed, one of my hands clasped in his. It made my heart ache.

"Well, I know you're hurting," my mom said, rising cautiously from the bed. I had no idea if she was talking about my physical or emotional pain. "Get some sleep. I know we both need it."

It was both comforting and uncomfortable with Tripod sleeping beside me like a furry, immovable log. Whenever I tried to get him to adjust, he just groaned and snuggled in.

I'd gotten a few hours of sleep, but now my pain medicine was wearing thin, and I sent a text to my mom.

> Cassidy: Can you bring me something
> to drink? I'm ready for some
> more drugs.

> Mom: Good, you're awake. Are you up
> for visitors?

It had to be Lilith. My mom texted her when I went in for surgery, and my best friend had wanted to come by the hospital. I'd foolishly thought I'd get to go home last night and had told her not to worry about it.

> Cassidy: Yeah, send her up.

Footsteps creaked on the stairs, causing both Polly and Tripod to lift their heads toward the sound. My door pushed open without a knock, and in strolled a boy, a can of Dr. Pepper in his hand.

God, again?

THIRTY-FOUR

Tripod was off the bed in a heartbeat, darting around Preston's legs in that joyful dance only dogs do when excited to see new people. *Traitor*, I wanted to yell to my dog. Polly had my back. She glared at Preston, and as he cautiously approached the bed, she hissed.

Today, I was most definitely a cat person.

I eyed Preston while he set the unopened can on my nightstand like it was a peace offering.

"No," I growled.

Tripod froze, sensing the tension, and hightailed it back to my bed.

"I just need two minutes." His voice was quiet and pleading.

"Well, whatever you need," I patronized. I stared at my ex-boyfriend, wondering why the hell my mother let him up. I'd told her he'd stopped by this morning and our conversation had been tense.

He glanced around my room, and though he'd been here countless times, he looked at the space like it was new. Perhaps it was. I'd removed all traces of him after my birthday. I didn't need to see his face or the reminder of how much he looked like his dad.

"I'm sorry." He turned in his spot, looking at me directly. "I didn't mean to hurt you. That day I screwed up, it was supposed to be a group of us, but everyone bailed—including you—except Stacy. So, I'd had a couple of beers, and we got into the hot tub because—"

"I don't want to know," I snapped.

He straightened and ran his fingers through his hair. His mannerisms were just like his father. "I didn't fuck her. It didn't get that far."

"I don't want to know." I couldn't be clearer than I'd been already. The angriest part of me wondered if sex hadn't happened because Greg had caught them. "And I don't want your apology. Just go."

Unlike last time, he looked lost, and very much like the boy I'd loved once. But my heart didn't work like it used to.

"Okay. I didn't come here to make it worse. I was trying to fix it."

Had he lost his damn mind? "Fix it? You can't fix this."

"That came out wrong," he answered quickly. "I'm trying to fix *me*. I've been an asshole to everyone, but most of all, to you." He put his hands on his hips and sighed. "I got to the point where it was so bad, I didn't even notice how awful I was anymore."

Something had changed in him, like his eyes were wide open again. "What happened?"

"When he got home from work, my dad and I had a beer together."

My dad, he'd said. Not Greg. I waited for Preston to elaborate, but he didn't. "Must have been one magical fucking beer."

Preston shifted in his stance, visibly agitated. Like last time, he didn't want to be having this conversation. How had his father gotten him to attempt it a second time?

"Look, I spent most of my first year here being mad at him, so we never really talked. After a while, we just moved past it. I told myself I didn't want his apology, but I was . . . wrong. I didn't know I needed it until he actually said it today."

Everything went still. The moment in the hospital room had been the first time he'd truly heard his father's apology.

He took a sudden step toward the bed, and Polly let out a low, guttural warning. If it had been in human speak, it would have been a threat to rip his face to shreds.

"Okay, Polly. Chill." He turned his focus back to me. "Like I said, I fucked up. You might not want my apology now, but I need to say it in case you do someday. I'm sorry. You didn't deserve what I did or how I treated you, and I'm sorry."

What was I supposed to say? I opened my mouth, but words failed me. "Uh . . ."

He was sincere. He'd come to apologize, not to make himself feel better, but for me. Preston's first selfless act in a long, long time. Maybe it had been magical beer.

I went with what was easiest. He'd said what he needed to, and I had to acknowledge it. "Okay."

I shifted gingerly on the bed. What was supposed to happen now? I accepted his apology, but he wasn't exactly forgiven, and there were other things I was still upset about.

He walked over to my desk and leaned against it, his expression odd. "He was a different person last night, after your surgery. You should have seen him." He folded his arms over his chest. "He was scared, and it freaked me the fuck out."

Alarm coasted through me. "Scared of what?"

"Losing me. Losing you." Preston's eyes weren't quite as dark as his father's. Maybe they'd grow to be that way. He just hadn't seen as much as Greg had yet. But Preston's eyes were beautiful all the same and trapped me under his intense gaze. "He told me today he's spent the last ten years trying to dig himself out of the hole he made when he was my age, and he wasn't going to let me do the same."

A faint, embarrassed smile glanced over his lips and vanished as quickly as it had appeared.

"Then," he continued, "my dad laid into me about all the shit he'd let me get away with, because he thought going easy on me was his best chance to earn forgiveness. He told me he was going to, quote, 'take away my shovel.'"

I blinked.

Preston straightened from the desk. "You know, so I couldn't dig my own hole?"

"I got it," I said dryly.

"So, we talked about—fuck, everything. And I'm going to try to do better."

I couldn't help but be dubious. "Starting today."

"Yeah." His gaze drifted away from mine. "I had to find out you were in the hospital from my dad."

"Was I supposed to tell you? Honestly, I didn't think you'd care."

He deflated. "What I mean is, you were my best friend, and I took you for granted. I didn't realize how much I did until you were with . . . someone else."

The statement dropped the big, fat elephant right between us, where we couldn't ignore it any longer.

"You mean, the someone you took away from me?"

He gave me an annoyed look. "You think walking in on that was easy? Sorry if I wasn't immediately cool with seeing you fuck my dad."

My cheeks burned, and I dropped my gaze to my lap. "I'm sorry you found out that way, but we were going to tell you."

"Yeah, I know. He pointed out I'd done stuff behind your back and kept it a secret, so I guess I don't really have any room to complain." He exhaled loudly, his shoulders dropping. "Honestly, Cassidy, I don't get it. You and my dad together? It's a little fucked up."

Anger swelled inside me. "You don't—"

He held up a hand. "I'm not done. I don't understand it, and I don't like it, but that doesn't matter because it's not always about me."

My heart tripped, stumbling over itself. "What are you saying?"

"It's selfish of me to get in the way of you two. If you want to be together. So, I guess I'm not going to do it anymore." He grimaced. "But I can't promise it's not going to be awkward as fuck."

My chest tightened. "Really?"

"Yeah, it's super weird. He's twenty years older than you."

I made a face. "No, I meant—oh."

Preston's expression said he'd been messing with me. Then he turned sincere. "If we hadn't gone through this whole mess, my dad and I would still be where we were, stuck in a holding pattern."

Shock wasn't a strong enough word for what I was feeling. "You've forgiven him?"

He shrugged. "I dunno. I'm getting there."

"Preston," I said, trying not to gasp, "that's huge."

"Yeah, it is." He nodded and gave me such a deep look, I felt the weight of it. "You played a big part in that."

I put my hand to the center of my chest to keep his words from knocking me out. After everything, I still cared about him, and it meant so much that he'd taken this step.

"So, I'm gonna go now. I should probably tell you my dad's downstairs with your mom, and the air was kind of frosty between them."

I didn't know which part to focus on first. "Your dad's here?"

"We both wanted to see you. I got to go first."

"Of course, you did." I wasn't sure if he'd know this time I meant it as a joke, or how he'd handle it, or if it was too soon. But I hoped one day we could go back to being friends, and we had to start somewhere.

The corner of his mouth twitched into a smile. "I hope you feel better soon."

Did he mean it on more than one level? Because I already felt a lifetime better.

THIRTY-FIVE

My mouth went dry as the stairs groaned. Greg was about to walk into my room, and I had to look like garbage. I hadn't showered since—oh, God—Thursday. I finger-combed my bedhead as fast as my wounds would allow, trying to look presentable.

Preston had left my door open when he'd gone, so there wasn't a knock, only Greg's voice from the hallway. "Cassidy?"

"In here." Could he hear how tight my voice was?

He stepped into the room and was instantly greeted by Tripod. The dog's outward excitement was mirrored inside me. Greg looked how he usually did. Dark jeans, fitted t-shirt, expensive watch on his wrist. His hair was styled as normal, his beard trim.

But he was more appealing than I'd ever seen him. The lines at the corners of his eyes were less pronounced. As he watched Tripod's ridiculous fit of excitement at his feet, Greg was quick to smile.

"This dog is missing a leg," he said.

"He is? I hadn't noticed."

As he looked at me, the connection between us was so strong, I worried I might melt. "And you want to be a vet," he teased.

I swallowed a lump in my throat. Everything was so different now.

His gaze drifted around my room, taking in the lavender paint I'd had on the walls since I was five. At least I'd gotten rid of most of the high school junk.

"Are you making house calls now?" I asked.

"I'm not here as your doctor." His expression was coy. "How did your conversation go with Preston?"

I snagged my bottom lip between my teeth for a moment. "It . . . went."

He mentally stumbled, probably expecting me to offer up more, but wires crossed in my brain. It was confusing having Greg in my bedroom. Preston had lifted the restraint on Greg and me, but I still felt it there between us.

Plus, I'd told him I was falling in love, so I needed him to make the next move.

One footstep was all he got before Polly lifted her head and hissed at the intruder.

"Your cat only has one eye."

"Would you feel more comfortable if I put on her eye patch?" I said. "She doesn't really like wearing it."

My joke died as he approached, his shadow falling over me. All I could see was him. His tone was strong, yet soft. "I made you a promise yesterday."

My heart rate climbed as I recalled his words. He swore it wouldn't be the last time he touched me. But he'd also fulfilled this promise, hadn't he? My mom said he'd held my hand. Was he going to remind me of that?

"Did you come to collect?"

He reached out, skimming his fingertips along my cheek-bone, his voice as soft as his touch. "I did."

The caress of his fingers sent sparks raining across my skin. His hand moved along my cheek, sliding gently into my hair, and tilted my head back. My eyes fluttered closed as he lowered in and sealed his mouth over mine.

The kiss was so passionate, I was surprised it didn't blow the doors off the house. His lips moved against mine, swallowing the small cry I gave, and kept on delivering a nuclear kiss I didn't even know existed until now. He shifted the angle, adjusting to taste me better, and I reached up, gripping his face between my palms. Did he notice my hands were shaking?

He lowered to sit beside me on the bed, deepening the kiss. Polly wasn't having it. Her hiss this time was laced with malice, followed by her low, angry growl.

"What is that cat's deal?" he asked between kisses.

"She hates people."

He cradled my face in a hand, holding me steady as his mouth roamed down the column of my throat. I squeezed my eyes shut, trying to hold back the shiver I knew he'd cause.

"She likes you," he argued.

I stroked my palms down his t-shirt covered chest, enjoying the feel of the hard muscles beneath them. I loved having him back in my hands. "I have my moments."

Greg's traveling kiss ventured back up to my lips, where he lingered for a long moment. As he drew back, it came from him in a burst. "I might be in love with you too."

My eyes flew wide open, and I gasped. As I searched his expression, I saw everything in his eyes. He was nervous about admitting it, but it was the truth. Dr. Gregory Lowe was in love with me. How crazy was that?

I couldn't stop the grin that spread across my face. "Oh, Doctor. What are we going to do about this?"

He planted a searing kiss on me. "I'm sure we'll figure it out."

FOUR MONTHS LATER

The headlights of Greg's car cut through the night as we sped through the rural side streets on our way back to his house. My phone chimed with a text message, and I dug it out of my clutch.

Lilith: How was dinner with Daddy?

Cassidy: Ugh, please stop
calling him that.

I pictured her on the other end of the phone, amused with herself.

"Who are you texting?" Greg asked. His eyes stayed on the road, thankfully not shifting to see what she'd sent.

"Lilith," I said. "She wanted to know how the fundraiser was."

Cassidy: The event was fine. Glad
it's over.

The hospital held an annual dinner a few weeks before Christmas that was part party for staff, and part fundraiser. It'd been dry chicken, medical jargon I only half-understood, and plenty of raised eyebrows. I wasn't an idiot. Most of Greg's colleagues saw me as a trophy girlfriend or thought the age difference was scandalous.

"How was it for you?" He asked it like he hadn't been by my side all evening, even though he had.

"It was about what I expected. Lots of stares." I loved the cute black cocktail dress I'd bought for the event but spent the entire night uncomfortable from all the strangers' judgement.

"Fuck 'em," he said. "Most of them are just jealous."

As I stared at him in his sexy suit and tie, the faint lines of silver threading his hair, I understood. If I was any other woman, I'd be jealous of me too. But I was Greg's first choice, and he was mine.

"I know you didn't want to go," he added, "so thanks. I appreciate it." He took a hand off the steering wheel and set it on my knee.

It made me feel warm and fuzzy inside, which was good. My formal coat wasn't very warm, and the outside temperature was closing in on freezing.

"You doctors sure fall into the stereotype of loving golf. So much conversation about 'playing the back nine.' I pretended they were using a euphemism for anal just to keep it interesting."

Greg's mouth fell open into an incredulous grin. "Dirty girl."

I shrugged. He wasn't wrong.

We made it home, and while Greg was hanging our coats up in the entryway closet, I went into the kitchen just as Preston appeared at the top of the stairs.

"Hey," he said.

I strived for a bright, casual tone. "Hi."

Would it ever not be weird seeing each other? Vanderbilt was a big school, so we rarely ran into each other on campus, and winter break was the only reason Preston was home now.

He hadn't been home alone, though. There was a girl on the landing of the stairs, standing beside him. She was pretty, with big eyes, full lips, and glossy blonde hair I was envious of.

"This is Iris," he said. "We were just heading out to see a movie." He gestured to me. "Iris, this is Cassidy, my dad's girlfriend."

Surprise splashed on her face.

Preston said it all like it was no big deal. "Yeah, she's young. We used to date. Whatever, it's weird." He slipped his hand behind Iris's back and pressed her forward. "We need to go or we're going to be late."

"Nice meeting you," she said automatically, not done processing all the info he'd just dumped on her.

"You too," I lobbed back as they went out the door to the garage.

Sometimes I wondered if he had adjusted better than I had.

Four months ago, Greg had told me we'd figure it out, and we had, for the most part. There were some days that were hard. I only saw him once over Thanksgiving break, due to his job. I still wasn't twenty-one, which occasionally was a pain when we wanted to go out.

Plus, he'd forced me to watch the movie *Alien*.

My mom was warming to Greg, ever so slowly. I knew she'd get there eventually. He made me happy, and wasn't that what really mattered?

"You meet Iris?" Greg asked as he reappeared, ushering me toward the kitchen.

"Yeah. She's cute." I opened the fridge and grinned when I saw the cans of Dr. Pepper beside a bottle of white wine. "What are we doing tonight?" I asked casually.

He matched my tone. "I don't know. What do you want to do?"

"Christmas movie?" I volunteered.

"Okay. *Gremlins* or *Die Hard*?"

I rolled my eyes. "I've seen *Die Hard*."

He made an exaggerated sigh. "Damn. I kind of wanted to watch that again."

I plucked the wine from the fridge, closed the door, and set the bottle down on the island with a thump. "Or we could drink this, and you could play the back nine."

He laughed and grabbed my waist, lifted, and seated me on the granite counter top, my legs spread on either side of his hips. "I like this plan much better."

I grinned as he buried his mouth in the side of my neck, causing goosebumps to burst down my legs.

"I'm crazy in love with you, you know that?" he murmured.

"I love you too," I whispered back.

I was still young and had things to learn, but on him I was certain. We'd taken a strange path to come together, but in the end, it was worth it.

He was so absolutely worth it.

THANK YOU

To my perfect (and crazy hot) husband, whose support makes my dream possible. You're not only my alpha reader, you're my everything!

To my story editors Andrea Lefkowitz and Nikki Terrill. I love you with every inch of my cold, black heart!

To my beta readers Joscelyn Fussell, Rebecca Nebel and Veronica Larsen. I so appreciate your invaluable feedback! Don't worry, the next book won't be as bad. #famouslastwords

To my editor Lori Whitwam. Your comments on the manuscript are both hilarious and amazing. Thanks for making me look good.

To my publicist Heather Roberts. Thanks for all your pimping!

As always, the most important *thanks* goes to YOU, reader, for choosing to read my work. I've been writing for a few years now, but I will never get used to the excitement I have when my book winds up in someone else's hands. (Especially when they're not related to me.) I am forever grateful and honored you want to spend time with my characters and sexy words.

MORE FROM NIKKI SLOANE

THE BLINDFOLD CLUB SERIES

IT *takes* TWO

THREE *simple* RULES

THREE *hard* LESSONS

THREE *little* MISTAKES

THREE *dirty* SECRETS

THREE *sweet* NOTHINGS

ONE *more* RULE

THE SORDID SERIES

SORDID

TORRID

SPORTS ROMANCE

THE RIVALRY

ABOUT NIKKI SLOANE

Nikki Sloane landed in graphic design after her careers as a waitress, a screenwriter, and a ballroom dance instructor fell through. For eight years she worked for a design firm in that extremely tall, black, and tiered building in Chicago that went through an unfortunate name change during her time there. Now she lives in Kentucky, is married and has two sons. She is a three-time Romance Writers of America RITA® Finalist, also writes romantic suspense under the name Karyn Lawrence, and couldn't be any happier that people enjoy reading her sexy words.

www.NikkiSloane.com

www.twitter.com/AuthorNSloane

www.facebook.com/NikkiSloaneAuthor

www.instagram.com/nikkisloane